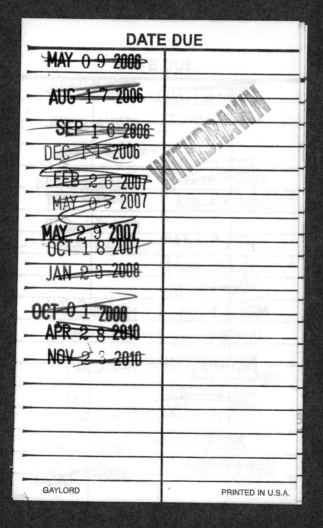

INDEMNITY ONLY

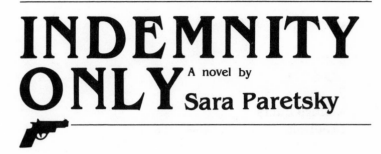

INDEMNITY ONLY

A novel by

Sara Paretsky

Delacorte Press

Published by
Delacorte Press
Bantam Doubleday Dell Publishing Group, Inc.
666 Fifth Avenue
New York, New York 10103

Library of Congress Cataloging in Publication Data

Paretsky, Sara.
    Indemnity only : a novel / by Sara Paretsky.
        p.   cm.
    ISBN 0-385-30260-6
    I. Title.
    PS3566.A647I5   1991
    813'.54—dc20   90-40139
                                                  CIP

Manufactured in the United States of America

Published simultaneously in Canada

March 1991

10 9 8 7 6 5 4 3 2 1
BVG

For Stuart Kaminsky. Thanks.

A NOTE FROM
THE AUTHOR

On New Year's Eve, flushed with champagne, I made a secret resolution to write a novel in 1979 or send that fantasy packing along with my daydreams of singing at La Scala or dancing with Nureyev. The next day I began:

> I looked hopefully in my wallet, but found only the two greasy singles which had been there in the morning. I could get a sandwich, or a pack of cigarettes and a cheap shot of scotch. I sighed and looked down at the Wabash Avenue el tracks.

Nine months later, I'd added about fifty pages to this unpromising opening and thought I should resign myself to a life of selling computers to insurance agents. At that point a co-worker named Mary Hogan, who knew about my efforts, showed me the Northwestern University fall extension catalog. Stuart Kaminsky was teaching an evening course called "Writing Detective Fiction for Publication." I felt like Alice finding the mushroom—just what I needed to get to be the right size.

Stuart read my puny story with great care. He gave me essential advice for thinking about my character and my story. In the process V. I. stopped smoking and took up my whisky, Black Label. Most important, Stuart became the voice I needed to hear, the voice that said, "You can write. You can do this thing." Without Stuart I would not have had the confidence to push the story through to the end. That is why *Indemnity Only* is dedicated to him.

Whenever I read the memoirs of a writer like Sartre, who says he knew from childhood he was "destined for words," or Bellow, who knew he "was born to be a performing or interpretive creature," I wonder what unacknowledged voice spoke to them as children. Sartre actually tells us it was his mother and his grandfather who bound his childish effusions as novels and passed them with much outspoken pride around the neighborhood. Without his family creating in him that vision of himself, young Jean-Paul could not have grown up with such a sense of destiny. His cousins, told at the same age they were fated to be engineers, became engineers.

I wrote from my earliest childhood, but for myself only. Like the heroine of *Dream Girl*, I spent vast amounts of my waking hours imagining myself inside different stories; when they acquired some kind of shape, I wrote them down. But I thought my stories were a sign of the sickness afflicting the woman in the play, and that true love would cure me as it did her, for I grew up in a time and place where little girls were destined to be wives and mothers.

I did find true love, but my husband, Courtenay Wright, convinced me that my stories were worth telling, that my dreams signaled not sickness but a lively mind. His support has not wavered from that cold New Year's Day to the present hot June in which I struggle with my seventh V. I. novel. I have had some years of terrible pain and disability in between; Courtenay has held on to me and kept me from losing that essential core from which my stories come. In a way, every word I write is dedicated to Courtenay.

When I finished the manuscript in May 1980, with the first weak paragraph and limp chapter exchanged for the current one, Stuart Kaminsky sent it to his agent, Dominick Abel, in New York. Dominick took on V. I. and me and has stuck with us ever since. I don't want to turn this introduction into a volume of the Talmud, so I'll only say of Dominick, in the old Chinese words, that I would send him for horses.

It took him a year to find a publisher for *Indemnity Only*. Indeed, when I'm getting too conceited with myself, I pull out the file of rejection letters from that year and read that I'm "too talky"; have "wooden characters"; wrote a "derivative story"; and that *Indemnity Only* was a "marginal book which we can't afford to take on." The file is a nice fat one and a good antidote for vanity. In the face of so much negativism, I'm especially grateful to Nancy van Itallie and the Dial Press for taking the gamble on publishing me.

The Dial Press is no more, and that is sad. But after almost a decade of wandering I've found my proper home at Delacorte. Jackie Farber and Carole Baron provide the kind of editorial and publishing support most writers only dream about.

Indemnity Only came to life so precariously that it remains very precious to me. Sometimes I look at it with amazement—amazed that I did find the strength to write a book, amazed that someone actually published it. And now that Delacorte is bringing out a new edition I look at it with a lot of pride. I was tempted to go through and polish up the writing, change those flaws I wasn't alert enough to see in 1979. But I decided it would be unethical to tamper with the text. With the exception of two very small corrections this is the same book I sent Dominick Abel ten years ago.

Sara Paretsky
Chicago
June 1990

INDEMNITY ONLY

ONE
SUMMERTIME

The night air was thick and damp. As I drove south along Lake Michigan, I could smell rotting alewives like a faint perfume on the heavy air. Little fires shone here and there from late-night barbecues in the park. On the water a host of green and red running lights showed people seeking relief from the sultry air. On shore traffic was heavy, the city moving restlessly, trying to breathe. It was July in Chicago.

I got off Lake Shore Drive at Randolph Street and swung down Wabash under the iron arches of the elevated tracks. At Monroe I stopped the car and got out.

Away from the lake the city was quieter. The South Loop, with no entertainment beyond a few peepshows and the city lockup, was deserted—a drunk weaving uncertainly down the street was my only companion. I crossed Wabash and went into the Pulteney Building next to the Monroe Street Tobacco Store. At night it looked like a terrible place to have an office. The hall's mosaic-tiled walls were chipped an dirty. I wondered if anyone ever washed the scuffed linoleum floor. The lobby must create a reassuring impression on potential clients.

I pushed the elevator button. No response. I tried again. Again no response. I shoved open the heavy stairwell door, climbing slowly to the fourth floor. It was cool in the stairwell and I lingered there a few minutes before moving on down the badly lit hallway to the east end, the end where rents are cheaper because all the offices look out on the Wabash el. In the dim light I could read the inscription on the door: "V. I. Warshawski. Private Investigator."

I had called my answering service from a filling station on

the North Side, just a routine check on my way home to a shower, air conditioning, and a late supper. I was surprised when they told me I had a caller, and unhappy when they said he'd refused to give a name. Anonymous callers are a pain. They usually have something to hide, often something criminal, and they don't leave their names just so you can't find out what they're hiding ahead of time.

This guy was coming at 9:15, which didn't even give me time to eat. I'd spent a frustrating afternoon in the ozone-laden heat trying to track down a printer who owed me fifteen hundred dollars. I'd saved his firm from being muscled out by a national chain last spring and now I was sorry I'd done it. If my checking account hadn't been so damned anemic, I'd have ignored this phone call. As it was, I squared my shoulders and unlocked the door.

With the lights on my office looked Spartan but not unpleasant and I cheered up slightly. Unlike my apartment, which is always in mild disarray, my office is usually tidy. I'd bought the big wooden desk at a police auction. The little Olivetti portable had been my mother's, as well as a reproduction of the Ufizzi hanging over my green filing cabinet. That was supposed to make visitors realize that mine was a high-class operation. Two straight-backed chairs for clients completed the furniture. I didn't spend much time here and didn't need any other amenities.

I hadn't been in for several days and had a stack of bills and circulars to sort through. A computer firm wanted to arrange a demonstration of what computers could do to help my business. I wondered if a nice little desk-top IBM could find me paying customers.

The room was stuffy. I looked through the bills to see which ones were urgent. Car insurance—I'd better pay that. The others I threw out—most were first-time bills, a few second-time. I usually only pay bills the third time they come around. If they want the money badly, they won't forget you. I stuffed the insurance into my shoulder bag, then turned to the window and switched the air conditioner onto "high." The room went dark. I'd blown a fuse in the Pulteney's uncertain electrical system. Stupid. You can't turn an air conditioner right onto "high" in a building like this. I cursed myself and the building management equally and wondered whether the storeroom with the fuse boxes was open at night. During the years I'd spent in the building, I'd learned how to repair most of what could go wrong with it, including the bathroom on the seventh floor, whose toilet backed up about once a month.

I made my way back down the hall and down the stairs to the basement. A single naked bulb lit the bottom of the stairs. It showed a padlock on the supply-room door. Tom Czarnik, the building's crusty superintendent, didn't trust anyone. I can open some locks, but I didn't have time now for an American padlock. One of those days. I counted to ten in Italian, and started back upstairs with even less enthusiasm than before.

I could hear a heavy tread ahead of me and guessed it was my anonymous visitor. When I got to the top, I quietly opened the stairwell door and watched him in the dim light. He was knocking at my office door. I couldn't see him very well, but got the impression of a short stocky man. He held himself aggressively, and when he got no answer to his knocking, he opened the door without hesitation and went inside. I walked down the hallway and went in after him.

A five-foot-high sign from Arnie's Steak Joynt flashed red and yellow across the street, providing spasms of light to my office. I saw my visitor whirl as I opened the door. "I'm looking for V. I. Warshawski," he said, his voice husky but confident—the voice of a man used to having his own way.

"Yes," I said, going past him to sit behind my desk.

"Yes, what?" he demanded.

"Yes, I'm V. I. Warshawski. You call my answering service for an appointment?"

"Yeah, but I didn't know it would mean walking up four

flights of stairs to a dark office. Why the hell doesn't the elevator work?"

"The tenants in this building are physical fitness nuts. We agreed to get rid of the elevator—climbing stairs is well known as a precaution against heart attacks."

In one of the flashes from Arnie's I saw him make an angry gesture. "I didn't come here to listen to a comedienne," he said, his husky voice straining. "When I ask questions I expect to hear them answered."

"In that case, ask reasonable questions. Now, do you want to tell me why you need a private investigator?"

"I don't know. I need help all right, but this place—Jesus—and why is it so dark in here?"

"The lights are out," I said, my temper riding me. "You don't like my looks, leave. I don't like anonymous callers, either."

"All right, all right," he said placatingly. "Simmer down. But do we have to sit in the dark?"

I laughed. "A fuse blew a few minutes before you showed up. We can go over to Arnie's Steak Joynt if you want some light." I wouldn't have minded getting a good look at him myself.

He shook his head. "No, we can stay here." He fidgeted around some, then sat in one of the visitors' chairs.

"You got a name?" I asked, to fill in the pause while he collected his thoughts.

"Oh, yeah, sorry," he said, fumbling in his wallet. He pulled out a card and passed it across the desk. I held it up to read in a flash from Arnie's. "John L. Thayer. Executive Vice-President, Trust, Ft. Dearborn Bank and Trust." I pursed my lips. I didn't make it over to La Salle Street very often, but John Thayer was a very big name indeed at Chicago's biggest bank. Hot diggity, I thought. Play this fish right, Vic, I urged myself. Here come de rent!

I put the card in my jeans pocket. "Yes, Mr. Thayer. Now what seems to be the problem?"

"Well, it's about my son. That is, it's about his girl friend.
At least she's the one who—" He stopped. A lot of people,
especially men, aren't used to sharing their problems, and it
takes them a while to get going. "You know, I don't mean any
offense, but I'm not sure I should talk to you after all. Not
unless you've got a partner or something."

I didn't say anything.

"You got a partner?" he persisted.

"No, Mr. Thayer," I said evenly. "I don't have a partner."

"Well, this really isn't a job for a girl to take on alone."

A pulse started throbbing in my right temple. "I skipped
dinner after a long day in the heat to meet you down here."
My voice was husky with anger. I cleared my throat and tried
to steady myself. "You wouldn't even identify yourself until I
pushed you to it. You pick at my office, at me, but you can't
come out and ask anything directly. Are you trying to find
out whether I'm honest, rich, tough, or what? You want
some references, ask for them. But don't waste my time like
this. I don't need to argue you into hiring my services—it was
you who insisted on making an appointment for the middle
of the night."

"I'm not questioning your honesty," he said quickly. "Look,
I'm not trying to get your goat. But you are a girl, and things
may get heavy."

"I'm a woman, Mr. Thayer, and I can look out for myself.
If I couldn't, I wouldn't be in this kind of business. If things
get heavy, I'll figure out a way to handle them—or go down
trying. That's my problem, not yours. Now, you want to tell
me about your son, or can I go home where I can turn on an
air conditioner?"

He thought some more, and I took some deep breaths to
calm myself, ease the tension in my throat.

"I don't know," he finally said. "I hate to, but I'm running
out of options." He looked up, but I couldn't see his face.
"Anything I tell you has to be strictly in confidence."

"Righto, Mr. Thayer," I said wearily. "Just you, me, and Arnie's Steak Joynt."

He caught his breath but remembered he was trying to be conciliatory. "It's really Anita, my son's girl friend. Not that Pete—my son, that is—hasn't been a bit of a problem, too."

Dope, I thought morosely. All these North Shore types think about is dope. If it was a pregnancy, they'd just pay for an abortion and be done with it. However, mine was not to pick and choose, so I grunted encouragingly.

"Well, this Anita is not really a very desirable type, and ever since Pete got mixed up with her he's been having some peculiar ideas." The language sounded strangely formal in his husky voice.

"I'm afraid I only detect things, Mr. Thayer. I can't do too much about what the boy thinks."

"No, no, I know that. It's just that—they've been living together in some disgusting commune or other—did I tell you they're students at the University of Chicago? Anyway, he, Pete, he's taken to talking about becoming a union organizer and not going to business school, so I went down to talk to the girl. Make her see reason, kind of."

"What's her last name, Mr. Thayer?"

"Hill. Anita Hill. Well, as I said, I went down to try to make her see reason. And—right after that she disappeared."

"It sounds to me like your problem's solved."

"I wish it was. The thing is, now Pete's saying I bought her off, paid her to disappear. And he's threatening to change his name and drop out of sight unless she turns up again."

Now I've heard everything, I thought. Hired to find a person so her boyfriend would go to business school.

"And were you responsible for her disappearance, Mr. Thayer?"

"Me? If I was, I'd be able to get her back."

"Not necessarily. She could have squeezed fifty grand out of you and gone off on her own so you couldn't get it back. Or you could have paid her to disappear completely. Or you may have killed her or caused her to be killed and want someone else to take the rap for you. A guy like you has a lot of resources."

He seemed to laugh a little at that. "Yeah, I suppose all that could be true. Anyway, I want you to find her—to find Anita."

"Mr. Thayer, I don't like to turn down work, but why not get the police—they're much better equipped than I for this sort of thing."

"The police and I—" he started, then broke off. "I don't feel like advertising my family problems to the police," he said heavily.

That had the ring of truth—but what had he started to say? "And why were you so worried about things getting heavy?" I wondered aloud.

He shifted in his chair a bit. "Some of those students can get pretty wild," he muttered. I raised my eyebrows skeptically, but he couldn't see that in the dark.

"How did you get my name?" I asked. Like an advertising survey—did you hear about us in *Rolling Stone* or through a friend?

"I found your name in the Yellow Pages. And I wanted someone in the Loop and someone who didn't know—my business associates."

"Mr. Thayer, I charge a hundred and a quarter a day, plus expenses. And I need a five-hundred-dollar deposit. I make progress reports, but clients don't tell me how to do the job— any more than your widows and orphans tell you how to run the Fort Dearborn's Trust Department."

"Then you will take the job?" he asked.

"Yes," I said shortly. Unless the girl was dead, it shouldn't be too hard to find her. "I'll need your son's address at the university," I added. "And a picture of the girl if you have one."

He hesitated over that, seemed about to say something, but then gave it to me: 5462 South Harper. I hoped it was the right place. He also produced a picture of Anita Hill. I couldn't make it out in the spasmodic light, but it looked like a yearbook snap. My client asked me to call him at home to report progress, rather than at the office. I jotted his home number on the business card and put it back in my pocket.

"How soon do you think you'll know something?" he asked.

"I can't tell you until I've looked at it, Mr. Thayer. But I'll get on the case first thing tomorrow."

"Why can't you go down there tonight?" he persisted.

"Because I have other things to do," I answered shortly. Like dinner and a drink.

He argued for a bit, not so much because he thought I'd change my mind as because he was used to getting his own way. He finally gave up on it and handed me five hundred-dollar bills.

I squinted at them in the light from Arnie's. "I take checks, Mr. Thayer."

"I'm trying to keep people at the office from knowing I've been to a detective. And my secretary balances my checkbook."

I was staggered, but not surprised. An amazing number of executives have their secretaries do that. My own feeling was that only God, the IRS, and my bank should have access to my financial transactions.

He got up to go and I walked out with him. By the time I'd locked the door, he had started down the stairs. I wanted to get a better look at him, and hurried after him. I didn't want to have to see every man in Chicago under a flashing neon sign to recognize my client again. The stairwell lighting wasn't that good, but under it his face appeared square and rugged. Irish-looking, I would have said, not what I would have thought of as second-in-command at the Fort Dearborn. His suit was expensive and well cut, but he looked more as if he'd stepped from an Edward G. Robinson movie than the nation's eighth largest bank. But then, did I look like a detective? Come to think of it, most people don't try to guess what women do for a living by the way they look—but they are usually astounded to find out what I do.

My client turned east, toward Michigan Avenue. I shrugged and crossed the street to Arnie's. The owner gave me a double Johnnie Walker Black and a sirloin from his private collection.

TWO
DROPPING
OUT OF SCHOOL

I woke up early to a day that promised to be as hot and steamy as the one before. Four days out of seven, I try to force myself to get some kind of exercise. I'd missed the previous two days, hoping that the heat would break, but I knew I'd better get out this morning. When thirty is a fond memory, the more days that pass without exercise, the worse you feel going back to it. Then, too, I'm undisciplined in a way that makes it easier to exercise than to diet, and the running helps keep my weight down. It doesn't mean I love it, though, especially on mornings like this.

The five hundred dollars John Thayer had given me last night cheered me up considerably, and I felt good as I put on cutoffs and a T-shirt. The money helped take my mind off the thick air when I got outside. I did five easy miles—over to the lake and around Belmont Harbor and back to my large, cheap apartment on Halsted. It was only 8:30, but I was sweating freely from running in the heat. I drank a tall glass of orange juice and made coffee before taking a shower. I left my running clothes on a chair and didn't bother with the bed. After all, I was on a job and didn't have time—besides, who was going to see it?

Over coffee and some smoked herring I tried to decide how to approach Peter Thayer about his missing girl friend. If his family disapproved of her, he would probably resent his father hiring a private detective to look into her disappearance. I'd have to be someone connected with the university—maybe in one of her classes wanting to borrow some notes?

I looked pretty old for an undergraduate—and what if she wasn't registered for the summer quarter? Maybe I'd be from an underground journal, wanting her to do an article on something. Something on labor unions—Thayer had said she was trying to push Peter into being a union organizer.

I stacked my dishes by the sink and eyed them thoughtfully: one more day and I'd have to wash them. I took the garbage out, though—I'm messy but not a slob. Newspapers had been piling up for some time, so I took a few minutes to carry them out next to the garbage cans. The building super's son made extra money recycling paper.

I put on jeans and a yellow cotton top and surveyed myself in the mirror with critical approval. I look my best in the summer. I inherited my Italian mother's olive coloring, and tan beautifully. I grinned at myself. I could hear her saying, "Yes, Vic, you are pretty—but pretty is no good. Any girl can be pretty—but to take care of yourself you must have brains. And you must have a job, a profession. You must work." She had hoped I would be a singer and had trained me patiently; she certainly wouldn't have liked my being a detective. Nor would my father. He'd been a policeman himself, Polish in an Irish world. He'd never made it beyond sergeant, due partly to his lack of ambition, but also, I was sure, to his ancestry. But he'd expected great things of me. . . . My grin went a little sour in the mirror and I turned away abruptly.

Before heading to the South Side, I walked over to my bank to deposit the five hundreds. First things first. The teller took them without a blink—I couldn't expect everyone to be as impressed with them as I was.

It was 10:30 when I eased my Chevy Monza onto the Belmont entrance to Lake Shore Drive. The sky was already bleached out, and the waves reflected back a coppery sheen. Housewives, children, and detectives were the only people out this time of day; I coasted to Hyde Park in twenty-three minutes and parked on the Midway.

I hadn't been on campus in ten years, but the place hadn't

changed much, not as much as I had. I'd read somewhere that the dirty, poverty-stricken collegiate appearance was giving way to the clean-cut look of the fifties. That movement had definitely passed Chicago by. Young people of indeterminate sex strolled by hand-in-hand or in groups, hair sticking out, sporting tattered cutoffs and torn work shirts— probably the closest contact any of them had with work. Supposedly a fifth of the student body came from homes with an annual income of fifty thousand dollars or more, but I'd hate to use looks to decide which fifth.

I walked out of the glare into cool stone halls and stopped at a campus phone to call the registrar. "I'm trying to locate one of your students, a Miss Anita Hill." The voice on the other end, old and creaky, told me to wait. Papers rustled in the background. "Could you spell that name?" I obliged. More rustling. The creaky voice told me they had no student by that name. Did that mean she wasn't registered for the summer quarter? It meant they had no student by that name. I asked for Peter Thayer and was a little surprised when she gave me the Harper address—if Anita didn't exist, why should the boy?

"I'm sorry to be so much trouble, but I'm his aunt. Can you tell me what classes he might be in today? He's not home and I'm only in Hyde Park for the day." I must have sounded benevolent, for Ms. Creaky condescended to tell me that Peter was not registered this summer, but that the Political Science Department in the college might be able to help me find him. I thanked her benevolently and signed off.

I frowned at the phone and contemplated my next move. If there was no Anita Hill, how could I find her? And if there was no Anita Hill, how come someone was asking me to find her? And why had he told me the two were students at the university, when the registrar showed no record of the girl? Although maybe he was mistaken about her being at the University of Chicago—she might go to Roosevelt and live in

Hyde Park. I thought I should go to the apartment and see if anyone was home.

I went back to my car. It was stifling inside and the steering wheel burned my fingers. Among the papers on the backseat was a towel I'd taken to the beach a few weeks ago. I rummaged for it and covered the steering wheel with it. It had been so long since I'd been in the neighborhood that I got confused in the one-way streets, but I eventually made it to Harper. 5462 was a three-story building that had once been yellow brick. The entryway smelled like an el station—musty, with a trace of urine in the air. A bag labeled "Harold's Chicken Shack" had been crumpled and thrown in a corner, and a few picked bones lay near it. The inner door hung loosely in its frame. It probably hadn't had a lock for some time. Its paint, once brown, had chipped and peeled badly. I wrinkled my nose. I couldn't blame the Thayers too much if they didn't like the place their son lived in.

The names on the bell panel had been hand-printed on index cards and taped to the wall. Thayer, Berne, Steiner, McGraw, and Harata occupied a third-floor apartment. That must be the disgusting commune that had angered my client. No Hill. I wondered if he'd gotten Anita's last name wrong, or if she was using an assumed name. I rang the bell and waited. No response. I rang again. Still no answer.

It was noon now and I decided to take a break. The Wimpy's I remembered in the nearby shopping center had been replaced by a cool, attractive, quasi-Greek restaurant. I had an excellent crabmeat salad and a glass of Chablis and walked back to the apartment. The kids probably had summer jobs and wouldn't be home until five, but I didn't have anything else to do that afternoon besides trying to find my welching printer.

There was still no answer, but a scruffy-looking young man came out as I was ringing. "Do you know if anyone in the Thayer-Berne apartment is home?" I asked. He looked at me in a glazed way and mumbled that he hadn't seen any of them for several days. I pulled Anita's picture from my pocket and told him I was trying to track down my niece. "She should be home right now, but I'm wondering if I have the right address," I added.

He gave me a bored look. "Yeah, I think she lives here. I don't know her name."

"Anita," I said, but he'd already shuffled outside. I leaned against the wall and thought for a few minutes. I could wait until tonight to see who showed up. On the other hand, if I went in now, I might find out more on my own than I could by asking questions.

I opened the inside door, whose lock I'd noticed that morning was missing, and climbed quickly to the third floor. Hammered on the Thayer-Berne apartment door. No answer. Put my ear to it and heard the faint hum of a window air conditioner. Pulled a collection of keys from my pocket and after a few false starts found one that turned the lock back.

I stepped inside and quietly shut the door. A small hallway opened directly onto a living room. It was sparsely furnished with some large denim-covered pillows on the bare floor and a stereo system. I went over and looked at it—Kenwood turntable and JBL speakers. Someone here had money. My client's son, no doubt.

The living room led to a hallway with rooms on either side of it, boxcar style. As I moved down it, I could smell something rank, like stale garbage or a dead mouse. I poked my head into each of the rooms but didn't see anything. The hall ended in a kitchen. The smell was strongest there, but it took me a minute to see its source. A young man slumped over the kitchen table. I walked over to him. Despite the window air conditioner his body was in the early stages of decomposition.

The smell was strong, sweet, and sickening. The crabmeat and Chablis began a protest march in my stomach, but I fought back my nausea and carefully lifted the boy's shoulders. A small hole had been put into his forehead. A trickle of blood had come out of it and dried across his face, but his face wasn't damaged. The back of his head was a mess.

I lowered him carefully to the table. Something, call it my woman's intuition, told me I was looking at the remains of Peter Thayer. I knew I ought to get out of the place and call the cops, but I might never have another chance to look over the apartment. The boy had clearly been dead for some time—the police could wait another few minutes for him.

I washed my hands at the sink and went back down the hall to explore the bedrooms. I wondered just how long the body had been there and why none of the inmates had called the police. The second question was partially answered by a list taped up next to the phone giving Berne's, Steiner's, and Harata's summer addresses. Two of the bedrooms containing books and papers but no clothes must belong to some combination of those three.

The third room belonged to the dead boy and a girl named Anita McGraw. Her name was scrawled in a large, flowing hand across the flyleaves of numerous books. On the dilapidated wooden desk was an unframed photo of the dead boy and a girl out by the lake. The girl had wavy auburn hair and a vitality and intenseness that made the photo seem almost alive. It was a much better picture than the yearbook snap my client had given me last night. A boy might give up far more than business school for a girl like that. I wanted to meet Anita McGraw.

I looked through the papers, but they were impersonal—flyers urging people to boycott non-union–made sheets, some Marxist literature, and the massive number of notebooks and term papers to be expected in a student apartment. I found a couple of recent pay stubs made out to Peter Thayer from the Ajax Insurance Company stuffed in one drawer. Clearly the boy had had a summer job. I balanced them on my hand for a minute, then pushed them into my back jeans pocket. Wedged behind them were some other papers, including a voter registration card with a Winnetka address on it. I took that, too. You never know what may come in handy. I picked up the photograph and left the apartment.

Once outside I took some gulping breaths of the ozone-laden air. I never realized it could smell so good. I walked back to the shopping center and called the twenty-first police district. My dad had been dead for ten years, but I still knew the number by heart.

"Homicide, Drucker speaking," growled a voice.

"There's a dead body at Fifty-four sixty-two South Harper, apartment three," I said.

"Who are you?" he snapped.

"Fifty-four sixty-two South Harper, apartment three," I repeated. "Got that?" I hung up.

I went back to my car and left the scene. The cops might be all over me later for leaving, but right now I needed to sort some things out. I made it home in twenty-one minutes and took a long shower, trying to wash the sight of Peter Thayer's head from my mind. I put on white linen slacks and a black silk shirt—clean, elegant clothes to center me squarely in the world of the living. I pulled the assortment of stolen papers from my back jeans pocket and put them and the photograph into a big shoulder bag. I headed back downtown to my office, ensconced my evidence in my wall safe, then checked in with my answering service. There were no messages, so I tried the number Thayer had given me. I rang three times and a woman's voice answered: "The number you have dialed—674-9133—is not in service at this time. Please check your number and dial again." That monotonous voice destroyed whatever faith I still had in the identity of my last night's visitor. I was certain he was not John Thayer. Who was he, then, and why had he wanted me to find that body? And why had he brought the girl into it, then given her a phony name?

With an unidentified client and an identified corpse, I'd been wondering what my job was supposed to be—fall girl for finding the body, no doubt. Still . . . Ms. McGraw had not been seen for several days. My client might just have wanted me to find the body, but I had a strong curiosity about the girl.

My job did not seem to include breaking the news of Peter's death to his father, if his father didn't already know. But before I completely wrote off last night's visitor as John Thayer, I should get his picture. "Clear as you go" has ever been my motto. I pulled on my lower lip for a while in an agony of thought and finally realized where I could get a picture of the man with a minimum of fuss and bother—and with no one knowing I was getting it.

I locked the office and walked across the Loop to Monroe and La Salle. The Fort Dearborn Trust occupied four massive buildings, one on each corner of the intersection. I picked the one with gold lettering over the door, and asked the guard for the PR department.

"Thirty-second floor," he mumbled. "You got an appointment?" I smiled seraphically and said I did and sailed up thirty-two stories while he went back to chewing his cigar butt.

PR receptionists are always trim, well-lacquered, and dressed in the extreme of fashion. This one's form-fitting lavender jumpsuit was probably the most outlandish costume in the bank. She gave me a plastic smile and graciously tendered a copy of the most recent annual report. I stuck on my own plastic smile and went back to the elevator, nodded beneficently to the guard, and sauntered out.

My stomach still felt a little jumpy, so I took the report over to Rosie's Deli to read over ice cream and coffee. John L. Thayer, Executive Vice-President, Trust Division, was pictured prominently on the inside cover with some other bigwigs. He was lean, tanned, and dressed in banker's gray, and I did not have to see him under a neon light to know that he bore no resemblance to my last night's visitor.

I pulled some more on my lip. The police would be interviewing all the neighbors. One clue I had that they didn't, because I had taken it with me, was the boy's pay stubs. Ajax Insurance had its national headquarters in the Loop, not far from where I was now. It was three in the afternoon, not too late for business calls.

Ajax occupied all sixty floors of a modern glass-and-steel skyscraper. I'd always considered it one of the ugliest buildings downtown from the outside. The lower lobby was drab, and nothing about the interior made me want to reverse my first impression. The guard here was more aggressive than the one at the bank, and refused to let me in without a security pass. I told him I had an appointment with Peter Thayer and asked what floor he was on.

"Not so fast, lady," he snarled. "We call up, and *if* the gentleman is here, he'll authorize you."

"Authorize me? You mean he'll authorize my entry. He doesn't have any authority over my existence."

The guard stomped over to his booth and called up. The news that Mr. Thayer wasn't in today didn't surprise me. I demanded to talk to someone in his office. I was tired of being feminine and conciliatory, and made myself menacing enough that I was allowed to speak to a secretary.

"This is V. I. Warshawski," I said crisply. "Mr. Thayer is expecting me."

The soft female voice at the other end apologized, but "Mr. Thayer hasn't been in all week. We've even tried calling him at home, but no one answers."

"Then I think I'd better talk to someone else in your office." I kept my voice hard. She wanted to know what my business was.

"I'm a detective," I said. "Something rotten's going on which young Thayer wanted to talk to me about. If he's not in, I'll talk to someone else who knows his job." It sounded pretty thin to me, but she put me on hold and went off to consult someone. Five minutes later, the guard still glaring at me and fingering his gun, the soft-voiced female came back on the line, rather breathless. Mr. Masters, the Claim Department vice-president, would talk to me.

The guard hated letting me go up—he even called back up to Ms. Softy, in hopes I was lying. But I finally made it to the fortieth floor. Once off the elevator, my feet sank deep into green pile. I made my way through it to a reception area at the south end of the hall. A bored receptionist left her novel and shunted me to the soft-voiced young woman, seated at a teak desk with a typewriter to one side. She in turn ushered me in to see Masters.

Masters had an office big enough for the Bears to work out in, with a magnificent view of the lake. His face had the well-filled, faintly pink look a certain type of successful business-man takes on after forty-five, and he beamed at me above a well-cut gray summer suit. "Hold my calls, Ellen," he said to the secretary as she walked out.

I gave him my card as we exchanged firm handshakes.

"Now what was it you wanted, Miss—ah—?" He smiled patronizingly.

"Warshawski. I want to see Peter Thayer, Mr. Masters. But as he's apparently not in and you've agreed to see me, I'd like to know why the boy felt he needed a private detective."

"I really couldn't tell you that, Miss—ah—do you mind if I call you—" He looked at the card. "What does the V stand for?"

"My first name, Mr. Masters. Maybe you can tell me what Mr. Thayer does here."

"He's my assistant," Masters obliged genially. "Jack Thayer is a good friend of mine, and when his boy—who's a student at the University of Chicago—needed summer work, I was glad to help out." He adjusted his features to look sorrowful. "Certainly if the boy is in the kind of trouble that it takes a detective to solve, I think I should know about it."

"What kinds of things does Mr. Thayer do as your assistant? Settle claims?"

"Oh, no," he beamed. "That's all done at our field locations.

No, we handle the business side of the business—budgets, that kind of thing. The boy adds up figures for me. And he does good staff work—reviews reports, et cetera. He's a good boy—I hope he's not in trouble with those hippies he runs around with down there." He lowered his voice. "Between you and me, Jack says they've given him a bad idea of the business world. The big point about this summer job was to give him a better picture of the business world from the inside."

"And has it?" I asked.

"I'm hopeful, Miss—ah—I'm hopeful." He rubbed his hands together. "I certainly wish I could help you. . . . If you could give me a clue about what was bothering the boy?"

I shook my head. "He didn't say . . . Just called me and asked if I could stop by this afternoon. There wouldn't be anything going on here that he'd feel would require a detective, would there?"

"Well, a department head often doesn't know what's going on in his own department." Masters frowned importantly. "You're too remote—people don't confide in you." He smiled again. "But I'd be very surprised."

"Why did you want to see me?" I asked.

"Oh, I promised Jack Thayer I'd keep an eye on his boy, you know. And when a private detective comes around, it sounds kind of serious. Still, I wouldn't worry about it too much, Miss—ah—although maybe we could hire you to find out where Peter's gone." He chuckled at his joke. "He hasn't been in all week, you know, and we can't reach him at home. I haven't told Jack yet—he's disappointed enough in the boy as it is."

He ushered me down the hall and back to the elevator. I rode down to the thirty-second floor, got off, and rode back up. I strolled back down the hall.

"I'd like to see where young Thayer sits," I told Ellen. She looked at Masters's door for guidance, but it was shut.

"I don't think—"

"Probably not," I interrupted. "But I'm going to look around his desk anyway. I can always get someone else to tell me where it is."

She looked unhappy, but took me over to a partitioned cubicle. "You know, I'm going to be in trouble if Mr. Masters comes out and finds you here," she said.

"I don't see why," I told her. "It's not your fault. I'll tell him you did your best to force me off the floor."

Peter Thayer's desk was unlocked. Ellen stood watching me for a few minutes as I pulled open the drawers and sorted through the papers. "You can search me on my way out to see if I've taken anything," I told her without looking up. She sniffed, but walked back to her own desk.

These papers were as innocuous as those in the boy's apartment. Numerous ledger sheets with various aspects of the department's budget added up, a sheaf of computer printouts that dealt with Workers Compensation case estimates, correspondence to Ajax claim handlers—"Dear Mr. So-and-So, please verify the case estimates for the following claimants." Nothing you'd murder a boy for.

I was scratching my head over these slim pickings, wondering what to do next, when I realized someone was watching me. I looked up. It wasn't the secretary.

"You're certainly a lot more decorative than young Thayer," my observer remarked. "You taking his place?"

The speaker was in his shirt-sleeves, a man in his thirties who didn't have to be told how good-looking he was. I appreciated his narrow waist and the way his Brooks Brothers trousers fit.

"Does anyone around here know Peter Thayer at all well?" I asked.

"Yardley's secretary is making herself sick over him, but I don't know whether she knows him." He moved closer. "Why the interest? Are you with the IRS? Has the kid omitted taxes on some of the vast family holdings deeded to him? Or absconded with Claim Department funds and made them over to the revolutionary committee?"

"You're in the right occupational ball park," I conceded, "and he has, apparently, disappeared. I've never talked to him," I added carefully. "Do you know him?"

"Better than most people around here." He grinned cheerfully and seemed likable despite his arrogance. "He supposedly did legwork for Yardley—Yardley Masters—you were just seen talking to him. I'm Yardley's budget manager."

"How about a drink?" I suggested.

He looked at his watch and grinned again.

"You've got a date, little lady."

His name was Ralph Devereux. He was a suburbanite who had only recently moved to the city, following a divorce that left his wife in possession of their Downers Grove house, he informed me in the elevator. The only Loop bar he knew was Billy's, where the Claim Department hung out. I suggested the Golden Glow a little farther west, to avoid the people he knew. As we walked down Adams Street, I bought a *Sun-Times*.

The Golden Glow is an oddity in the South Loop. A tiny saloon dating back to the last century, it still has a mahogany horseshoe-shaped bar where serious drinkers sit. Eight or nine little tables and booths are crammed in along the walls, and a couple of real Tiffany lamps, installed when the place was built, provide a homey glow. Sal, the bartender, is a magnificent black woman, close to six feet tall. I've watched her break up a fight with just a word and a glance—no one messes with Sal. This afternoon she wore a silver pantsuit. Stunning.

She greeted me with a nod and brought a shot of Black Label to the booth. Ralph ordered a gin-and-tonic. Four o'clock is a little early, even for the Golden Glow's serious-drinking clientele, and the place was mostly deserted.

Devereux placed a five-dollar bill on the table for Sal. "Now tell me why a gorgeous lady like yourself is interested in a young kid like Peter Thayer."

I gave him back his money. "Sal runs a tab for me," I explained. I thumbed through the paper. The story hadn't come in soon enough for the front page, but they'd given it two quarter columns on page seven. RADICAL BANKING HEIR SHOT, the headline read. Thayer's father was briefly mentioned in the last paragraph; his four roommates and their radical activities were given the most play. The Ajax Insurance Company was not mentioned at all.

I folded the paper back and showed the column to Devereux. He glanced at it briefly, then did a double take and snatched the paper from me. I watched him read the story. It was short and he must have gone through it several times. Then he looked up at me, bewildered.

"Peter Thayer? Dead? What is this?"

"I don't know. I'd like to find out."

"You knew when you bought the paper?"

I nodded. He glanced back down at the story, then at me. His mobile face looked angry.

"How did you know?"

"I found the body."

"Why the hell didn't you tell me over at Ajax instead of putting me through this charade?" he demanded.

"Well, anyone could have killed him. You, Yardley Masters, his girl friend . . . I wanted to get your reaction to the news."

"Who the hell *are* you?"

"My name's V. I. Warshawski. I'm a private detective and I'm looking into Peter Thayer's death." I handed him a business card.

"You? You're no more a detective than I am a ballet dancer," he exclaimed.

"I'd like to see you in tights and a tutu," I commented,

pulling out the plastic-encased photostat of my private investigator's license. He studied it, then shrugged without speaking. I put it back in my wallet.

"Just to clear up the point, Mr. Devereux, did you kill Peter Thayer?"

"No, I goddamn did not kill him." His jaw worked angrily. He kept starting to talk, then stopping, unable to put his feelings into words.

I nodded at Sal and she brought us a couple more drinks. The bar was beginning to fill up with precommute drinkers. Devereux drank his second gin and relaxed somewhat. "I'd like to have seen Yardley's face when you asked him if he killed Peter," he commented dryly.

"I didn't ask him. I couldn't figure out why he wanted to talk to me, though. Was he really very protective of Thayer? That's what he intimated."

"No." He considered the question. "He didn't pay much attention to him. But there was the family connection. . . . If Peter was in trouble, Yardley'd feel he owed it to John Thayer to look after him. . . . Dead . . . he was a hell of a nice boy, his radical ideas notwithstanding. Jesus, this is going to cut up Yardley. His old man, too. Thayer didn't like the kid living where he did—and now, shot by some junkie . . ."

"How do you know his father didn't like it?"

"Oh, it wasn't any secret. Shortly after Pete started with us, Jack Thayer came storming in showing his muscle and bellowing around like a vice-president in heat—how the kid was betraying the family with his labor-union talk, and why couldn't he live in a decent place—I guess they'd bought a condo for him down there, if you can believe that. I must say, the boy took it very well—didn't blow up back or anything."

"Did he work with any—well, highly confidential—papers at Ajax?"

Devereux was surprised. "You're not trying to link his death with Ajax, are you? I thought it was pretty clear that he was shot by one of those drug addicts who are always killing people in Hyde Park."

"You make Hyde Park sound like the site of the Tong Wars, Mr. Devereux. Of the thirty-two murders in the twenty-first police district last year, only six were in Hyde Park—one every two months. I don't think Peter Thayer is just the neighborhood's July–August statistic."

"Well, what makes you think it's connected with Ajax, then?"

"I don't think so. I'm just trying to eliminate possibilities. . . . Have you ever seen a dead body—or at least a body that got that way because of a bullet?" He shook his head and moved defensively in his chair. "Well, I have. And you can often tell from the way the body lies whether the victim was trying to fight off the attacker. Well, this boy was sitting at his kitchen table in a white shirt—probably ready to come down here Monday morning—and someone put a little hole smack in the middle of his head. Now a professional might have done that, but even so, he'd have to bring along someone whom the boy knew to get his confidence. It could've been you, or Masters, or his father, or his girl friend. . . . I'm just trying to find out why it couldn't be you."

He shook his head. "I can't do anything to prove it. Except that I don't know how to handle a gun—but I'm not sure I could prove that to you."

I laughed. "You probably could. . . . What about Masters?"

"Yardley? Come on! The guy's one of the most respected people you could hope to find at Ajax."

"That doesn't preclude his being a murderer. Why don't you let me know more about what Peter did there."

He protested some more, but he finally agreed to tell me about his work and what Peter Thayer had done for him. It just didn't seem to add up to murder. Masters was responsible for the financial side of the claim operation, reserving and so on, and Peter had added up numbers for him, checking office copies of issued drafts against known reserves for various claims, adding up overhead items in the field offices to see where they were going over budget, and all the dull day-to-day activities that businesses need in order to keep on going. And yet . . . and yet . . . Masters had agreed to see me, an unknown person, and a detective besides, on the spur of the moment. If he hadn't known Peter was in trouble—or even, maybe, known he was dead—I just couldn't believe his obligation to John Thayer would make him do that.

I contemplated Devereux. Was he just another pretty face, or did he know anything? His anger had seemed to me the result of genuine shock and bewilderment at finding out the boy was dead. But anger was a good cover for other emotions too. . . . For the time being I decided to classify him as an innocent bystander.

Devereux's native Irish cockiness was starting to return—he began teasing me about my job. I felt I'd gotten all I could from him until I knew enough to ask better questions, so I let the matter drop and moved on to lighter subjects.

I signed the bar tab for Sal—she sends me a bill once a month—and went on to the Officer's Mess with Devereux for a protracted meal. It's Indian, and to my mind one of the most romantic restaurants in Chicago. They make a very nice Pimm's Cup, too. Coming on top of the Scotch, it left me with a muzzy impression of dancing at a succession of North Side discos. I might have had a few more drinks. It was after one when I returned, alone, to my apartment. I was glad just to fling my clothes onto a chair and fall into bed.

THREE
THAT PROFESSIONAL TOUCH

Peter Thayer was protesting capitalist oppression by running wildly up and down the halls at Ajax, while Anita McGraw stood to one side carrying a picket sign and smiling. Ralph Devereux came out of his office and shot Thayer. The shot reverberated in the halls. It kept ringing and ringing and I tried seizing the gun from Devereux and throwing it away, but the sound continued and I jerked awake. The doorbell was shrilling furiously. I slid out of bed and pulled on jeans and a shirt as a loud knock sounded. The fuzziness in my mouth and eyes told me I'd had one or two Scotches too many too late in the evening before. I stumbled to the front room and looked through the peephole as heavy fists hammered the door again.

Two men were outside, both beefy, with jacket sleeves too short and hair crew-cut. I didn't know the younger one on the right, but the older one on the left was Bobby Mallory, Homicide lieutenant from the twenty-first district. I fumbled the lock open and tried to smile sunnily.

"Morning, Bobby. What a nice surprise."

"Good morning, Vicki. Sorry to drag you out of bed," Mallory said with heavy humor.

"Not at all, Bobby—I'm always glad to see you." Bobby Mallory had been my dad's closest friend on the force. They'd started on the same beat together back in the thirties, and Bobby hadn't forgotten Tony even after promotions had moved him out of my dad's work life. I usually have Thanksgiving dinner with him and Eileen, his warmly maternal wife. And his six children and four grandchildren.

Most of the time Bobby tries to pretend I'm not working, or at least not working as an investigator. Now he was looking past me, not at me. "This is Sergeant John McGonnigal," he said heartily, waving his arm loosely in McGonnigal's direction. "We'd like to come in and ask you a few questions."

"Certainly," I said politely, wishing my hair weren't sticking out in different directions all over my head. "Nice to meet you, Sergeant. I'm V. I. Warshawski."

McGonnigal and I shook hands and I stood back to let them into the small entryway. The hallway behind us leads straight back to the bathroom, with the bedroom and living rooms opening off to the right, and the dining room and kitchen to the left. This way in the mornings I can stumble straight from bedroom to bathroom to kitchen.

I took Bobby and McGonnigal to the kitchen and put on some coffee. I casually whisked some crumbs off the kitchen table and rummaged in the refrigerator for pumpernickel and cheddar cheese. Behind me, Bobby said, "You ever clean up this dump?"

Eileen is a fanatical housekeeper. If she didn't love to watch people eat, you'd never see a dirty dish in their house. "I've been working," I said with what dignity I could muster, "and I can't afford a housekeeper."

Mallory looked around in disgust. "You know, if Tony had turned you over his knee more often instead of spoiling you rotten, you'd be a happy housewife now, instead of playing at detective and making it harder for us to get our job done."

"But I'm a happy detective, Bobby, and I made a lousy housewife." That was true. My brief foray into marriage eight years ago had ended in an acrimonious divorce after fourteen months: some men can only admire independent women at a distance.

"Being a detective is not a job for a girl like you, Vicki—it's not fun and games. I've told you this a million times. Now you've got yourself messed up in a murder. They were going to send Althans out to talk to you, but I pulled my rank to get the assignment. That still means you've got to talk. I want to know what you were doing messing around with the Thayer boy."

"Thayer boy?" I echoed.

"Grow up, Vicki," Mallory advised. "We got a pretty good description of you from that doped-out specimen on the second floor you talked to on your way into the building. Drucker, who took the squeal, thought it might be your voice when he heard the description. . . . And you left your thumbprint on the kitchen table."

"I always said crime didn't pay, Bobby. You guys want some coffee or eggs or anything?"

"We already ate, clown. Working people can't stay in bed like sleeping beauty."

It was only 8:10, I noticed, looking at the wooden clock next to the back door. No wonder my head felt so woolly. I methodically sliced cheese, green peppers, and onions, put them on the pumpernickel, and put the open-faced sandwich under the broiler. I kept my back to Bobby and the sergeant while I waited for the cheese to melt, then transferred the whole thing to a plate and poured myself a cup of coffee. From his breathing I could tell Bobby's temper was mounting. His face was red by the time I put my food on the table and straddled a chair opposite him.

"I know very little about the Thayer boy, Bobby," I apologized. "I know he used to be a student at the University of Chicago, and that he's dead now. And I knew he's dead because I read it in the *Sun-Times*."

"Don't be cute with me, Vicki; you know he's dead because you found the body."

I swallowed a mouthful of toasted cheese and green pepper. "Well, I assumed after reading the *Sun-Times* story that the boy was Thayer, but I certainly didn't know that when I saw the body. To me, he seemed to be just another corpse. Snuffed out in the springtime of life," I added piously.

"Spare me his funeral oration and tell me what brought you down there," Mallory demanded.

"You know me, Bobby—I have an instinct for crime. Where evil flourishes, there I will be, on my self-appointed mission to stamp it out."

Mallory turned redder. McGonnigal coughed diffidently and changed the subject before his boss hemorrhaged. "Do you have a client of some kind, Miss Warshawski?" he asked.

Of course I'd seen this one coming, but I still wasn't sure what I wanted to do. However, she who hesitates is lost in the detective biz, so I opted for partial disclosure.

"I was hired to get Peter Thayer to agree to go to business school." Mallory choked. "I'm not lying, Bobby," I said earnestly. "I went down there to meet the kid. And the door to his apartment was open, so I—"

"When you got there or after you'd picked the lock?" Mallory interrupted.

"So I went in," I continued. "Anyway, I guess I failed in my assignment, since I don't think Peter Thayer will ever go to business school. I'm not sure I still have a client."

"Who hired you, Vicki?" Mallory was talking more quietly now. "John Thayer?"

"Now why would John Thayer want to hire me, Bobby?"

"You tell me that, Vicki. Maybe he wanted some dirt to use as a lever to pry the kid off those potheads down there."

I swallowed the rest of my coffee and looked at Mallory squarely. "A guy came to me night before last and told me he was John Thayer. He wanted me to find his son's girl friend, Anita. Anita Hill."

"There's no Anita Hill in that setup," McGonnigal volunteered. "There's an Anita McGraw. It looks like he was sharing a room with a girl, but the whole setup is so unisex you can't tell who was with who."

"Whom," I said absently. McGonnigal looked blank. "You can't tell who was with *whom*, Sergeant," I explained. Mallory made explosive noises. "Anyway," I added hastily, "I was beginning to suspect that the guy had sent me on a wild-goose chase when I found there was no Anita Hill at the university. Later I was sure of it."

"Why?" Mallory demanded.

"I got a copy of Thayer's picture from the Fort Dearborn Bank and Trust. He wasn't my client."

"Vicki," Mallory said. "I think you're a pain in the butt. I think Tony would turn in his grave if he knew what you were doing. But you're not a fool. Don't tell me you didn't ask for any identification."

"He gave me his card and his home phone and a retainer. I figured I could get back to him."

"Let me see the card," Mallory demanded. Suspicious bastard.

"It's his card," I said.

"Could I please see it anyway." Tone of father barely restraining himself with recalcitrant child.

"It won't tell you anything it didn't tell me, Bobby."

"I don't believe he gave you a card," Mallory said. "You knew the guy and you're covering for him."

I shrugged and went to the bedroom and got the card out of my top drawer. I wiped it clean of prints with a scarf and brought it back to Mallory. The Fort Dearborn logo was in the lower left-hand corner. "John L. Thayer, Executive Vice-President, Trust" was in the middle, with his phone number. On the bottom I had scribbled the alleged home number.

Mallory grunted with satisfaction and put it in a plastic bag. I didn't tell him the only prints on it at this point were mine. Why spoil one of his few pleasures?

Mallory leaned forward. "What are you going to do next?"

"Well, I don't know. I got paid some money to find a girl and I feel like I ought to find her."

"You going to ask for a revelation, Vicki?" Mallory said with heavy humor. "Or do you have something to go on?"

"I might talk to some people."

"Vicki, if you know anything that you're not telling me in connection with this murder—"

"You'll be the first to know, Bobby," I promised. That wasn't exactly a lie, because I didn't know for sure that Ajax was involved in the murder—but we all have our own ideas on what's connected to what.

"Vicki, we're on the case. You don't have to prove anything to me about how cute or clever you are. But do me a favor— do a favor for Tony—let Sergeant McGonnigal and me find the murderer."

I stared limpidly at Bobby. He leaned forward earnestly. "Vicki, what did you notice about the body?"

"He'd been shot, Bobby. I didn't do a postmortem."

"Vicki, for two cents I'd kick you in your cute little behind. You've made a career out of something which no nice girl would touch, but you're no dummy. I know when you—got yourself into that apartment—and we'll overlook just how you got in there right now—you didn't scream or throw up, the way any decent girl would. You looked the place over. And if something didn't strike you straight off about that corpus, you deserve to go out and get your head blown off."

I sighed and slouched back in the chair. "Okay, Bobby: the kid was set up. No dope-crazed radical fired that shot. Some-one he knew, whom he would invite to sit down for a cup of coffee, had to be there. To my mind, a pro fired the shot, because it was perfectly done—just one bullet and right on the target—but someone he knew had to be along. Or it could have been an acquaintance who's a heck of a marks-man. . . . You looking into his family?"

Mallory ignored my question. "I figured you'd work that out. It's because you're smart enough to see how dangerous this thing could be that I'm asking you to leave it alone." I yawned. Mallory was determined not to lose his temper.

"Look, Vicki, stay out of that mess. I can smell organized crime, organized labor, a whole lot of organizations that you shouldn't mess with."

"You figure because the boy's got radical friends and waves some posters he's glued into organized labor? Come on, Bobby!"

Mallory's struggle between the desire to get me out of the Thayer case and the need to keep police secrets to himself showed on his face. Finally he said, "We have evidence that the kids were getting some of their posters from a firm which does most of the printing for the Knifegrinders."

I shook my head sorrowfully. "Terrible." The International Brotherhood of Knifegrinders was notorious for their underworld connections. They'd hired muscle in the rough-and-tumble days of the thirties and had never been able to get rid of them since. As a result most of their elections and a lot of their finances were corrupt and—and suddenly it dawned on me who my elusive client was, why Anita McGraw's name sounded familiar, and why the guy had picked me out of the Yellow Pages. I leaned farther back in my chair but said nothing.

Mallory's face turned red. "Vicki, if I find you crossing my path on this case, I'm going to run you in for your own good!" He stood so violently that his chair turned over. He motioned to Sergeant McGonnigal and the two slammed the door behind them.

I poured myself another cup of coffee and took it into the bathroom with me where I dumped a generous dollop of Azuree mineral salts into the tub and ran myself a hot bath. As I sank into it, the aftereffects of my late-night drinking seeping out of my bones, I recalled a night more than twenty years ago. My mother was putting me to bed when the doorbell rang and the man who lived in the apartment below us staggered in. A burly man my dad's age, maybe younger—all big men seem old to little girls. I'd peeped around the door because everyone was making such a commotion and seen him covered with blood before my mother rounded on me and hustled me into the bedroom. She stayed there with me and together we heard snatches of conversation: The man had been shot, possibly by management-hired thugs, but he was afraid to go to the police officially because he'd hired thugs himself, and would my dad help him.

Tony did, fixing up the wound. But he ordered him—unusual in a man usually so gentle—to leave the neighborhood and never come around to us again. The man was Andrew McGraw.

I'd never seen him again, never even connected him with the McGraw who was now president of Local 108 and hence, in effect, of the whole union. But he'd obviously remembered my dad. I guessed he'd tried to reach Tony at the police and, when he'd learned my dad was dead, had pulled me out of the Yellow Pages, assuming I would be Tony's son. Well, I wasn't: I was his daughter, and not the easygoing type my dad had been. I had my Italian mother's drive, and I try to emulate her insistence on fighting battles to the finish. But regardless of what kind of person *I* was, McGraw might be finding himself now in trouble of the kind that not even easygoing Tony would have helped him out of.

I drank some more coffee and flexed my toes in the water. The bath shimmered turquoise, but clear. I peered through it at my feet, trying to figure out what I knew. McGraw had a daughter. She probably loved him, since she seemed dedicated to the labor movement. Children usually do not espouse causes or careers of parents they hate. Had she disappeared, or was he hiding her? Did he know who had killed young Peter and had she run away because of this? Or did he think she'd killed the boy? Most murders, I reminded myself, were committed between loved ones, which made her statistically the odds-on favorite. What were McGraw's connections with the hired muscle with whom the International Brotherhood lived so cozily? How easily could he have hired someone to fire that shot? He was someone the boy would let in and talk to, no matter what their feelings for each other were, because McGraw was his girl friend's father.

The bathwater was warm, but I shivered as I finished my coffee.

FOUR

YOU CAN'T SCARE ME (I'M STICKING TO THE UNION)

The headquarters of the International Brotherhood of Knife-grinders, Shear Edgers, and Blade Sharpeners is located on Sheridan Road just south of Evanston. The ten-story building was put up about five years ago, and is sided with white Italian marble. The only other building in Chicago built with such opulence is the headquarters for Standard of Indiana; I figured that put the brotherhood's excess profits on a par with those of the oil industry.

Local 108 headquarters was on the ninth floor. I gave the floor receptionist my card. "Mr. McGraw is expecting me," I told her. I was shunted down the north corridor. McGraw's secretary was guarding the entrance to a lakeside office in an antechamber that would have done Louis XIV proud. I wondered how the International Brothers felt when they saw what their dues had built for them. Or maybe there were some beaten-up offices lower down for entertaining the rank-and-file.

I gave my card to the secretary, a middle-aged woman with gray sausage curls and a red-and-white dress that revealed an unlovely sag in her upper arms. I keep thinking I should lift five-pound weights to firm up my triceps. Looking at her, I wondered if I would have time to stop at Stan's Sporting Goods on my way home to pick up some barbells.

"I have an appointment with Mr. McGraw."

"You're not in the book," she said abruptly, not really looking at me. I had on my navy raw silk suit, with the blouson jacket. I look stunning in this outfit and thought I deserved a little more attention. Must be those sagging triceps.

I smiled. "I'm sure you know as well as I do that Mr. McGraw conducts some of his business on his own. He arranged to see me privately."

"Mr. McGraw may sometimes take up with whores," she said, her face red, her eyes on her desk top, "but this is the first time he's ever asked one up to his office."

I restrained an impulse to brain her with her desk lamp. "Good-looking lady like you in his front office, he doesn't need outside talent. . . . Now will you please inform Mr. McGraw that I'm here?"

Her shapeless face shook under the thick pancake. "Mr. McGraw is in conference and can't be disturbed." Her voice trembled. I felt like a creep—I couldn't find a girl or a murderer, but I sure knew how to rough up middle-aged secretaries.

McGraw's office was soundproofed, but noise of the conference came into the antechamber. Quite a conference. I was about to announce my intention of sitting and waiting when one sentence rose above the din and penetrated the rosewood door.

"Goddamnit, you set my son up!"

How many people could possibly have sons who might have been set up in the last forty-eight hours and be connected with the Knifegrinders? Maybe more than one, but the odds were against it. With the sausage curls protesting loudly, I opened the door into the inner office.

Not as large as Masters's, but by no means shabby, it overlooked Lake Michigan and a nice little private beach. At the moment it was none too peaceful. Two men had been sitting at a round table in the corner, but one was on his feet yelling to make his point. Even with his face distorted by anger I didn't have any trouble recognizing the original of the picture in the Fort Dearborn Trust's annual report. And rising to his feet and yelling back as I entered was surely my client. Short, squat without being fat, and wearing a shiny gray suit.

They both stopped cold as they saw me.

"What the hell are you doing in here!" my client roared. "Mildred?"

Sausage curls waddled in, her eyes gleaming. "I told her you wouldn't want to see her, but no, she has to come barging in like she's—"

"Mr. McGraw, I am V. I. Warshawski." I pitched my voice to penetrate the din. "And you may not want to see me, but I look like an angel compared to a couple of homicide dicks who're going to be after you pretty soon. . . . Hi, Mr. Thayer," I added, holding out a hand. "I'm sorry about your son—I'm the person who found the body."

"It's all right, Mildred," McGraw said weakly. "I know this lady and I do want to talk to her." Mildred gave me a furious look, then turned and stalked out, shutting the door with what seemed unnecessary violence.

"Mr. Thayer, what makes you think Mr. McGraw set your son up?" I asked conversationally, seating myself in a leather armchair in a corner.

The banker had recovered himself. The anger had smoothed out of his face, leaving it dignified and blank. "McGraw's daughter was going out with my son," he said, smiling a little. "When I learned my boy was dead, had been shot, I just stepped in to see if McGraw knew anything about it. I don't think he set Peter up."

McGraw was too angry to play along with Thayer. "The hell you say," he yelled, his husky voice rising. "Ever since Annie started hanging around with that whey-faced, North Shore pipsqueak, you've been coming around here, calling her names, calling me names. Now the kid is dead, you're trying to smear her! Well, by God you won't get away with it!"

"All right!" Thayer snapped. "If that's the way you want to play ball, that's how we'll play it. Your daughter—I saw the kind of girl she was the first time I set eyes on her. Peter never had a chance—innocent young kid, high ideals, giving up everything his mother and I had planned for him for the sake of a girl who'd hop into bed with—"

"Watch what names you call my daughter," McGraw growled.

"I practically begged McGraw here to leash his daughter," Thayer continued. "I might as well have saved my pride. This type of person doesn't respond to any human feeling. He and his daughter had earmarked Peter for some kind of setup because he came from a wealthy family. Then, when they couldn't get any money out of him, they killed him."

McGraw was turning purple. "Have you shared this theory with the police, Mr. Thayer?" I asked.

"If you have, Thayer, I'll have your ass in court for slander," McGraw put in.

"Don't threaten me, McGraw," Thayer growled. John Wayne impersonation.

"Have you shared this theory with the police, Mr. Thayer?" I repeated.

He flushed slightly under his careful tan. "No, I didn't want it blurted all over the newspapers—I didn't want any of my neighbors to see what the boy was up to."

I nodded. "But you're really convinced that Mr. McGraw here—and/or his daughter—set up Peter and had him shot."

"Yes, I am, damnit!"

"And have you any evidence to support this allegation?" I asked.

"No, he doesn't, goddamnit!" McGraw yelled. "No one could support such a goddamn asshole statement! Anita was in love with that North Shore snot. I told her that it was a colossal mistake. Get involved with the bosses and you get your ass burned. And now look what's happened."

It seemed to me that the bosses had been the ones to get

burned in this case, but I didn't think it would do any good to mention it.

"Did you give Mr. McGraw one of your business cards when you were here before?" I asked Thayer.

"I don't know," he said impatiently. "I probably gave one to his secretary when I arrived. Anyway, what business is it of yours?"

I smiled. "I'm a private investigator, Mr. Thayer, and I'm investigating a private matter for Mr. McGraw here. He showed me one of your business cards the other night, and I wondered where he got it."

McGraw shifted uncomfortably. Thayer stared at him with a look of disbelief. "You showed her one of my cards? Why the hell did you do that? For that matter, why were you talking to a private investigator at all?"

"I had my reasons." McGraw looked embarrassed, but he also looked mean.

"I bet you did," Thayer said heavily. He turned to me. "What are you doing for McGraw?"

I shook my head. "My clients pay for privacy."

"What kinds of things do you investigate?" Thayer asked. "Divorces?"

"Most people think of divorce when they meet a private detective. Frankly divorce is pretty slimy. I do a lot of industrial cases. . . . You know Edward Purcell, the man who used to be chairman of Transicon?"

Thayer nodded. "I know of him anyway."

"I did that investigation. He hired me because his board was pressuring him to find out where the disposable assets were going. Unfortunately he didn't cover his tracks well enough before he hired me." Purcell's subsequent suicide and the reorganization of a badly damaged Transicon had been a ten-day wonder in Chicago.

Thayer leaned over me. "In that case, what are you doing for McGraw?" He lacked McGraw's raw menace, but he, too, was a powerful man, used to intimidating others. The force of his personality was directed at me and I sat up straight to resist it.

"What business is it of yours, Mr. Thayer?"

He gave me the frown that got obedience from his junior trust officers. "If he gave you my card, it's my business."

"It didn't have anything to do with you, Mr. Thayer."

"That's right, Thayer," McGraw growled. "Now get your ass out of my office."

Thayer turned back to McGraw and I relaxed slightly. "You're not trying to smear me with any of your dirty business are you, McGraw?"

"Watch it, Thayer. My name and my operation have been cleared in every court in this country. In Congress too. Don't give me that crap."

"Yeah, Congress cleared you. Lucky, wasn't it, the way Derek Bernstein died right before the Senate hearings began."

McGraw walked right up to the banker. "You SOB. You get out of here now or I'll get some people to throw you out in a way that'll pop your high-and-mighty executive dignity for you."

"I'm not afraid of your thugs, McGraw; don't threaten me."

"Oh, come on," I snapped. "Both of you are tough as all get out, and you're both frightening me to pieces. So can you cut out this little-boy stuff? Why do you care so much about it, Mr. Thayer? Mr. McGraw here may have tossed a business card of yours around—but he hasn't tried to smear your name with his dirty business—if he's got dirty business. You got something on your conscience that's making you so upset? Or do you just have to prove you're the toughest guy in any crowd you're in?"

"Watch what you say to me, young lady. I've got a lot of powerful friends in this city, and they can—"

"That's what I mean," I interrupted. "Your powerful friends can take away my license. No doubt. But why do you care?"

He was silent for a minute. Finally he said, "Just be careful what you get into with McGraw here. The courts may have cleared him, but he's into a lot of ugly business."

"All right; I'll be careful."

He gave me a sour look and left.

McGraw looked at me approvingly. "You handled him just right, Warshawski."

I ignored that. "Why did you give me a fake name the other night, McGraw? And why did you give your daughter a different phony one?"

"How'd you find me, anyway?"

"Once I saw the McGraw name, it began stirring in the back of my mind. I remembered you from the night you were shot—it came back to me when Lieutenant Mallory mentioned the Knifegrinders. Why'd you come to me to begin with? You think my dad might help you out the way he did back then?"

"What are you talking about?"

"Oh, can it, McGraw. I was there. You may not remember me—but I remember you. You came in absolutely covered with blood and my dad fixed up your shoulder and got you out of the building. Did you think he'd help you out of whatever trouble you're in this time, until you found out he was dead? Then what—you found my name in the Yellow Pages and thought maybe I was Tony's son? Now, why did you use Thayer's name?"

The fight died down in him a bit. "I wasn't sure you'd do a job for me if you knew who I was."

"But why Thayer? Why drag in the senior guy in Chicago's biggest bank? Why not just call yourself Joe Blow?"

"I don't know. It was just an impulse, I guess."

"Impulse? You're not that dumb. He could sue you for slander or something, dragging his name in like that."

"Then why the hell did you let him know I'd done it? You're on my payroll."

"No, I'm not. You've hired me to do some independent

professional work, but I'm not on your payroll. Which brings us to the original question: what'd you hire me for, anyway?"

"To find my daughter."

"Then why did you give her a false name? How could I possibly look for her? No. I think you hired me to find the body."

"Now, look here, Warshawski—"

"You look, McGraw. It's so obvious you knew the kid was dead. When did you find out? Or did you shoot him yourself?"

His eyes disappeared in his heavy face and he pushed close to me. "Don't talk smart with me, Warshawski."

My heart beat faster but I didn't back away. "When did you find the body?"

He stared at me another minute, then half-smiled. "You're no softie. I don't object to a lady with guts. . . . I was worried about Anita. She usually calls me on Monday evening, and when she didn't, I thought I should go down and check up on her. You know what a dangerous neighborhood that is."

"You know, Mr. McGraw, it continues to astonish me the number of people who think the University of Chicago is in an unsafe neighborhood. Why parents ever send their children to school there at all amazes me. Now let's have a little more honesty. You knew Anita had disappeared when you came to see me, or you would never have given me her picture. You are worried about her, and you want her found. Do you think she killed the boy?"

That got an explosive reaction. "No, I don't, goddamnit. If you must know, she came home from work Tuesday night and found his dead body. She called me in a panic, and then she disappeared."

"Did she accuse you of killing him?"

"Why should she do that?" He was bellicose but uncomfortable.

"I can think of lots of reasons. You hated young Thayer,

thought your daughter was selling out to the bosses. So in a mistaken fit of paternal anxiety, you killed the kid, thinking it would restore your daughter to you. Instead—"

"You're crazy, Warshawski! No parent is that cuckoo."

I've seen lots of kookier parents but decided not to argue that point. "Well," I said, "you don't like that idea, try this one. Peter somehow got wind of some shady, possibly even criminal, activities that you and the Knifegrinders are involved in. He communicated his fears to Anita, but being in love he wouldn't welch on you to the cops. On the other hand, being young and idealistic, he had to confront you. And he couldn't be bought. You shot him—or had him shot—and Anita knew it had to be you. So she did a bunk."

McGraw's nerves were acting up again, but he blustered and bellowed and called me names. Finally he said, "Why in Sam Hill would I want you to find my daughter if all she'd do is finger me?"

"I don't know. Maybe you were playing the odds—figuring you've been close and she wouldn't turn on you. Trouble is, the police are going to be making the connection between you and Anita before too long. They know the kids had some tie-in with the brotherhood because there was some literature around the house created by your printer. They're not dummies, and everyone knows you're head of the union and they know there was a McGraw in the apartment.

"When they come around, they're not going to care about your daughter, or your relationship with her. They've got a murder to solve, and they'll be happy to tag you with it—especially with a guy in Thayer's position pressuring them. Now if you tell me what you know, I may—no promises, but *may*—be able to salvage you and your daughter—if you're not guilty, of course."

McGraw studied the floor for a while. I realized I'd been clutching the arms of the chair while I was talking and carefully relaxed my muscles. Finally he looked up at me and said, "If I tell you something, will you promise not to take it to the police?"

I shook my head. "Can't promise anything, Mr. McGraw. I'd lose my license if I kept knowledge of a crime to myself."

"Not that kind of knowledge, damnit! Goddamnit, Warshawski, you keep acting like I committed the goddamn murder or something." He breathed heavily for a few minutes. Finally he said, "I just want to tell you about—you're right. I did—I was—I did find the kid's body." He choked that out, and the rest came easier. "Annie—Anita—called me Monday night. She wasn't in the apartment, she wouldn't say where she was." He shifted a bit in his chair. "Anita's a good, levelheaded kid. She never got any special pampering as a child, and she grew up knowing how to be independent. She and I are, well, we're pretty close, and she's always been union all the way, but she's no clinging daddy's girl. And I never wanted her to be one.

"Tuesday night I hardly recognized her. She was pretty damn near hysterical, yelling a lot of half-assed stuff which didn't make any sense at all. But she didn't mention the kid's murder."

"What was she yelling?" I asked conversationally.

"Oh, just nonsense, I couldn't make anything out of it."

"Same song, second verse," I remarked.

"What?"

"Same as the first," I explained. "A little bit louder and a little bit worse."

"Once and for all, she didn't accuse me of killing Peter Thayer!" he yelled at the top of his lungs.

We weren't moving too quickly.

"Okay, she didn't accuse you of murdering Peter. Did she tell you about his being dead?"

He stopped for a minute. If he said yes, the next question was, why had the girl done a bunk if she didn't think McGraw had committed the murder? "No, like I said, she was just hysterical. She— Well, later, after I saw the body, I figured she was calling because of—of, well, that." He stopped again, but this time it was to collect some memories. "She hung up and I tried calling back, but there wasn't any answer, so I went down to see for myself. And I found the boy."

"How'd you get in?" I asked curiously.

"I have a key. Annie gave it to me when she moved in, but I'd never used it before." He fumbled in his pocket and pulled out a key. I looked at it and shrugged.

"That was Tuesday night?" He nodded. "And you waited 'til Wednesday night to come to see me?"

"I waited all day hoping that someone else would find the body. When no report came out—you were right, you know." He smiled ruefully, and his whole face became more attractive. "I hoped that Tony was still alive. I hadn't talked to him for years, he'd warned me off good and proper over the Stellinek episode—didn't know old Tony had it in him—but he was the only guy I could think of who might help me."

"Why didn't you call the cops yourself?" I asked.

His face closed up again. "I didn't want to," he said shortly.

I thought about it. "You probably wanted your own source of information on the case, and you didn't think your police contacts could help you." He didn't disagree.

"Do the Knifegrinders have any pension money tied up with the Fort Dearborn Trust?" I asked.

McGraw turned red again. "Keep your goddamn mitts out of our pension fund, Warshawski. We have enough snoopers smelling around there to guarantee it grade A pure for the next century. I don't need you, too."

"Do you have any financial dealings with the Fort Dearborn Trust?"

He was getting so angry I wondered what nerve I'd touched, but he denied it emphatically.

"What about the Ajax Insurance Company?"

"Well, what about them?" he demanded.

"I don't know, Mr. McGraw—do you buy any insurance from them?"

"I don't know." His face was set and he was eyeing me hard and cold, the way he no doubt had eyed young Timmy Wright of Kansas City Local 4318 when Timmy had tried to talk to him about running a clean election down there. (Timmy had shown up in the Missouri River two weeks later.) It was much more menacing than his red-faced bluster. I wondered.

"Well, what about your pensions? Ajax is big in the pension business."

"Goddamnit, Warshawski, get out of the office. You were hired to find Anita, not to ask a lot of questions about something that isn't any of your goddamned business. Now get out and don't come back."

"You want me to find Anita?" I asked.

McGraw suddenly deflated and put his head in his hands. "Oh, jeez, I don't know what to do."

I looked at him sympathetically. "Someone got you in the squeeze?"

He just shook his head but wouldn't answer. We sat it out in silence for a while. Then he looked at me, and he looked gray. "Warshawski, I don't know where Annie is. And I don't want to know. But I want you to find her. And when you do, just let me know if she's all right. Here's another five hundred dollars to keep you on for a whole week. Come to me when it runs out." It wasn't a formal apology, but I accepted it and left.

I stopped at Barb's Bar-B-Q for some lunch and called my answering service. There was a message from Ralph Devereux at Ajax; would I meet him at the Cartwheel at 7:30 tonight. I called him and asked if he had discovered anything about Peter Thayer's work.

"Look," he said, "will you tell me your first name? How the hell can I keep on addressing someone as 'V.I.'?"

"The British do it all the time. What have you found out?"

"Nothing. I'm not looking—there's nothing to find. That kid wasn't working on sensitive stuff. And you know why— V.I.? Because insurance companies don't run to sensitive stuff. Our product, how we manufacture it, and what we charge for it are only regulated by about sixty-seven state and federal agencies."

"Ralph, my first name is Victoria; my friends call me Vic. Never Vicki. I know insurance isn't your high-sensitivity business—but it offers lots of luscious opportunities for embezzlement."

A pregnant silence. "No," he finally said, "at least—not here. We don't have any check-signing or authorizing responsibility."

I thought that one over. "Do you know if Ajax handles any of the Knifegrinders' pension money?"

"The Knifegrinders?" he echoed. "What earthly connection does that set of hoodlums have with Peter Thayer?"

"I don't know. But do you have any of their pension money?"

"I doubt it. This is an insurance company, not a mob hangout."

"Well, could you find out for me? And could you find out if they buy any insurance from you?"

"We sell all kinds of insurance, Vic—but not much that a union would buy."

"Why not?"

"Look," he said, "it's a long story. Meet me at the Cartwheel at seven thirty and I'll give you chapter and verse on it."

"Okay," I agreed. "But look into it for me, anyway. Please?"

"What's the I stand for?"

"None of your goddamn business." I hung up. I stood for Iphigenia. My Italian mother had been devoted to Victor Emmanuel. This passion and her love of opera had led her to burden me with an insane name.

I drank a Fresca and ordered a chef's salad. I wanted ribs and fries, but the memory of Mildred's sagging arms stopped me. The salad didn't do much for me. I sternly put French fries out of my mind and pondered events.

Anita McGraw had called up and—at a minimum—told her father about the murder. My bet was she'd accused him of being involved. Ergo, Peter had found out something disreputable about the Knifegrinders and had told her. He probably found it out at Ajax, but possibly from the bank. I loved the idea of pensions. The Loyal Alliance Pension Fund got lots of publicity for their handling, or mishandling, of Knifegrinder pension money, but twenty million or so could easily have been laid off on a big bank or insurance company. And pension money gave one so much scope for fraudulent activity.

Why had McGraw gone down to the apartment? Well, in the first place, he knew whatever discreditable secret Thayer had uncovered. He was afraid that Anita was probably in on it—young lovers don't keep much to themselves. And if she called up because she'd found her boyfriend with a hole in his head, McGraw probably figured she'd be next, daughter or no daughter. So he went racing down to Hyde Park, terrified he'd find her dead body too. Instead she'd vanished. So far, so good.

Now if I could find Anita, I'd know the secret. Or if I found the secret, I could publicize it, which would take the heat off the girl and maybe persuade her to return. It sounded good.

What about Thayer, though? Why had McGraw used his card, and why had this upset him so much? Just the principle of the thing? I ought to talk to him alone.

I paid my bill and headed back to Hyde Park. The college Political Science Department was on the fourth floor of one of the older campus buildings. On a hot summer afternoon the hallways were empty. Through the windows along the stairwell I could see knots of students lying on the grass, some reading, some sleeping. A few energetic boys were playing Frisbee. An Irish setter loped around, trying to catch the disk.

A student was tending the desk in the department office. He looked about seventeen, his long blond hair hanging over his forehead, but no beard—he didn't appear ready to grow one yet. He was wearing a T-shirt with a hole under the left arm and was sitting hunched over a book. He looked up reluctantly when I said hello but kept the book open on his lap.

I smiled pleasantly and told him I was looking for Anita McGraw. He gave me a hostile look and turned back to his book without speaking.

"Come on. What's wrong with asking for her? She's a student in the department, right?" He refused to look up. I felt my temper rising, but I wondered if Mallory had been here before me. "Have the police been around asking for her?"

"You ought to know," he muttered, not looking up.

"You think just because I'm not wearing sloppy blue jeans I'm with the police?" I asked. "How about digging out a departmental course list for me?"

He didn't move. I stepped around to his side of the desk and pulled open a drawer.

"Okay, okay," he said huffily. He put the book spine up on the desk top. *Capitalism and Freedom,* by Marcuse. I might have guessed. He rummaged through the drawer and pulled out a nine-page list, typed and mimeographed, labeled "College Time Schedule: Summer 1979."

I flipped through it to the Political Science section. Their summer schedule filled a page. Class titles included such things as "The Concept of Citizenship in Aristotle and Plato"; "Idealism from Descartes Through Berkeley"; and "Superpower Politics and the Idea of *Weltverschwinden.*" Fascinating. Finally I found one that sounded more promising: "The Capitalist Standoff: Big Labor Versus Big Business." Someone who taught a course like that would surely attract a young labor organizer like Anita McGraw. And might even know who some of her friends were. The instructor's name was Harold Weinstein.

I asked the youth where Weinstein's office was. He hunched further into Marcuse and pretended not to hear. I came around the desk again and sat on it facing him, and grabbed his shirt collar and jerked his face up so that I could see his eyes. "I know you think you're doing the revolution a great service by not revealing Anita's whereabouts to the pigs," I said pleasantly. "Perhaps when her body is found in a car trunk you will invite me to the party where you celebrate upholding your code of honor in the face of unendurable oppression." I shook him a bit. "Now tell me where to find Harold Weinstein's office."

"You don't have to tell her anything, Howard," someone said behind me. "And you," he said to me, "don't be surprised when students equate police with fascism—I saw you roughing up that boy."

The speaker was thin with hot brown eyes and a mop of unruly hair. He was wearing a blue work shirt tucked neatly into a pair of khaki jeans.

"Mr. Weinstein?" I said affably, letting go of Howard's shirt. He stared at me with his hands on his hips, brooding. It looked pretty noble. "I'm not with the police—I'm a private detective. And when I ask anyone a civil question, I like to get a civil answer, not an arrogant shrug of the shoulders.

"Anita's father, Andrew McGraw, hired me to find her. I have a feeling, which he shares, that she may be in bad trouble. Shall we go somewhere and talk about it?"

"You have a feeling, do you," he said heavily. "Well, go feel about it somewhere else. We don't like police—public or private—on this campus." He turned to stalk back down the corridor.

"Well executed," I applauded. "You've been studying Al Pacino. Now that you've finished emoting, could we talk about Anita?"

The back of his neck turned red, and the color spread to his ears, but he stopped. "What about her?"

"I'm sure you know she's disappeared, Mr. Weinstein. You may also know that her boyfriend, Peter Thayer, is dead. I am trying to find her in the hopes of keeping her from sharing his fate." I paused to let him absorb it. "My guess is that she's hiding out someplace and she thinks she won't be found by whoever killed him. But I'm afraid she's crossed the path of an ugly type of killer. The kind that has a lot of money and can buy his way past most hideouts."

He turned so that I could see his profile. "Don't worry, Philip Marlowe—they won't bribe me into revealing her whereabouts."

I wondered hopefully if he could be tortured into talking. Aloud, I said, "Do you know where she is?"

"No comment."

"Do you know any of her good friends around here?"

"No comment."

"Gee, you're helpful, Mr. Weinstein—you're my favorite prof. I wish you'd taught here when I went to school." I pulled out my card and gave it to him. "If you ever feel like commenting, call me at this number."

Back outside in the heat I felt depressed. My navy silk suit was stunning, but too heavy for the weather; I was sweating, probably ruining the fabric under the arms. Besides, I seemed to be alienating everyone whose path I crossed. I wished I'd smashed in Howard's face.

A circular stone bench faced the college building. I walked over to it and sat down. Maybe I'd give up on this stupid case. Industrial espionage was more my speed, not a corrupt union and a bunch of snotty kids. Maybe I'd use the thousand dollars McGraw had given me to spend the summer on the Michigan peninsula. Maybe that would make him angry enough to send someone after me with cement leggings.

The Divinity School was just behind me. I sighed, pulled myself to my feet, and moved into its stone-walled coolness.

A coffee shop used to serve overboiled coffee and tepid lemonade in the basement. I made my way downstairs and found the place still in operation. There was something reassuring in this continuity and in the sameness of the young faces behind the makeshift counter. Kindly and naive, they preached a lot of violent dogma, believed that burglars had a right to the goods they took because of their social oppression, and yet would be rocked to their roots if someone ever required them to hold a machine gun themselves.

I took a Coke and retired to a dark corner with it. The chairs weren't comfortable, but I pulled my knees up to my chin and leaned against the wall. About a dozen students were seated around the wobbly tables, some of them trying to read in the dim light, most of them talking. Snatches of conversation reached me. "Of course if you're going to look at it dialectically, the only thing they can do is—" "I told her if she didn't put her foot down he'd—" "Yeah, but Schopenhauer says—" I dozed off.

I was jerked awake a few seconds later by a loud voice saying, "Did you *hear* about Peter Thayer?" I looked up. The speaker, a plump young woman with wild red hair, wearing an ill-fitting peasant blouse, had just come into the room. She dumped her book bag on the floor and joined a table of three in the middle of the room. "I was just coming out of class when Ruth Yonkers told me."

I got up and bought another Coke and sat down at a table behind the redhead.

A thin youth with equally wild but dark hair was saying, "Oh, yeah, the cops were all over the Political Science Office this morning. You know, he was living with Anita McGraw, and she hasn't been seen since Sunday. Weinstein really told them off," he added admiringly.

"Do they think she killed him?" the redhead asked.

A dark, somewhat older woman snorted. "Anita McGraw? I've known her for two years. She might off a cop, but she wouldn't shoot her boyfriend."

"Do you know him, Mary?" the redhead breathed.

"No," Mary answered shortly. "I never met him. Anita belongs to University Women United—that's how I know her. So does Geraldine Harata, her other roommate, but Geraldine's away for the summer. If she wasn't, the cops would probably suspect her. They always pick on women first."

"I'm surprised you let her into UWU if she has a boyfriend," a bearded young man put in. He was heavy and sloppy—his T-shirt gaped, revealing an unlovely expanse of stomach.

Mary looked at him haughtily and shrugged.

"Not everyone in UWU is a lesbian," the redhead bristled.

"With so many men like Bob around, it's hard to understand why not," Mary drawled. The fat youth flushed and muttered something, of which "castrating" was the only word I caught.

"But I never met Anita," the redhead continued. "I only started going to UWU meetings in May. Has she really disappeared, Mary?"

Mary shrugged again. "If the pigs are trying to put Peter Thayer's death off on her, I wouldn't be surprised."

"Maybe she went home," Bob suggested.

"No," the thin youth said. "If she'd done that, the police wouldn't have been around here looking for her."

"Well," Mary said, "I, for one, hope they don't catch up with her." She got up. "I have to go listen to Bertram drone on about medieval culture. One more crack about witches as hysterical women and he'll find himself attacked by some after class."

She hoisted a knapsack over her left shoulder and ambled off. The others settled closer to the table and switched to an animated discussion of homo- versus heterosexual relationships. Poor Bob favored the latter, but didn't seem to get many opportunities for actively demonstrating it. The thin boy vigorously defended lesbianism. I listened in amusement. College students had enthusiastic opinions about so many topics. At four the boy behind the counter announced he was closing. People started gathering up their books. The three I was listening to continued their discussion for a few minutes until the counterman called over, "Hey, folks, I want to get out of here."

They reluctantly picked up their book bags and moved toward the stairs. I threw out my paper cup and slowly followed them out. At the top of the stairs I touched the redhead's arm. She stopped and looked at me, her face friendly and ingenuous.

"I heard you mention UWU," I said. "Can you tell me where they meet?"

"Are you new on campus?" she asked.

"I'm an old student, but I find I have to spend some time down here this summer," I answered truthfully.

"Well, we have a room in a building at fifty-seven thirty-five University. It's one of those old homes the university has taken over. UWU meets there on Tuesday nights, and other women's activities go on during the rest of the week."

I asked her about their women's center. It was clearly not large, but better than nothing at all, which was what we'd had in my college days when even women radicals treated women's liberation as a dirty phrase. They had a women's health counseling group, courses on self-defense, and they sponsored rap groups and the weekly University Women United meetings.

We had been moving across campus toward the Midway, where my car was parked. I offered her a ride home and she flung herself puppylike into the front seat, talking vigorously if ingenuously about women's oppression. She wanted to know what I did.

"Free-lance work, mostly for corporations," I said, expecting more probing, but she took that happily enough, asking if I would be taking photographs. I realized she assumed that I must be a free-lance writer. I was afraid if I told her the truth, she would tell everyone at UWU and make it impossible for me to find any answers about Anita. Yet I didn't want to tell glaring lies, because if the truth did come out, these young radical women would be even more hostile. So I said "no photographs" and asked her if she did any photography herself. She was still chattering cheerfully when we pulled up in front of her apartment.

"I'm Gail Sugarman," she announced as she struggled clumsily out of the car.

"How do you do, Gail," I replied politely. "I'm V. I. Warshawski."

"Veeyai!" she exclaimed. "What an unusual name. Is it African?"

"No," I answered gravely, "it's Italian." Driving off, I could see her in the rearview mirror, scrambling up the front steps of her apartment. She made me feel incredibly old. Even at twenty I had never possessed that naive, bouncing friendliness; and now it made me feel cynical and remote. In fact, I felt a bit ashamed of deceiving her.

FIVE

GOLD COAST BLUES

Lake Shore Drive, long one large pothole, was being dug up and repaired. Only two northbound lanes were open and the traffic was backed up for miles. I decided to cut off onto the Stevenson Expressway going west, and then back north on the Kennedy, which went up the industrial North Side toward the airport. The rush-hour traffic was exacerbated by the load of people trying to get out of town on a stifling Friday night. It took me over an hour to fight my way to the Belmont exit, and then fifteen blocks east to my apartment. By the time I got there, all I could think of was a tall, cool drink and a long, soothing shower.

I hadn't noticed anyone coming up the stairs behind me, and was turning my key in the lock when I felt an arm on my shoulder. I'd been mugged once before in this hallway. Whirling reflexively, I snapped my knee and kicked in one motion, delivering directly onto my assailant's exposed shinbone. He grunted and backed off but came back with a solid punch aimed at my face. I ducked and took it on the left shoulder. A lot of the zip was gone, but it shook me a little and I drew away.

He was a short, stocky man, wearing an ill-fitting plaid jacket. He was panting a little, which pleased me: it meant he was out of shape, and a woman has better odds against an out-of-shape man. I waited for him to move or run away. Instead he drew a gun. I stood still.

"If this is a holdup, I only have thirteen dollars in my purse. Not worth killing for."

"I'm not interested in your money. I want you to come with me."

"Come with you where?" I asked.

"You'll find out when we get there." He waved the gun at me and pointed down the stairs with his other arm.

"Beats me why well-paid hoods always dress so sloppily," I commented. "Your jacket doesn't fit, your shirt's untucked—you look like a mess. Now if you were a policeman, I could understand it; they—"

He cut me off with an enraged bellow. "I don't need a god-damn broad to tell me how to dress!" He seized my arm with unnecessary force and started to hustle me down the stairs. He was holding me too close, though. I was able to turn slightly and bring my hand up with a short, strong chop under his gun wrist. He let go of me but didn't drop the gun. I followed through with a half-turn that brought my right elbow under his armpit and made a wedge of my right fist and forearm. I drove it into his ribs with my left hand, palm open, and heard a satisfying *pop* that told me I'd hit home between the fifth and sixth ribs and separated them. He yelled in pain and dropped the gun. I reached for it, but he had enough sense to step on my hand. I butted him in the stomach with my head and he let go, but I was off balance and sat down hard. Someone was clattering up the stairs behind me and I only had time to swing my foot and kick the gun away before turning to see who it was.

I thought it might be a neighbor, roused by the noise, but it seemed to be a partner, dressed nearly to match the first hood but bigger. He saw his buddy leaning against the wall, moaning, and hurled himself onto me. We rolled and I got both hands under his chin, forcing his neck back. He let go, but clobbered me on the right side of my head. It shook me all the way down my back, but I didn't give in to it. I kept rolling and leaped up with my back to the wall. I didn't want to give him time to draw a gun, so I grasped the paneling behind me for leverage and swung my feet at his chest, knocking him off balance, but falling on top of him. He got another good punch in, to my shoulder, just missing the jaw, before I wiggled away. He was stronger, but I was in better shape and more agile, and I was on my feet way in advance of him, kicking him hard over his left kidney. He collapsed at that, and I was hauling back to do it again when his partner recovered himself enough to pick up his gun and clip me under the left ear. My kick connected at the same time and then I was falling, falling, but remembering to fall rolling, and rolling off the edge of the world.

I wasn't out long but long enough for them to hustle me downstairs. Good work for two partially disabled men. I guessed any neighbors alerted by the sound had turned up their TVs to drown it out.

I regained a sickly sort of consciousness as they pushed me into the car, fought to hold it, threw up on one of them, and went under again. I came back more slowly the second time. We were still moving. The one with the separated ribs was driving; I'd thrown up on the other one, and the smell was rather strong. His face was very set and I thought he might be close to tears. It's not nice for two men to go after one woman and only get her after losing a rib and a kidney, and then to have her vomit down your jacket front and not be able to move or clean it off—I wouldn't have liked it, either. I fumbled in my jacket pocket for some Kleenex. I still felt sick, too sick to talk and not much like cleaning him up, either, so I dropped the tissues on him and leaned back. He gave a little squeal of rage and knocked them to the floor.

When we stopped, we were close to North Michigan Avenue, just off Astor on Division, in the area where rich people live in beautiful old Victorian houses and apartments or enormous high-rise modern condominiums. My right-hand partner flung himself out the door, took off his jacket, and dropped it in the street.

"Your gun's showing," I told him. He looked down at it, then at his jacket. His face turned red. "You goddamn bitch," he said. He leaned into the car to take another poke at me, but the angle wasn't good and he couldn't get much leverage behind his arm.

Ribs spoke up. "Come on, Joe—it's getting late and Earl don't like to be kept waiting." This simple statement worked powerfully on Joe. He stopped swinging and yanked me out of the car, with Ribs pushing me from the side.

We went into one of the stately old houses that I always thought I'd like to own if I ever rescued an oil-tanker billionaire from international kidnappers and got set up for life as my reward. It was dull red brick, with elegant wrought-iron railing up the steps and around the front windows. Originally built as a single-family home, it was now a three-flat apartment. A cheerful black-and-white patterned wallpaper covered the entry hall and stairwell. The bannister was carved wood, probably walnut, and beautifully polished. The three of us made an ungainly journey up the carpeted stairs to the second floor. Ribs was having trouble moving his arms, and Joe seemed to be limping from his kidney kicks. I wasn't feeling very well myself.

The second-floor apartment was opened by yet another gun-carrier. His clothes fit him better, but he didn't really look like the class of person that belonged in this neighborhood. He had a shock of black hair that stood up around his head in a wiry bush. On his right cheek was a deep red scar, cut roughly like a Z. It was so dark that it looked as though someone had painted him with lipstick.

"What kept you two so long? Earl's getting angry," he demanded, ushering us into a wide hallway. Plush brown carpet on the floor, a nice little Louis Quinze side table, and a few pictures on the walls. Charming.

"Earl warned us this goddamn Warshawski bitch was a wise-ass, but he didn't say she was a goddamn karate expert." That was Ribs. He pronounced my name "Worchotsi." I looked down at my hands modestly.

"Is that Joe and Freddie?" a nasal tenor squeaked from inside. "What the hell took you guys so long?" Its owner appeared in the doorway. Short, pudgy, and bald, he was familiar to me from my early days in Chicago law enforcement.

"Earl Smeissen. How absolutely delightful. But you know, Earl, if you'd called me up and asked to see me, we could have gotten together with a lot less trouble."

"Yeah, Warchoski, I just bet we would've," he said heavily. Earl had carved himself a nice little niche on the North Side with classy prostitution setups for visiting conventioneers, and a little blackmail and extortion. He had a small piece of the drug business, and the rumor was that he would arrange a killing to oblige a friend if the price was right.

"Earl, this is quite a place you've got. Inflation must not be hurting business too much."

He ignored me. "Where the hell's your jacket, Joe? You been walking around Chicago showing your gun to every cop on the beat?"

Joe turned red again and started to mutter something. I intervened. "I'm afraid that's my fault, Earl. Your friends here jumped me in my own hallway without introducing themselves or saying they had come from you. We had a bit of a fracas, and Freddie's ribs got separated—but he pulled himself together nicely and knocked me out. When I came to, I was sick on Joe's jacket. So don't blame the poor fellow for ditching it."

Earl turned outraged to Freddie, who shrank back down the hall. "You let a goddamn dame bust your ribs?" he yelled, his voice breaking to a squeak. "The money I pay you and you can't do a simple little job like fetch a goddamn broad?"

One of the things I hate about my work is the cheap swearing indulged in by cheap crooks. I also hate the word *broad*. "Earl, could you reserve your criticisms of your staff until I'm not here? I have an engagement this evening—I'd appreciate it if you told me why you wanted to see me so badly you sent two hoods to get me, so I can get there on time."

Earl gave Freddie a vicious look and sent him off to see a doctor. He motioned the rest of us into the living room, and noticed Joe limping. "You need a doctor, too? She break your leg?" he asked sarcastically.

"Kidneys," I replied modestly. "It all comes from knowing how."

"Yeah, I know about you, Warchoski. I know what a wise-ass you are, and I heard how you offed Joe Correl. If Freddie knocked you out, I'll give him a medal. I want you to understand you can't mess around with me."

I sank down into a wide armchair. My head was throbbing and it hurt to focus on him. "I'm not messing around with you, Earl," I said earnestly. "I'm not interested in prostitution or juice loans or—"

He hit me across the mouth. "Shut up." His voice rose to a squeak and his eyes got smaller in his pudgy face. In a detached way I felt some blood dribbling down my chin—he must have caught me with his ring.

"Is this a general warning, then? Are you hauling in all the private eyes in Chicago and saying 'Now hear this—don't mess around with Earl Smeissen!'?"

He swung at me again, but I blocked him with my left arm. He looked at his hand in surprise, as if he wondered what had happened to it.

"Don't clown with me, Warchoski—I can call in plenty of people to wipe that smirk off your face."

"I don't think it would take very many," I said, "but I still don't have any idea what part of your turf I'm messing in."

Earl signaled to the doorman, who came and held my shoulders against the chair. Joe was hovering in the background, a lascivious look on his face. My stomach turned slightly.

"Okay, Earl, I'm terrified," I said.

He hit me again. I was going to look like absolute hell to-morrow, I thought. I hoped I wasn't shaking; my stomach was knotted with nervousness. I took several deep diaphragm breaths to try to relieve the tension.

The last slap seemed to satisfy Earl. He sat down on a dark couch close to my chair.

"Warchoski," he squeaked, "I called you down here to tell you to lay off the Thayer case."

"You kill the boy, Earl?" I asked.

He was on his feet again. "I can mark you good, so good that no one will ever want to look at your face again," he shouted. "Now just do what I say and keep your mitts outta that."

I decided not to argue with him—I didn't feel in any shape to take on both him and the doorman, who continued to hold my shoulders back. I wondered if his scar had turned redder with all the excitement but voted against asking him.

"Suppose you do scare me off? What about the police?" I objected. "Bobby Mallory's hot on the trail, and whatever his faults, you can't buy Bobby."

"I'm not worried about Mallory," Earl's voice was back in its normal register, so I concluded the brainstorm was passing. "And I'm not buying you—I'm telling you."

"Who got you involved, Earl? College kids aren't part of your turf—unless young Thayer was cutting into your dope territory?"

"I thought I'd just told you not to pry into my affairs," he said, getting up again. Earl was determined to pound me. Maybe it would be better to get it over with quickly and get out, rather than let him go on for hours. As he came at me, I pulled my foot back and kicked him squarely in the crotch. He howled in anguish and collapsed in a heap on the couch. "Get her, Tony, get her," he squealed.

I didn't have a chance against Tony, the doorman. He was trained in the art of working over loan defaulters without showing a mark. When he finished, Earl came hobbling over from the couch. "This is just a taste, Warchoski," he hissed. "You lay off the Thayer case. Agreed?"

I looked at him without speaking. He really could kill me and get away with it—he'd done it to others. He had good connections with City Hall and probably in the police department too. I shrugged and winced. He seemed to accept that as agreement. "Get her out, Tony."

Tony dumped me unceremoniously outside the front door. I sat for a few minutes on the stairs, shivering in the heat and trying to pull myself together. I was violently ill over the railing, which cleared my headache a bit. A woman walking by with a man said, "Disgusting so early in the evening. The police should keep people like that out of this neighborhood." I agreed. I got to my feet, rather wobbly, but I could walk. I felt my arms. They were sore, but nothing was broken. I staggered over to the inner drive, parallel to Lake Shore Drive and only a block away, and hailed a taxi home. The first one pulled off after a look at me, but the second one took me. The driver clucked and fussed like a Jewish mother, wanting to know what I'd done to myself and offering to take me to a hospital or the police or both. I thanked him for his concern but assured him I was all right.

SIX

IN THE COOL
OF THE NIGHT

I'd dropped my purse by my door when Freddie and I were scuffling, and asked the cabdriver to come upstairs with me to get paid off. Living at the top of the building, I was pretty confident that my bag would still be there. It was, and my keys were still in the door.

The driver tried one last protest. "Thanks," I said, "but I just need a hot bath and a drink and I'll be all right."

"Okay, lady." He shrugged. "It's your funeral." He took his money, looked at me one last time, and went downstairs.

My apartment lacked the splendor of Earl's. My little hallway had a small rug, not wall-to-wall carpeting, and an umbrella stand rather than a Louis Quinze table. But it also wasn't filled with thugs.

I was surprised to find it was only seven. It had been only an hour and a half since I had come up the stairs the first time that evening. I felt as though I'd moved into a different time zone. I ran a bath for the second time that day and poured myself an inch of Scotch. I soaked in water as hot as I could bear it, lying in the dark with a wet towel wrapped around my head. Gradually my headache dissipated. I was very, very tired.

After thirty minutes of soaking and reheating the tub, I felt able to cope with some motion. Wrapping a large towel around me, I walked through the apartment, trying to keep my muscles from freezing on me. All I really wanted to do was sleep, but I knew if I did that now I wouldn't be able to

walk for a week. I did some exercises, gingerly, fortifying myself with Black Label. Suddenly I caught sight of a clock and
remembered my date with Devereux. I was already late and
wondered if he was still there.

With an effort I found the restaurant's name in the phone
book and dialed their number. The maître d'hôtel was very
cooperative and offered to look for Mr. Devereux in the bar.
A few minutes passed, and I began to think he must have
gone home when he came onto the line.

"Hello, Ralph."

"This had better be good."

"If I tried explaining it, it would take hours and you still
wouldn't believe me," I answered. "Will you give me another
half hour?"

He hesitated; I guessed he was looking for the pride to say
no—good-looking guys aren't used to being stood up. "Sure,"
he said finally. "But if you're not here by eight thirty, you can
find your own way home."

"Ralph," I said, controlling my voice carefully, "this has
been one absolute zero of a day. I'd like to have a pleasant
evening, learn a little bit about insurance, and try to forget
what's gone before. Can we do that?"

He was embarrassed. "Sure, Vicki—I mean Vic. See you in
the bar."

We hung up and I looked through my wardrobe for something elegant enough for the Cartwheel, but loose and flowing, and found a string-colored Mexican dress that I'd
forgotten about. It was two-piece, with a long full skirt and a
woven, square-necked top that tied at the waist and bloused
out below. The long sleeves covered my puffy arms and I
didn't have to wear pantyhose or a slip. Cork sandals completed the costume.

Surveying my face under the bathroom light made me
want to reconsider going out in public. My lower lip was
swollen where Earl's pinky ring had sliced it, and a purple

smudge was showing on my left jaw, extending veinous red lines like a cracked egg along my cheek to the eye.

I tried some makeup; my base wasn't very heavy and didn't conceal the worst of the purple but did cover the spidery red marks. Heavy shadow took the focus from an incipient black eye, and dark lipstick, applied more strongly than my usual style, made the swollen lip look pouty and sexy—or might if the lights were dim enough.

My legs were stiffening up, but my daily runs seemed to be paying off—I negotiated the stairs without more than minor tremors. A taxi was going by on Halsted; it dropped me in front of the Hanover House Hotel on Oak Street at 8:25.

This was my first visit to the Cartwheel. To me it typified the sterile place where bright, empty North Siders with more money than sense liked to eat. The bar, to the left of the entrance, was dark, with a piano amplified too loudly, playing songs that bring tears to the eyes of Yale graduates. The place was crowded, Friday night in Chicago. Ralph sat at the end of the bar with a drink. He looked up as I came in, smiled, sketched a wave, but didn't get up. I concentrated on walking smoothly, and made it to where he sat. He looked at his watch. "You just made it."

In more ways than one, I thought. "Oh, you'd never have left without finishing your drink." There weren't any empty stools. "How about proving you're a more generous soul than I and letting me have that seat and a Scotch?"

He grinned and grabbed me, intending to pull me onto his lap. A spasm of pain shot through my ribs. "Oh, Jesus, Ralph! Don't!"

He let go of me at once, got up stiffly and quietly, and offered me the barstool. I stood, feeling awkward. I don't like scenes, and I didn't feel like using the energy to calm Ralph down. He'd seemed like a guy made for sunshine; maybe his divorce had made him insecure with women. I saw I'd have to tell him the truth and put up with his sympathy. And I didn't want to reveal how badly Smeissen had shown me up that afternoon. It was no comfort that he would limp in pain for a day or two.

I dragged my attention back to Ralph. "Would you like me to take you home?" he was asking.

"Ralph, I'd like a chance to explain some things to you. I know it must look as though I don't want to be here, showing up an hour late and all. Are you too upset for me to tell you about it?"

"Not at all," he said politely.

"Well, could we go someplace and sit down? It's a little confusing and hard to do standing up."

"I'll check on our table." When he went off, I sank gratefully onto the barstool and ordered a Johnnie Walker Black. How many could I drink before they combined with my tired muscles and put me to sleep?

Ralph came back with the news that our table was a good ten-minute wait away. The ten stretched into twenty, while I sat with my uninjured cheek propped on my hand and he stood stiffly behind me. I sipped my Scotch. The bar was over-air-conditioned. Normally the heavy cotton of the dress would have kept me plenty warm, but now I started to shiver slightly.

"Cold?" Ralph asked.

"A little," I admitted.

"I could put my arms around you," he offered tentatively.

I looked up at him and smiled. "That would be very nice," I said. "Just do it gently, please."

He crossed his arms around my chest. I winced a little at first, but the warmth and the pressure felt good. I leaned back against him. He looked down at my face, and his eyes narrowed.

"Vic, what's wrong with your face?"

I raised an eyebrow. "Nothing's wrong."

"No, really," he said, bending closer, "you've gotten cut— and that looks like a bruise and swelling on your cheek."

"Is it really bad?" I asked. "I thought the makeup covered it pretty well."

"Well, they're not going to put you on the cover of *Vogue* this week, but it's not too awful. It's just that as an old claims man I've seen lots of accident victims. And you look like one."

"I feel like one too," I agreed, "but really, this wasn't—"

"Have you been to a doctor about this?" he interrupted.

"You sound just like the cabbie who took me home this afternoon. He wanted to rush me to Passavant—I practically expected him to come in with me and start making me chicken soup."

"Was your car badly damaged?" he asked.

"My car is not damaged at all." I was beginning to lose my temper—irrationally, I knew—but the probing made me feel defensive.

"Not damaged," he echoed, "then how—"

At that moment our table was announced in the bar. I got up and went over to the headwaiter, leaving Ralph to pay for drinks. The headwaiter led me off without waiting for Ralph, who caught up with us just as I was being seated. My spurt of temper had infected him; he said, "I hate waiters who haul off ladies without waiting for their escorts." He was just loud enough for the maître d' to hear. "I'm sorry, sir—I didn't realize you were with madame," he said with great dignity before moving off.

"Hey, Ralph, take it easy," I said gently. "A little too much ego-jockeying is going on—my fault as much as yours. Let's stop and get some facts and start over again."

A waiter materialized. "Would you care for a drink before dinner?"

Ralph looked up in irritation. "Do you know how many hours we've spent in the bar waiting for this table? No, we don't want a drink—at least, I don't." He turned to me. "Do you?"

"No, thanks," I agreed. "Any more and I'll fall asleep—

which will probably ruin forever any chance I have of making you believe that I'm not trying to get out of an evening with you."

Were we ready to order? the waiter persisted. Ralph told him roundly to go away for five minutes. My last remark had started to restore his native good humor, however. "Okay, V. I. Warshawski—convince me that you really aren't trying to make this evening so awful that I'll never ask you out again."

"Ralph," I said, watching him carefully, "do you know Earl Smeissen?"

"Who?" he asked uncomprehendingly. "Is this some kind of detective guessing game?"

"Yeah, I guess so," I answered. "Between yesterday afternoon and this afternoon I've talked to a whole lot of different people who either knew Peter Thayer or his girl friend—the gal who's vanished. You and your boss, among others.

"Well, when I got home late this afternoon, two hired thugs were waiting for me. We fought. I was able to hold them off for a while, but one of them knocked me out. They took me to Earl Smeissen's home. If you don't know Earl, don't try to meet him. He was just starting to muscle to the top of his racket—extortion, prostitution—when I was with the Public Defender ten years ago, and he seems to have kept right on trucking since then. He now has a stable of tough guys who all carry guns. He is not a nice person."

I stopped to marshal my presentation. From the corner of my eye I saw the waiter shimmering up again, but Ralph waved him away. "Anyway, he ordered me off the Thayer case, and set one of his tame goons on me to back it up." I stopped. What had happened next in Earl's apartment was very raw in my mind. I had calculated it carefully at the time, decided that it was better to get everything over at once and convince Earl that I was scared than to sit there all evening while he took increasingly violent shots at me. Nonetheless, the thought of being so helpless, the memory of Tony beating me, like a disloyal whore or a welching loan customer—to be so vulnerable was close to unbearable. Unconsciously, my left hand had clenched, and I realized I was slicing it against the tabletop. Ralph was watching me, an uncertain look on his face. His business and suburban life hadn't prepared him for this kind of emotion.

I shook my head and tried for a lighter touch. "Anyway, my rib cage is a little sore—which is why I winced and yelled when you grabbed hold of me in the bar. The question that's exercising me, though, is who told Earl that I'd been around asking questions. Or more precisely, who cared so much that I'd been around that he asked—or paid—Earl to frighten me off."

Ralph was still looking a little horrified. "Have you been to the police about this?"

"No," I said impatiently. "I can't go to the police about this kind of thing. They know I'm interested in the case—they've asked me to get off, too, although more politely. If Bobby Mallory—the lieutenant in charge of the case—knew I'd been beaten up by Earl, Smeissen would deny the whole thing, and if I could prove it in court, he could say it was a million things other than this that made him do it. And Mallory wouldn't give me an earful of sympathy—he wants me out of there anyway."

"Well, don't you think he's right? Murder really is a police matter. And this group seems pretty wild for you to be mixed up with."

I felt a quick surge of anger, the anger I get when I feel someone is pushing me. I smiled with an effort. "Ralph, I'm tired and I ache. I can't try explaining to you tonight why this is my job—but please believe that it is my job and that I can't give it to the police and run away. It's true I don't know specifically what's going on here, but I do know the temperament and reactions of a guy like Smeissen. I usually only deal with white-collar criminals—but when they're cornered, they're not much different from an extortion artist like Smeissen."

"I see." Ralph paused, thinking, then his attractive grin came. "I have to admit that I don't know much about crooks of any kind—except the occasional swindlers who try to rip off insurance companies. But we fight them in the courts, not with hand-to-hand combat. I'll try to believe you know what you're up to, though."

I laughed a little embarrassedly. "Thanks. I'll try not to act too much like Joan of Arc—getting on a horse and charging around in all directions."

The waiter was back, looking a little intimidated. Ralph ordered baked oysters and quail, but I opted for Senegalese soup and spinach salad. I was too exhausted to want a lot of food.

We talked about indifferent things for a while. I asked Ralph if he followed the Cubs. "For my sins, I'm an ardent fan," I explained. Ralph said he caught a game with his son every now and then. "But I don't see how anyone can be an ardent Cub fan. They're doing pretty well right now—cleaned out the Reds—but they'll fade the way they always do. No, give me the Yankees."

"Yankees!" I expostulated. "I don't see how anyone can root for them—it's like rooting for the Cosa Nostra. You know they've got the money to buy the muscle to win—but that doesn't make you cheer them on."

"I like to see sports played well," Ralph insisted. "I can't stand the clowning around that Chicago teams do. Look at the mess Veeck's made of the White Sox this year."

We were still arguing about it when the waiter brought the first course. The soup was excellent—light, creamy, with a hint of curry. I started feeling better and ate some bread and butter, too. When Ralph's quail arrived, I ordered another bowl of soup and some coffee.

"Now explain to me why a union wouldn't buy insurance from Ajax."

"Oh, they could," Ralph said, his mouth full. He chewed and swallowed. "But it would only be for their head-quarters—maybe fire coverage on the building, Workers Compensation for the secretaries, things like that. There wouldn't be a whole lot of people to cover. And a union like the Knifegrinders—see, they get their insurance where they work. The big thing is Workers Comp, and that's paid for by the company, not the union."

"That covers disability payments, doesn't it?" I asked.

"Yes, or death if it's job-related. Medical bills even if there isn't lost time. I guess it's a funny kind of setup. Your rates depend on the kind of business you conduct—a factory pays more than an office, for instance. But the insurance company can be stuck with weekly payments for years if a guy is dis-abled on the job. We have some cases—not many, fortu-nately—that go back to 1927. But see, the insured doesn't pay more, or not that much more, if we get stuck with a whole lot of disability payments. Of course, we can cancel the insurance, but we're still required to cover any disabled workers who are already collecting.

"Well, this is getting off the subject. The thing is, there are lots of people who go on disability who shouldn't—it's pretty cushy and there are plenty of corrupt doctors—but it's hard to imagine a full-scale fraud connected with it that would do anyone else much good." He ate some more quail. "No, your real money is in pensions, as you suggested, or maybe life insurance. But it's easier for an insurance company to com-mit fraud with life insurance than for anyone else. Look at the Equity Funding case."

"Well, could your boss be involved in something like that? Rigging phony policies with the Knifegrinders providing dummy policyholders?" I asked.

"Vic, why are you working so hard to prove that Yardley's

a crook? He's really not a bad guy—I've worked for him for three years, and I've never heard anything against him."

I laughed at that. "It bugs me that he agreed to see me so easily. I don't know a lot about insurance, but I've been around big corporations before. He's a department head, and they're like gynecologists—their schedules are always booked for about twice as many appointments as they can realistically handle."

Ralph clutched his head. "You're making me dizzy, Vic, and you're doing it on purpose. How can a claim department head possibly be like a gynecologist!"

"Yeah, well, you get the idea. Why would he agree to see me? He'd never heard of me, he has wall-to-wall appointments—but he didn't even take phone calls while we were talking."

"Yes, but you knew Peter was dead, and he didn't—so you were expecting him to behave in a certain guilty way and that's what you saw," Ralph objected. "He might have been worried about him, about Peter, because he'd promised Jack Thayer that he'd be responsible for the boy. I don't really see anything so surprising in Yardley's talking to you. If Peter had been just a stray kid, I might—but an old family friend's son? The kid hadn't been in for four days, he wasn't answering the phone—Yardley felt responsible as much as annoyed."

I stopped, considering. What Ralph said made sense. I wondered if I had gotten carried away, whether my instinctive dislike of over-hearty businessmen was making me see ghosts where there were none.

"Okay, you could be right. But why couldn't Masters be involved in a life-insurance fiddle?"

Ralph was finishing off his quail and ordering coffee and dessert. I asked for a large dish of ice cream. "Oh, that's the way insurance companies are set up," he said when the waiter had disappeared again. "We're big—third largest in total premiums written, which is about eight point four billion dollars a year. That includes all lines, and all of the thirteen companies that make up the Ajax group. For legal reasons, life insurance can't be written by the same company that writes property and casualty. So the Ajax Assurance Company does all our life and pension products, while the Ajax Casualty and some of the smaller ones do property and casualty."

The waiter returned with our desserts. Ralph was having some kind of gooey torte. I decided to get Kahlua for my ice cream.

"Well, with a company as big as ours," Ralph continued, "the guys involved in casualty—that's stuff like Workers Comp, general liability, some of the auto—anyway, guys like Yardley and me don't know too much about the life side of the house. Sure, we know the people who run it, eat with them now and then, but they have a separate administrative structure, handle their own claims and so on. If we got close enough to the business to analyze it, let alone commit fraud with it, the political stink would be so high we'd be out on our butts within an hour. Guaranteed."

I shook my head reluctantly and turned to my ice cream. Ajax did not sound promising, and I'd been pinning hopes to it. "By the way," I said, "did you check on Ajax's pension money?"

Ralph laughed. "You are persistent, Vic, I'll grant you that. Yeah, I called a friend of mine over there. Sorry, Vic. Nothing doing. He says he'll look into it, see whether we get any third-hand stuff laid off on us—" I looked a question. "Like the Loyal Alliance people give some money to Dreyfus to manage and Dreyfus lays some of it off on us. Basically though, this guy says Ajax won't touch the Knifegrinders with a ten-foot pole. Which doesn't surprise me too much."

I sighed and finished my ice cream, feeling suddenly tired again. If things came easily in this life, we would never feel pride in our achievements. My mother used to tell me that, standing over me while I practiced the piano. She'd probably disapprove of my work, if she were alive, but she would never let me slouch at the dinner table grumbling because it wasn't turning out right. Still, I was too tired tonight to try to grapple with the implications of everything I'd learned today.

"You look like your adventures are catching up with you," Ralph said.

I felt a wave of fatigue sweep over me, almost carrying me off to sleep with it. "Yeah, I'm fading," I admitted. "I think I'd better go to bed. Although in a way I hate to go to sleep, I'll be so sore in the morning. Maybe I could wake up enough to dance. If you keep moving, it's not so bad."

"You look like you'd fall asleep on a disco floor right now, Vic, and I'd be arrested for beating you or something. Why does exercise help?"

"If you keep the blood circulating, it keeps the joints from stiffening so much."

"Well, maybe we could do both—sleep and exercise, I mean." The smile in his eyes was half embarrassed, half pleased.

I suddenly thought that after my evening with Earl and Tony, I'd like the comfort of someone in bed with me. "Sure," I said, smiling back.

Ralph called to the waiter for the bill and paid it promptly, his hands shaking slightly. I considered fighting him for it, especially since I could claim it as a business expense, but decided I'd done enough fighting for one day.

We waited outside for the doorman to fetch the car. Ralph stood close to me, not touching me, but tense. I realized he had been planning this ending all along and hadn't been sure he could carry it off, and I smiled a little to myself in the dark. When the car came, I sat close to him on the front seat. "I live on Halsted, just north of Belmont," I said, and fell asleep on his shoulder.

He woke me up at the Belmont-Halsted intersection and asked for the address. My neighborhood is just north and west of a smarter part of town and there is usually good parking on the street; he found a place across from my front door.

It took a major effort to pull myself out of the car. The night air was warm and comforting and Ralph steadied me with shaking hands as we crossed the street and went into my front hallway. The three flights up looked very far away and I had a sudden mental flash of sitting on the front steps waiting for my dad to come home from work and carry me upstairs. If I asked Ralph to, he would carry me up. But it would alter the dependency balance in the relationship too much. I set my teeth and climbed the stairs. No one was lying in wait at the top.

I went into the kitchen and pulled a bottle of Martell from the liquor cupboard. I got two glasses down, two of my mother's Venetian glasses, part of the small dowry she had brought to her marriage. They were a beautiful clear red with twisted stems. It had been a long time since I had had anyone up to my apartment, and I suddenly felt shy and vulnerable. I'd been overexposed to men today and wasn't ready to do it again in bed.

When I brought the bottle and glasses back to the living room, Ralph was sitting on the couch, leafing through *Fortune* without reading it. He got up and took the glasses from me, admiring them. I explained that my mother had left Italy right before the war broke out on a large scale. Her own mother was Jewish and they wanted her out of harm's way. The eight red glasses she wrapped carefully in her underwear to take in the one suitcase she had carried, and they had always held pride of place at any festive meal. I poured brandy.

Ralph told me that his family was Irish. "That's why it's 'Devereux' without an *A*—the *A*s are French." We sat for a while without talking, drinking our brandy. He was a bit nervous, too, and it helped me relax. Suddenly he grinned, his face lighting, and said, "When I got divorced I moved into the city because I had a theory that that's where you meet the chicks—sorry, women. But to tell you the truth, you're the first woman I've asked out in the six months I've been here—and you're not like any woman I ever met before." He flushed a little. "I just wanted you to know that I'm not hopping in and out of bed every night. But I would like to get into bed with you."

I didn't answer him, but stood up and took his hand. Hand-in-hand, like five-year-olds, we walked into the bedroom. Ralph carefully helped me out of my dress and gently stroked my puffy arms. I unbuttoned his shirt. He took off his clothes and we climbed into the bed. I'd been afraid that I might have to help him along; recently divorced men sometimes have problems because they feel very insecure. Fortunately he didn't, because I was too tired to help anyone. My last memory was of his breath expelling loudly, and then I was asleep.

SEVEN
A LITTLE HELP
FROM A FRIEND

When I woke up, the room was full of the soft light of late morning, diffused through my heavy bedroom curtains. I was alone in the bed and lay still to collect my thoughts. Gradually the memory of yesterday's events returned, and I moved my head cautiously to look at the bedside clock. My neck was very stiff, and I had to turn my whole body to see the time— 11:30. I sat up. My stomach muscles were all right, but my thighs and calves were sore, and it was painful to stand upright. I did a slow shuffle to the bathroom, the kind you do the day after you run five miles when you haven't been out for a couple of months, and turned the hot water in the tub on full blast.

Ralph called to me from the living room. "Good morning," I called back. "If you want to talk to me, you'll have to come here—I'm not walking any farther." Ralph came into the bathroom, fully dressed, and joined me while I gloomily studied my face in the mirror over the sink. My incipient black eye had turned a deep blackish-purple, streaked with yellow and green. My uninjured left eye was bloodshot. My jaw had turned gray. The whole effect was unappealing.

Ralph seemed to share my feeling. I was watching his face in the mirror; he seemed a little disgusted. My bet was that Dorothy had never come home with a black eye—suburban life is so dull.

"Do you do this kind of thing often?" Ralph asked.

"You mean scrutinize my body, or what?" I asked.

He moved his hands vaguely. "The fighting," he said.

"Not as much as I did as a child. I grew up on the South Side. Ninetieth and Commercial, if you know the area—lots of Polish steelworkers who didn't welcome racial and ethnic newcomers—and the feeling was mutual. The law of the jungle ruled in my high school—if you couldn't swing a mean toe or fist, you might as well forget it."

I turned from the mirror. Ralph was shaking his head, but he was trying to understand, trying not to back away. "It's a different world," he said slowly. "I grew up in Libertyville, and I don't think I was ever in a real fight. And if my sister had come home with a black eye, my mother would have been hysterical for a month. Didn't your folks mind?"

"Oh, my mother hated it, but she died when I was fifteen, and my dad was thankful that I could take care of myself." That was true—Gabriella had hated violence. But she was a fighter, and I got my scrappiness from her, not from my big, even-tempered father.

"Did all the girls in your school fight?" Ralph wanted to know.

I climbed into the hot water while I considered this. "No, some of them just got scared off. And some got themselves boyfriends to protect them. The rest of us learned to protect ourselves. One girl I went to school with still loves to fight— she's a gorgeous redhead, and she loves going to bars and punching out guys who try to pick her up. Truly amazing."

I sank back in the water and covered my face and neck with hot wet cloths. Ralph was quiet for a minute, then said, "I'll make some coffee if you'll tell me the secret—I couldn't find any. And I didn't know whether you were saving those dishes for Christmas, so I washed them."

I uncovered my mouth but kept the cloth over my eyes. I'd forgotten the goddamn dishes yesterday when I left the house. "Thanks." What else could I say? "Coffee's in the freezer—whole beans. Use a tablespoon per cup. The grinder's by the stove—electric gadget. Filters are in the cupboard right over it, and the pot is still in the sink—unless you washed it."

He leaned over to kiss me, then went out. I reheated the washcloth and flexed my legs in the steamy water. After a while they moved easily, so I was confident they would be fine in a few days. Before Ralph returned with the coffee, I had soaked much of the stiffness out of my joints. I climbed out of the tub and enveloped myself in a large blue bath towel and walked—with much less difficulty—to the living room.

Ralph came in with the coffee. He admired my robe, but couldn't quite look me in the face. "The weather's broken," he remarked. "I went out to get a paper and it's a beautiful day—clear and cool. Want to drive out to the Indiana Dunes?"

I started to shake my head, but the pain stopped me. "No. It sounds lovely, but I've got some work to do."

"Come on, Vic," Ralph protested. "Let the police handle this. You're in rotten shape—you need to take the day off."

"You could be right," I said, trying to keep down my anger. "But I thought we went through all that last night. At any rate, I'm not taking the day off."

"Well, how about some company. Need someone to drive you?"

I studied Ralph's face, but all I saw was friendly concern. Was he just having an attack of male protectiveness, or did he have some special reason for wanting me to stay off the job? As a companion he'd be able to keep tabs on my errands. And report them to Earl Smeissen?

"I'm going to Winnetka to talk to Peter Thayer's father. Since he's a neighbor of your boss, I'm not sure it would look too good for you to come along."

"Probably not," he agreed. "Why do you have to see him?"

"It's like the man said about Annapurna, Ralph: because he's there." There were a couple of other things I needed to do, too, things I'd just as soon be alone for.

"How about dinner tonight?" he suggested.

"Ralph, for heaven's sake, you're beginning to act like a Seeing Eye dog. No. No dinner tonight. You're sweet, I appreciate it, but I want some time to myself."

"Okay, okay," he grumbled. "Just trying to be friendly."

I stood up and walked painfully over to the couch where he was sitting. "I know." I put an arm around him and gave him a kiss. "I'm just trying to be unfriendly." He pulled me onto his lap. The dissatisfaction smoothed out of his face and he kissed me.

After a few minutes I pulled myself gently away and hobbled back to the bedroom to get dressed. The navy silk was lying over a chair, with a couple of rents in it and a fair amount of blood and dirt. My cleaner could probably fix it up, but I didn't think I'd ever care to wear it again. I threw it out and put on my green linen slacks with a pale-lemon shirt and a jacket. Perfect for suburbia. I decided not to worry about my face. It would look even more garish with makeup in sunlight than as it was.

I fixed myself Cream of Wheat while Ralph ate toast and jam. "Well," I said, "time to head for suburbia."

Ralph walked downstairs with me, trying to hold out a supporting hand. "No, thanks," I said. "I'd better get used to doing this by myself." At the bottom he won points by not lingering over his good-byes. We kissed briefly; he sketched a cheerful wave and crossed the street to his car. I watched him out of sight, then hailed a passing cab.

The driver dropped me on Sheffield north of Addison, a neighborhood more decayed than mine, largely Puerto Rican. I rang Lotty Herschel's bell and was relieved when she answered it. "Who's there?" she squawked through the intercom. "It's me, Vic," I said, and pushed the front door while the buzzer sounded.

Lotty lived on the second floor. She was waiting for me in the doorway when I made it to the top of the stairs. "My dear

Vic—what on earth is wrong with you?" she greeted me, her thick black eyebrows soaring to punctuate her astonishment.

I'd known Lotty for years. She was a doctor, about fifty, I thought, but with her vivid, clever face and trim, energetic body it was hard to tell. Sometime in her Viennese youth she had discovered the secret of perpetual motion. She held fierce opinions on a number of things, and put them to practice in medicine, often to the dismay of her colleagues. She'd been one of the physicians who performed abortions in connection with an underground referral service I'd belonged to at the University of Chicago in the days when abortion was illegal and a dirty word to most doctors. Now she ran a clinic in a shabby storefront down the street. She'd tried running it for nothing when she first opened it, but found the neighborhood people wouldn't trust medical care they didn't have to pay for. Still, it was one of the cheapest clinics in the city, and I often wondered what she lived on.

Now she shut the door behind me and ushered me into her living room. Like Lotty herself, it was sparely furnished, but glowed with strong colors—curtains in a vivid red-and-orange print, and an abstract painting like fire on the wall. Lotty sat me on a daybed and brought me a cup of the strong Viennese coffee she lived on.

"So now, Victoria, what have you been doing that makes you hobble upstairs like an old woman and turns your face black-and-blue? I am sure not a car accident, that's too tame for you—am I right?"

"Right as always, Lotty," I answered, and gave her an abbreviated account of my adventures.

She pursed her lips at the tale of Smeissen but wasted no time arguing about whether I ought to go to the police or drop out of the case or spend the day in bed. She didn't always agree with me, but Lotty respected my decisions. She went into her bedroom and returned with a large, business-like black bag. She pulled my face muscles and looked at my

eyes with an ophthalmoscope. "Nothing time won't cure," she
pronounced, and checked the reflexes in my legs and the
muscles. "Yes, I see, you are sore, and you will continue to
be sore. But you are healthy, you take good care of yourself;
it will pass off before too long."

"Yes, I suspected as much," I agreed. "But I can't take the
time to wait for these leg muscles to heal. And they're sore
enough to slow me down quite a bit right now. I need something that will help me overlook the pain enough to do some
errands and some thinking—not like codeine that knocks you
out. Do you have anything?"

"Ah, yes, a miracle drug." Lotty's face was amused. "You
shouldn't put so much faith in doctors and drugs, Vic. However, I'll give you a shot of phenylbutazone. That's what they
give racehorses to keep them from aching when they run,
and it seems to me you're galloping around like a horse."

She disappeared for a few minutes, and I heard the refrigerator door open. She returned with a syringe and a small,
rubber-stoppered bottle. "Now, lie down; we'll do this in your
behind so it goes quickly to the bloodstream. Pull your slacks
down a bit, so; great stuff this, really, they call it 'bute' for
short, in half an hour you will be ready for the Derby, my
dear." As she talked, Lotty worked rapidly. I felt a small sting,
and it was over. "Now, sit. I'll tell you some stories about the
clinic. I'm going to give you some nepenthe to take away
with you. That's very strong, a painkiller; don't try to drive
while you're taking it, and don't drink. I'll pack up some bute
in tablets for you."

I leaned back against a big pillow and tried not to relax too
much. The temptation to lie down and sleep was very strong.
I forced myself to follow Lotty's quick, clever talk, asking
questions, but not debating her more outlandish statements.
After a while I could feel the drug taking effect. My neck
muscles eased considerably. I didn't feel like unarmed combat, but I was reasonably certain I could handle my car.

Lotty didn't try to stop my getting up. "You've rested for

close to an hour—you should do for a while." She packed the bute tablets in a plastic bottle and gave me a bottle of nepenthe.

I thanked her. "How much do I owe you?"

She shook her head. "No, these are all samples. When you come for your long-overdue checkup, then I'll charge you what any good Michigan Avenue doctor would."

She saw me to the door. "Seriously, Vic, if you get worried about this Smeissen character, you are always welcome in my spare room." I thanked her—it was a good offer, and one that I might need.

Normally I would have walked back to my car; Lotty was only about eight blocks from me. But even with the shot I didn't feel quite up to par, so I walked slowly down to Addison and caught a cab. I rode it down to my office, where I picked up Peter Thayer's voter card with the Winnetka address on it, then flagged another cab back to my own car on the North Side. McGraw was going to have quite a bill for expenses—all these cabs, and then the navy suit had cost a hundred and sixty-seven dollars.

A lot of people were out enjoying the day, and the clean fresh air lifted my spirits too. By two I was on the Edens Expressway heading toward the North Shore. I started singing a snatch from Mozart's *"Ch'io mi scordi di te,"* but my rib cage protested and I had to settle for a Bartok concerto on WFMT.

For some reason the Edens ceases to be a beautiful expressway as it nears the homes of the rich. Close to Chicago it's lined with greensward and neat bungalows, but as you go farther out, shopping centers crop up and industrial parks and drive-ins take over. Once I turned right onto Willow Road, though, and headed toward the lake, the view became more impressive—large stately homes set well back on giant, carefully manicured lawns. I checked Thayer's address and turned south onto Sheridan Road, squinting at numbers on mailboxes. His house was on the east side, the side where lots face Lake Michigan, giving the children private beaches and boat moorings when they were home from Groton or Andover.

My Chevy felt embarrassed turning through twin stone pillars, especially when it saw a small Mercedes, an Alfa, and an Audi Fox off to one side of the drive. The circular drive took me past some attractive flower gardens to the front door of a limestone mansion. Next to the door a small sign requested tradesmen to make deliveries in the rear. Was I a tradesman or -woman? I wasn't sure I had anything to deliver, but perhaps my host did.

I took a card from my wallet and wrote a short message on it: "Let's talk about your relations with the Knifegrinders." I rang the bell.

The expression on the face of the neatly uniformed woman who answered the door reminded me of my black eye: the bute had put it out of my mind for a while. I gave her the card. "I'd like to see Mr. Thayer," I said coolly.

She looked at me dubiously, but took the card, shutting the door in my face. I could hear faint shouts from beaches farther up the road. As the minutes passed, I left the porch to make a more detailed study of a flower bed on the other side of the drive. When the door opened, I turned back. The maid frowned at me.

"I'm not stealing the flowers," I assured her. "But since you don't have magazines in the waiting area, I had to look at something."

She sucked in her breath but only said, "This way." No "please," no manners at all. Still, this was a house of mourning. I made allowances.

We moved at a fast clip through a large entry room graced by a dull-green statue, past a stairway, and down a hall leading to the back of the house. John Thayer met us, coming from the other direction. He was wearing a white knit shirt and checked gray slacks—suburban attire but muted. His whole air was subdued, as if he were consciously trying to act like a mourning father.

"Thanks, Lucy. We'll go in here." He took my arm and moved me into a room with comfortable armchairs and packed bookcases. The books were lined up neatly on the shelves. I wondered if he ever read any of them.

Thayer held out my card. "What's this about, Warshawski?"

"Just what it says. I want to talk about your relations with the Knifegrinders."

He gave a humorless smile. "They are as minimal as possible. Now that Peter is—gone, I expect them to be non-existent."

"I wonder if Mr. McGraw would agree with that."

He clenched his fist, crushing the card. "Now we get to it. McGraw hired you to blackmail me, didn't he?"

"Then there is a connection between you and the Knifegrinders."

"No!"

"Then how can Mr. McGraw possibly blackmail you?"

"A man like that stops at nothing. I warned you yesterday to be careful around him."

"Look, Mr. Thayer. Yesterday you got terribly upset at learning that McGraw had brought your name into this. Today you're afraid he's blackmailing you. That's awfully suggestive."

His face was set in harsh, strained lines. "Of what?"

"Something was going on between you two that you don't want known. Your son found it out and you two had him killed to keep him quiet."

"That's a lie, Warshawski, a goddamned lie," he roared.

"Prove it."

"The police arrested Peter's killer this morning."

My head swam and I sat down suddenly in one of the leather chairs. "What?" My voice squeaked.

"One of the commissioners called me. They found a drug addict who'd tried to rob the place. They say Peter caught him at it and was shot."

"No," I said.

"What do you mean, no? They arrested the guy."

"No. Maybe they arrested him, but that wasn't the scene. No one robbed that place. Your son didn't catch anyone in the act. I tell you, Thayer, the boy was sitting at the kitchen table and someone shot him. That is not the work of a drug addict caught in a felony. Besides, nothing was taken."

"What are you after, Warshawski? Maybe nothing was taken. Maybe he got scared and fled. I'd believe that before I'd believe your story—that I shot my own son." His face was working with a strong emotion. Grief? Anger? Maybe horror?

"Mr. Thayer, I'm sure you've noticed what a mess my face is. A couple of punks roughed me up last night to warn me off the investigation into your son's death. A drug addict doesn't have those kinds of resources. I saw several people who might have engineered that—and you and Andy Mc-Graw were two of them."

"People don't like busybodies, Warshawski. If someone beat you up, I'd take the hint."

I was too tired to get angry. "In other words, you are involved but you figure you've got your ass covered. So that means I'll have to figure out a way to saw the barrel off your tail. It'll be a pleasure."

"Warshawski, I'm telling you for your own good: drop it." He went over to his desk. "I can see you're a conscientious girl—but McGraw is wasting your time. There's nothing to find." He wrote a check and handed it to me. "Here. You can give McGraw back whatever he's paid you and feel like you've done your duty."

The check was for $5,000. "You bastard. You accuse me of blackmail and then you try to buy me off?" A spurt of raw anger pushed my fatigue to one side. I ripped up the check and let the pieces fall to the floor.

Thayer turned white. Money was his raw nerve. "The police made an arrest, Warshawski. I don't need to buy you off. But if you want to act stupid about it, there's nothing more to say. You'd better leave."

The door opened and a girl came in. "Oh, Dad, Mother wants you to—" She broke off. "Sorry, didn't know you had company." She was an attractive teen-ager. Her brown, straight hair was well brushed and hung down her back, framing a small oval face. She was wearing jeans and a striped man's shirt several sizes too big for her. Maybe her brother's. Normally she probably had the confident, healthy air that money can provide. Right now she drooped a bit.

"Miss Warshawski was just leaving, Jill. In fact, why don't you show her out and I'll go see what your mother wants."

He got up and walked to the door, waiting until I followed him to say good-bye. I didn't offer to shake hands. Jill led me back the way I'd come earlier; her father walked briskly in the opposite direction.

"I'm very sorry about your brother," I said as we got to the greenish statue.

"So am I," she said, pulling her lips together. When we got to the front of the house, she followed me outside and stood staring up at my face, frowning a little. "Did you know Peter?" she finally asked.

"No, I never met him," I answered. "I'm a private investigator, and I'm afraid I'm the person who found him the other morning."

"They wouldn't let me look at him," she said.

"His face was fine. Don't have nightmares about him—his face wasn't damaged." She wanted more information. If he'd been shot in the head, how could his face look all right? I explained it to her in a toned-down, clinical way.

"Peter told me you could decide whether to trust people by their faces," she said after a minute. "But yours is pretty banged up so I can't tell. But you told me the truth about Peter and you're not talking to me as if I was a baby or something." She paused. I waited. Finally she asked, "Did Dad ask you to come out here?" When I replied, she asked, "Why was he angry?"

"Well, he thinks the police have arrested your brother's murderer, but I think they've got the wrong person. And that made him angry."

"Why?" she asked. "I mean, not why is he mad, but why do you think they got the wrong person?"

"The reasons are pretty complicated. It's not because I know who did it, but because I saw your brother, and the apartment, and some other people who've been involved, and they've reacted to my seeing them. I've been in this business for a while, and I have a feel for when I'm hearing the truth. A drug addict wandering in off the streets just doesn't fit with what I've seen and heard."

She stood on one foot, and her face was screwed up as if she were afraid she might start crying. I put an arm around her and pulled her to a sitting position on the shallow porch step.

"I'm okay," she muttered. "It's just—everything is so weird around here. You know, it's so terrible, Pete dying and everything. He—he—well—" She hiccuped back a sob. "Never mind. It's Dad who's crazy. Probably he always was but I never noticed it before. He's been raving on and on about how Anita and her father shot Pete for his money and dumb stuff like that, and then he'll start saying how it served Pete right, like he's glad he's dead or something." She gulped and ran her hand across her nose. "Dad was always in such a stew about Peter disgracing the family name, you know, but he wouldn't have—even if he'd become a union organizer he would have been a successful one. He liked figuring things out, he was that kind of person, figuring things out and trying to do them the best way." She hiccuped again. "And I like Anita. Now I suppose I'll never see her again. I wasn't supposed to meet her, but she and Pete took me out to dinner sometimes, when Mom and Dad were out of town."

"She's disappeared, you know," I told her. "You wouldn't know where she's gone, would you?"

She looked up at me with troubled eyes. "Do you think something's happened to her?"

"No," I said with a reassurance I didn't feel. "I think she got scared and ran away."

"Anita's really wonderful," she said earnestly. "But Dad and Mother just refused even to meet her. That was when Dad first started acting weird, when Pete and Anita began going together. Even today, when the police came, he wouldn't believe they'd arrested this man. He kept saying it was Mr. McGraw. It was really awful." She grimaced unconsciously. "Oh, it's been just horrible here. Nobody cares about Pete. Mother just cares about the neighbors. Dad is freaked out. I'm the only one who cares he's dead." Tears were streaming down her face now and she stopped trying to fight them. "Sometimes I even get the crazy idea that Dad just freaked out totally, like he does, and killed Peter."

This was the big fear. Once she'd said it, she started sobbing convulsively and shivering. I took off my jacket and wrapped it around her shoulders. I held her close for a few minutes and let her sob.

The door opened behind us. Lucy stood there, scowling. "Your father wants to know where you've gone to—and he doesn't want you standing around gossiping with the detective."

I stood up. "Why don't you take her inside and wrap her up in a blanket and get her something hot to drink: she's pretty upset with everything that's going on, and she needs some attention."

Jill was still shivering, but she'd stopped sobbing. She gave me a watery little smile and handed me my jacket. "I'm okay," she whispered.

I dug a card out of my purse and handed it to her. "Call me if you need me, Jill," I said. "Day or night." Lucy hustled her inside at top speed and shut the door. I was really toning down the neighborhood—good thing they couldn't see me through the trees.

My shoulders and legs were beginning to hurt again and I walked slowly back to my car. The Chevy had a crease in the front right fender where someone had sideswiped it in last winter's heavy snow. The Alfa, the Fox, and the Mercedes were all in mint condition. My car and I looked alike, whereas the Thayers seemed more like the sleek, scratchless Mercedes. There was a lesson in there someplace. Maybe too much urban living was bad for cars and people. Real profound, Vic.

I wanted to get back to Chicago and call Bobby and get the lowdown on this drug addict they'd arrested, but I needed to do something else while Lotty's painkiller was still holding me up. I drove back over to the Edens and went south to the Dempster exit. This road led through the predominantly Jewish suburb of Skokie, and I stopped at the Bagel Works delicatessen and bagel bakery there. I ordered a jumbo corned beef on rye and a Fresca, and sat in the car, eating while I tried to decide where to get a gun. I knew how to use them—my dad had seen too many shooting accidents in homes with guns. He'd decided the way to avoid one in our house was for my mother and me to learn how to use them. My mother had always refused: they gave her unhappy memories of the war and she would always say she'd use the time to pray for a world without weapons. But I used to go down to the police range with my dad on Saturday afternoons and practice target shooting. At one time I could clean and load and fire a .45 police revolver in two minutes, but since my father had died ten years ago, I hadn't been out shooting. I'd given his gun to Bobby as a memento when he'd died, and I'd never needed one since then. I had killed a man once, but that had been an accident. Joe Correl had jumped me outside a warehouse when I was looking into some inventory losses for a company. I had broken his hold and smashed his jaw in, and when he fell, he'd hit his head on the edge of a forklift. I'd broken his jaw, but it was his skull against the forklift that killed him.

But Smeissen had a lot of hired muscle, and if he was really pissed off, he could hire some more. A gun wouldn't completely protect me, but I thought it might narrow the odds.

The corned beef sandwich was delicious. I hadn't had one for a long time, and decided to forget my weight-maintenance program for one afternoon and have another. There was a phone booth in the deli, and I let my fingers do the walking through the Yellow Pages. The phone book showed four columns of gun dealers. There was one not too far from where I was in the suburb of Lincolnwood. When I called and described what I wanted, they didn't have it. After $1.20 worth of calls, I finally located a repeating, mediumweight Smith & Wesson on the far South Side of the city. My injuries were really throbbing by this time and I didn't feel like a forty-mile drive to the other end of the city. On the other hand, those injuries were why I needed the gun. I paid for the corned beef sandwich and with my second Fresca swallowed four of the tablets Lotty had given me.

The drive south should have taken only an hour, but I was feeling light-headed, my head and body not connected too strongly. The last thing I wanted was for one of Chicago's finest to pull me over. I took it slowly, swallowed a couple more tablets of bute, and put all my effort into holding my concentration.

It was close to five when I exited from I-57 to the south suburbs. By the time I got to Riley's, they were ready to close. I insisted on coming in to make my purchase.

"I know what I want," I said. "I called a couple of hours ago—a Smith & Wesson thirty-eight."

The clerk looked suspiciously at my face and took in the black eye. "Why don't you come back on Monday, and if you still feel you want a gun, we can talk about a model more suited to a lady than a Smith & Wesson thirty-eight."

"Despite what you may think I am not a wife-beating victim. I am not planning on buying a gun to go home and kill my husband. I'm a single woman living alone and I was attacked last night. I know how to use a gun, and I've decided I need one, and this is the kind I want."

"Just a minute," the clerk said. He hurried to the back of the store and began a whispered consultation with two men standing there. I went to the case and started inspecting guns and ammunition. The store was new, clean, and beautifully laid out. Their ad in the Yellow Pages proclaimed Riley's as Smith & Wesson specialists, but they had enough variety to please any kind of taste in shooting. One wall was devoted to rifles.

My clerk came over with one of the others, a pleasant-faced, middle-aged man. "Ron Jaffrey," he said. "I'm the manager. What can we do for you?"

"I called up a couple of hours ago asking about a Smith & Wesson thirty-eight. I'd like to get one," I repeated.

"Have you ever used one before?" the manager asked.

"No, I'm more used to the Colt forty-five," I answered. "But the S&W is lighter and better suited to my needs."

The manager walked to one of the cases and unlocked it. My clerk went to the door to stop another last-minute customer from entering. I took the gun from the manager, balanced it in my hand, and tried the classic police firing stance: body turned to create as narrow a target as possible. The gun felt good. "I'd like to try it before I buy it," I told the manager. "Do you have a target range?"

Jaffrey took a box of ammunition from the case. "I have to say you look as though you know how to handle it. We have a range in the back—if you decide against the gun, we ask you to pay for the ammo. If you take the gun, we throw in a box free."

"Fine," I said. I followed him through a door in the back, which led to a small range.

"We give lessons back here on Sunday afternoons, and let

people come in to practice on their own during the week. Need any help loading?"

"I may," I told him. "Time was when I could load and fire in thirty seconds, but it's been a while." My hands were starting to shake a bit from fatigue and pain and it took me several minutes to insert eight rounds of cartridges. The manager showed me the safety and the action. I nodded, turned to the target, lifted the gun, and fired. The action came as naturally as if ten days, not ten years, had passed, but my aim was way off. I emptied the gun but didn't get a bull's-eye, and only two in the inner ring. The gun was good, though, steady action and no noticeable distortion. "Let me try another lot."

I emptied the chambers and Jaffrey handed me some more cartridges. He gave me a couple of pointers. "You obviously know what you're doing, but you're out of practice and you've picked up some bad habits. Your stance is good, but you're hunching your shoulder—keep it down and only raise the arm."

I loaded and fired again, trying to keep my shoulder down. It was good advice—all but two shots got into the red and one grazed the bull's-eye. "Okay," I said. "I'll take it. Give me a couple of boxes of ammo, and a complete cleaning kit." I thought a minute. "And a shoulder holster."

We went back into the store. "Larry!" Jaffrey called. My clerk came over. "Clean and wrap this gun for the lady while I write up the bill." Larry took the gun, and I went with Jaffrey to the cash register. A mirror was mounted behind it, and I saw myself in it without recognition for a few seconds. The left side of my face was now completely purple and badly swollen while my right eye stared with the dark anguish of a Paul Klee drawing. I almost turned to see who this battered woman was before realizing I was looking at myself. No wonder Larry hadn't wanted to let me in the store.

Jaffrey showed me the bill. "Four hundred twenty-two dollars," he said. "Three-ten for the gun, ten for the second box of cartridges, fifty-four for the holster and belt, and twenty-eight for the cleaning kit. The rest is tax." I wrote a check out, slowly and laboriously. "I need a driver's license and two major credit cards or an interbank card," he said, "and I have to ask you to sign this register." He looked at my driver's license. "Monday you should go down to City Hall and register that gun. I send a list of all major purchases to the local police department, and they'll probably forward your name to the Chicago police."

I nodded and quietly put my identification back in my bill-fold. The gun took a big chunk out of the thousand dollars I'd had from McGraw, and I didn't think I could legitimately charge it to him as an expense. Larry brought me the gun in a beautiful velvet case. I looked at it and asked them to put it in a bag for me. Ron Jaffrey ushered me urbanely to my car, magnificently ignoring my face. "You live quite a ways from here, but if you want to come down and use the target, just bring your bill with you—you get six months' free practice with the purchase." He opened my car door for me. I thanked him, and he went back to the store.

The bute was still keeping the pain from crashing in on me completely, but I was absolutely exhausted. My last bit of energy had gone to buying the gun and using the target. I couldn't drive the thirty miles back to my apartment. I started the car and went slowly down the street, looking for a motel. I found a Best Western that had rooms backing onto a side street, away from the busy road I was on. The clerk looked curiously at my face but made no comment. I paid cash and took the key.

The room was decent and quiet, the bed firm. I uncorked the bottle of nepenthe Lotty had given me and took a healthy swallow. I peeled off my clothes, wound my watch and put it on the bedside table, and crawled under the covers. I debated calling my answering service but decided I was too tired to handle anything even if it had come up. The air conditioner, set on high, drowned out any street noises and made the room cold enough to enjoy snuggling under the blankets. I lay down and was starting to think about John Thayer when I fell asleep.

EIGHT
SOME VISITORS DON'T KNOCK

I came to slowly, out of a sound sleep. I lay quietly, not sure at first where I was, and dozed again lightly. When I woke up the second time, I was refreshed and aware. The heavy drapes shut out any outside light; I switched on the bedside lamp and looked at my watch—7:30. I had slept more than twelve hours.

I sat up and cautiously moved legs and neck. My muscles had stiffened again in my sleep, but not nearly as badly as the previous morning. I pulled myself from the bed and made it to the window with only minor twinges. Looking through a crack I pulled in the drapes, I saw bright morning sunlight.

I was puzzled by Thayer's account of a police arrest and wondered if there would be a story in the morning paper. I pulled on my slacks and shirt and went down to the lobby for a copy of the Sunday *Herald-Star*. Back upstairs I undressed again and ran a hot bath while I looked at the paper. DRUG ADDICT ARRESTED IN BANKING HEIR'S MURDER was on the lower right side of the front page.

Police have arrested Donald Mackenzie of 4302 S. Ellis in the murder of banking heir Peter Thayer last Monday. Asst. Police Commissioner Tim Sullivan praised the men working on the case and said an arrest was made early Saturday morning when one of the residents of the apartment where Peter Thayer lived identified Mackenzie as a man seen hanging around the building several times recently. It is believed that Mackenzie, allegedly addicted to cocaine, entered the Thayer apartment on Monday,

July 16, believing no one to be at home. When he found Peter Thayer eating breakfast in the kitchen, he lost his nerve and shot him. Commissioner Sullivan says the Browning automatic that fired the fatal bullet has not yet been traced but that the police have every hope of recovering the weapon.

The story was continued on page sixty-three. Here, a full page had been devoted to the case. Pictures of the Thayer family with Jill, another sister, and a chic Mrs. Thayer. A single shot of Peter in a baseball uniform for New Trier High School. A good candid picture of Anita McGraw. An accompanying story proclaimed LABOR LEADER'S DAUGHTER STILL MISSING. It suggested "now that the police have made an arrest, there is hope that Miss McGraw will return to Chicago or call her family. Meanwhile, her picture has been circulated to state police in Wisconsin, Indiana, and Michigan."

That seemed to be that. I lay back in the water and closed my eyes. The police were supposedly hunting high and low for the Browning, questioning Mackenzie's friends, and searching his hangouts. But I didn't think they'd find it. I tried to remember what Earl's goons had been carrying. Fred had had a Colt, but I thought Tony might have had a Browning. Why was Thayer so willing to believe Mackenzie had killed his son? According to Jill, he'd been insisting at first it was McGraw. Something nagged at the back of my mind, but I couldn't put a finger on it. Could there possibly be any proof that Mackenzie had done it? On the other hand, what proof did I have that he hadn't? My stiff joints, the fact that nothing had been touched in the apartment. . . . But what did it really add up to? I wondered if Bobby had made that arrest, whether he was among those diligent policemen whom Police Commissioner Sullivan unstintingly praised. I decided I needed to get back to Chicago and talk to him.

With this in mind I got dressed and left the motel. I realized I hadn't eaten since those two corned beef sandwiches yesterday afternoon and stopped at a little coffee shop for a cheese omelette, juice, and coffee. I was eating too much lately and not getting any exercise. I surreptitiously slid a finger around my waistband, but it didn't seem any tighter.

I took some more of Lotty's pills with my coffee and was feeling fine by the time I pulled off the Kennedy at Belmont. Sunday morning traffic was light and I made it to Halsted by a little after ten. There was a parking place across from my apartment, and a dark, unmarked car with a police antenna on it. I raised my eyebrows speculatively. Had the mountain come to Mohammed?

I crossed the street and looked into the car. Sergeant McGonnigal was sitting there alone with a newspaper. When he saw me, he put the paper down and got out of the car. He was wearing a light sports jacket and gray slacks and his shoulder holster made a little bulge under his right armpit. A southpaw, I thought. "Good morning, Sergeant," I said. "Beautiful day, isn't it?"

"Good morning, Miss Warshawski. Mind if I come up with you and ask you a few questions?"

"I don't know," I answered. "It depends on the questions. Bobby send you?"

"Yes. We got a couple of inquiries in and he thought I'd better come over to see if you're all right—that's quite a shiner you've picked up."

"Yes, it is," I agreed. I held the door to the building open for him and followed him in. "How long have you been here?"

"I stopped by last night, but you weren't home. I called a couple of times. When I stopped by this morning I just thought I'd wait until noon to see if you showed up. Lieutenant Mallory was afraid the captain would order an APB on you if I reported you missing."

"I see. I'm glad I decided to come home."

We got to the top of the stairs. McGonnigal stopped. "You usually leave your door open?"

"Never." I moved past him. The door was cracked open, hanging a bit drunkenly. Someone had shot out the locks to get in—they don't respond to forcing. McGonnigal pulled out his gun, slammed the door open, and rolled into the room. I drew back against the hall wall, then followed him in.

My apartment was a mess. Someone had gone berserk in it. The sofa cushions had been cut open, pictures thrown on the floor, books opened and dropped so that they lay with open spines and crumpling pages. We walked through the apartment. My clothes were scattered around the bedroom, drawers dumped out. In the kitchen all the flour and sugar had been emptied onto the floor, while pans and plates were everywhere, some of them chipped from reckless handling. In the dining room the red Venetian glasses were lying crazily on the table. Two had fallen off. One rested safely on the carpet, but the other had shattered on the wood floor. I picked up the seven whole ones and stood them in the breakfront and sat to pick up the pieces of the other. My hands were shaking and I couldn't handle the tiny shards.

"Don't touch anything else, Miss Warshawski." McGonnigal's voice was kind. "I'm going to call Lieutenant Mallory and get some fingerprint experts over here. They probably won't find anything, but we've got to try. In the meantime, I'm afraid you'll have to leave things the way they are."

I nodded. "The phone is next to the couch—what used to be the couch," I said, not looking up. Jesus, what next? Who the hell had been in here, and why? It just couldn't be a random burglar. A pro might take the place apart looking for valuables—but rip up the couch? Dump china onto the floor? My mother had carried those glasses from Italy in a suitcase and not a one had broken. Nineteen years married to a cop on the South Side of Chicago and not a one had broken. If I had become a singer, as she had wanted, this would never have happened. I sighed. My hands were calmer, so I picked up the little shards and put them in a dish on the table.

"Please don't touch anything," McGonnigal said again, from the doorway.

"Goddamnit, McGonnigal, shut up!" I snapped. "Even if you do find a fingerprint in here that doesn't belong to me or one of my friends, you think they're going to go all over these splinters of glass? And I'll bet you dinner at the Savoy that whoever came through here wore gloves and you won't find a damned thing, anyway." I stood up. "I'd like to know what you were doing when the tornado came through—sitting out front reading your newspaper? Did you think the noise came from someone's television? Who came in and out of the building while you were here?"

He flushed. Mallory was going to ask him the same question. If he hadn't bothered to find out, he was in hot water.

"I don't think this was done while I was here, but I'll go ask your downstairs neighbors if they heard any noise. I know it must be very upsetting to come home and find your apartment destroyed, but please, Miss Warshawski—if we're going to have a prayer of finding these guys we've got to fingerprint the place."

"Okay, okay," I said. He went out to check downstairs. I went to the bedroom. My canvas suitcase was lying open but fortunately had not been cut. I didn't think canvas would take fingerprints, so I put it on the dismantled box springs and packed, going through the array of clothes and lingerie on the floor. I put the wrapped box from Riley's in, too, and then called Lotty on the bedside phone.

"Lotty, I can't talk right now, but my apartment has been ravaged. Can I come and stay a few nights?"

"Naturally, Vic. Do you need me to come get you?"

"No, I'm okay. I'll be over in a while—I need to talk to the police first."

We hung up and I took the suitcase down to the car. McGonnigal was in the second-floor apartment; the door was half open and he was talking, with his back to the hallway. I put the suitcase in my trunk and was just unlocking the outer door to go back upstairs when Mallory came squealing up to the curb with a couple of squad cars hot behind him.

They double-parked, lights flashing, and a group of kids gathered at the end of the street, staring. Police like to create public drama—no other need for all that show.

"Hello, Bobby," I said as cheerily as I could manage.

"What the hell is going on here, Vicki?" Bobby asked, so angry that he forgot his cardinal rule against swearing in front of women and children.

"Not nice, whatever it is: someone tore my place up. They smashed one of Gabriella's glasses."

Mallory had been charging up the stairs, about to muscle me aside, but that stopped him—he'd drunk too many New Year's toasts out of those glasses. "Christ, Vicki, I'm sorry, but what the hell were you doing poking your nose into this business anyway?"

"Why don't you send your boys upstairs and we'll sit here and talk. There's no place to sit down up there and frankly, I can't stand to look at it."

He thought about it for a minute. "Yeah, why don't we go sit in my car, and you answer a few questions. Finchley!" he bellowed. A young black cop stepped forward. "Take the crew upstairs and fingerprint the place and search it if you can for any clues." He turned to me. "Anything valuable that might be missing?"

I shrugged. "Who knows what's valuable to a ransacker. A couple of good pieces of jewelry—my mother's; I never wear them, too old-fashioned—a single diamond pendant set in a white gold filigree with matching earrings. A couple of rings. There's a little silver flatware. I don't know—a turntable. I haven't looked for anything—just looked and looked away."

"Yeah, okay," Bobby said. "Go on." He waved a hand and the four uniformed men started up the stairs. "And send McGonnigal down to me," he called after them.

We went to Bobby's car and sat together in the front seat. His full, red face was set—angry, but not, I thought, with me. "I told you on Thursday to butt out of the Thayer case."

"I heard the police made an arrest yesterday—Donald Mackenzie. Is there still a Thayer case?"

Bobby ignored that. "What happened to your face?"

"I ran into a door."

"Don't clown, Vicki. You know why I sent McGonnigal over to talk to you?"

"I give up. He fell in love with me and you were giving him an excuse to come by and see me?"

"I can't deal with you this morning!" Bobby yelled, top volume. "A kid is dead, your place is a wreck, your face looks like hell, and all you can think of is getting my goat. Goddamnit, talk to me straight and pay attention to what I say."

"Okay, okay," I said pacifically. "I give up: why did you send the sergeant over to see me?"

Bobby breathed heavily for a few minutes. He nodded, as if to affirm that he'd recovered his self-control. "Because John Thayer told me last night that you'd been beaten up and you didn't believe that Mackenzie had committed the crime."

"Thayer," I echoed, incredulous. "I talked to him yesterday and he threw me out of his house because I wouldn't accept his word that Mackenzie was the murderer. Now why's he turning around telling you that? How'd you come to be talking to him, anyway?"

Bobby smiled sourly. "We had to go out to Winnetka to ask a few last questions. When it's the Thayer family, we wait on their convenience, and that was when it was convenient. . . . He believes it was Mackenzie but he wants to be sure. Now tell me about your face."

"There's nothing to tell. It looks worse than it is—you know how it is with black eyes."

Bobby drummed on the steering wheel in exaggerated patience. "Vicki, after I talked to Thayer, I had McGonnigal go through our reports to see if anyone had turned in anything on a battered woman. And we found a cabbie had stopped at the Town Hall Station and mentioned picking up a woman at Astor and the Drive and dropping her at your address. Quite a coincidence, huh? The guy was worried because you looked in pretty bad shape, but there wasn't anything anyone could do about it—you weren't filing a complaint."

"Right you are," I said.

Mallory tightened his lips but didn't lose his temper. "Now, Vicki," he continued. "McGonnigal wondered what you were doing down at Astor and the Drive looking so bloody. It's not really a mugger's spot. And he remembered how Earl Smeissen owns a condo down there on Astor, in from State Street—or Parkway they call it when it gets into the tony part of town. So now we want to know why Earl wanted to beat you up."

"It's your story. You're saying he beat me up, you give me a reason why."

"He probably had a bellyful of your clowning," Bobby said, his voice rising again. "For two cents, I'd black your other goddamn eye for you."

"Is that why you came over, to threaten me?"

"Vicki, I want to know why Earl beat you. The only reason I can think of is that he's tied to the Thayer boy—maybe had him shot when someone else fingered him."

"Then you don't think that Mackenzie is responsible?" Mallory was silent. "You make the arrest?"

"No," Mallory said stiffly. I could see this hurt. "Lieutenant Carlson did."

"Carlson? I don't know him. Who's he work for?"

"Captain Vespucci," Mallory said shortly.

I raised my eyebrows. "Vespucci?" I was beginning to sound like a parrot. Vespucci had been a colleague my father was ashamed to talk about. He'd been implicated in a number of departmental scandals over the years, most of them having to do with police bought off by the mob, or turning the other cheek to mob activities in their territory. There'd never been enough evidence to justify throwing him off the force—but that, too, the rumors said, was because he had the kind of connections that made you keep quiet.

"Carlson and Vespucci pretty close?" I asked.

"Yes," Bobby bit off.

I thought for a minute. "Did someone—like Earl, say— bring pressure on Vespucci to make an arrest? Is Donald Mackenzie another poor slob caught in a trap because he was wandering around the wrong part of town? Did he leave any prints in the apartment? Can you find the gun? Has he made a confession?"

"No, but he can't account for his time on Monday. And we're pretty sure he's been involved in some Hyde Park bur-glaries."

"But you don't agree that he's the killer?"

"As far as the department is concerned, the case is closed. I talked to Mackenzie myself this morning."

"And?"

"And nothing. My captain says it's a defensible arrest."

"Your captain owe anything to Vespucci?" I asked.

Mallory made a violent motion with his torso. "Don't talk like that to me, Vicki. We've got seventy-three unsolved hom-icides right now. If we wrap one up in a week, the captain has every right to be happy."

"All right, Bobby." I sighed. "Sorry. Lieutenant Carlson ar-rested Mackenzie, and Vespucci told your captain, who told you to lay off, the case was closed. . . . But you want to know why Earl beat me up." Mallory turned red again. "You can't have it both ways. If Mackenzie is the killer, why would Smeissen care about me and Peter Thayer? If he beat me up—and I mean *if*—it could have been for lots of reasons. He might've made a heavy pass I turned down. Earl doesn't like ladies who turn him down, you know—he's beaten a couple before. First time I ever saw Earl was when I was a starry-eyed rookie attorney on the Public Defender's roster. I was appearing for a lady whom Earl beat up. Nice young prostitute who didn't want to work for him. Sorry, I just committed slander: she alleged that Earl beat her up, but we couldn't make it stick."

"You're not going to ask for charges, then," Mallory said. "Figures. Now tell me about your apartment. I haven't seen it, but take it as read that it was torn apart—McGonnigal gave me a brief description. Someone was looking for something. What?"

I shook my head. "Beats me. None of my clients has ever given me the secret to the neutron bomb or even a new brand of toothpaste. I just don't deal with that kind of stuff. And anytime I do have volatile evidence, I leave it in a safe in my office . . ." My voice trailed off. Why hadn't I thought of that sooner? If someone had torn the apartment apart looking for something, they were probably down in my office now.

"Give me the address," Bobby said. I gave it to him and he got on the car radio and ordered a patrol car to go up and check. "Now, Vicki, I want you to be honest with me. This is off the record—no witnesses, no tapes. Tell me what you took out of that apartment that someone, call him Smeissen, wants back so badly." He looked at me in a kindly, worried, fatherly way. What did I have to lose by telling him about the picture and the pay stub?

"Bobby," I said earnestly, "I did look around the apartment, but I didn't see anything that smacked remotely of Earl or any other person in particular. Not only that, the place didn't look as though anyone else had searched it."

Sergeant McGonnigal came up to the car. "Hi, Lieutenant—Finchley said you wanted me."

"Yeah," Bobby said. "Who came in and out of the building while you were watching it?"

"Just one of the residents, sir."

"You sure of that?"

"Yes, sir. She lives in the second-floor apartment. I was just talking to her—Mrs. Alvarez—said she heard a lot of noise about three this morning, but didn't pay any attention to it—says Miss Warshawski often has strange guests and wouldn't thank her—Mrs. Alvarez—for interfering."

Thanks, Mrs. Alvarez, I thought. The city needs more neighbors like you. Glad I wasn't home at the time. But what, I wondered, was whoever ransacked my place looking for so desperately? That pay stub linked Peter Thayer to Ajax, but that was no secret. And the picture of Anita? Even if the police hadn't connected her to Andrew McGraw, the picture didn't do that, either. I had put them both in my inner safe at my office, a small bomb- and fireproof box built into the wall at the back of the main safe. I had kept current case papers in there ever since the chairman of Transicon had hired someone to retrieve evidence from my safe two years ago. But I just didn't think that was it.

Bobby and I discussed the break-in for another half hour, touching occasionally on my battle wounds. Finally I said, "Now you tell me something, Bobby: Why don't you believe it was Mackenzie?"

Mallory stared through the windshield. "I'm not doubting it. I believe it. I'd be happier if we had a gun or a fingerprint, but I believe it." I didn't say anything. Bobby continued to look forward with unseeing eyes. "I just wish I'd found him," he said at last. "My captain got a call from Commissioner Sullivan Friday afternoon saying he thought I was over-worked and he was asking Vespucci to assign Carlson to help me out. I went home under orders—to get some sleep. Not off the case. Just to sleep. And next morning there was an arrest." He turned to look at me. "You didn't hear that," he said.

I nodded agreement, and Bobby asked me a few more questions about the missing evidence, but his heart wasn't in it. At last he gave up. "If you won't talk, you won't. Just remember, Vicki: Earl Smeissen is a heavy. You know yourself the courts can't nail him. Don't try to play hardball with him—you're just not up to his weight at all."

I nodded solemnly. "Thanks, Bobby. I'll keep it in mind." I opened the door.

"By the way," Bobby said casually, "we got a call last night from Riley's Gun Shop down in Hazelcrest. Said a V. I. Warshawski had bought a small handgun down there and he was worried—she looked rather wild. That wouldn't be anyone you'd know, would it, Vicki?"

I got out of the car, shut the door, and looked in through the open window. "I'm the only one by that name in my family, Bobby—but there are some other Warshawskis in the city."

For once Bobby didn't lose his temper. He looked at me very seriously. "No one ever stopped you when you had your mind set on something, Vicki. But if you're planning on using that gun, get your ass down to City Hall first thing tomorrow morning and register it. Now tell Sergeant McGonnigal where you're going to be until your place is fixed up again."

While I was giving McGonnigal my address, a squawk came in on Mallory's radio about my office: the place had been ransacked. I wondered if my business-interruption insurance would cover this. "Remember, Vicki, you're playing hardball with a pro," Bobby warned. "Get in, McGonnigal." They drove off.

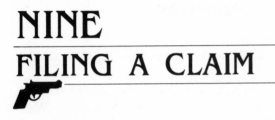

NINE
FILING A CLAIM

When I got to Lotty's it was afternoon. I had stopped on the way to call my answering service—a Mr. McGraw and a Mr. Devereux had both phoned, and left numbers. I copied them into my pocket phone book but decided not to call until I got to Lotty's. She greeted me with a worried head shake. "Not content with beating you, they beat your apartment. You run with a wild crowd, Vic." But no censure, no horror—one of the things I liked in Lotty.

She examined my face and my eye with her ophthalmoscope. "Coming along nicely. Much less swelling already. Headache? A bit? To be expected. Have you eaten? An empty stomach makes it worse. Come, a little boiled chicken—nice Eastern European Sunday dinner." She had eaten, but drank coffee while I finished the chicken. I was surprised at how hungry I was.

"How long can I stay?" I asked.

"I'm expecting no one this month. As long as you like until August tenth."

"I shouldn't be more than a week—probably less. But I'd like to ask the answering service to switch my home calls here."

Lotty shrugged. "In that case, I won't switch off the phone by the guest bed—mine rings at all hours—women having babies, boys being shot—they don't keep nine-to-five schedules. So you run the risk of answering my calls and if any come for you, I'll let you know." She got up. "Now I must leave you. My medical advice is for you to stay in, have a drink, relax—you're not in good shape and you've had a bad shock. But if you choose to disregard my professional advice, well, I'm not liable in a malpractice suit"—she chuckled slightly—"and keys are in the basket by the sink. I have an answering machine by my bedroom phone—turn it on if you decide to go out." She kissed the air near my face and left.

I wandered restlessly around the apartment for a few minutes. I knew I should go down to my office and assess the damage. I should call a guy I knew who ran a cleaning service to come and restore my apartment. I should call my answering service and get my calls transferred to Lotty's. And I needed to get back to Peter Thayer's apartment to see if there was something there that my apartment smashers believed I had.

Lotty was right: I was not in prime condition. The destruction of my apartment had been shocking. I was consumed with anger, the anger one has when victimized and unable to fight back. I opened my suitcase and got out the box with the gun in it. I unwrapped it and pulled out the Smith & Wesson. While I loaded it, I had a fantasy of planting some kind of hint that would draw Smeissen—or whomever—back to my apartment while I stood in the hallway and pumped them full of bullets. The fantasy was very vivid and I played it through several times. The effect was cathartic—a lot of my anger drained away and I felt able to call my answering service. They took Lotty's number and agreed to transfer my calls.

Finally I sat down and called McGraw. "Good afternoon, Mr. McGraw," I said when he answered. "I hear you've been trying to get in touch with me."

"Yes, about my daughter." He sounded a little ill-at-ease.

"I haven't forgotten her, Mr. McGraw. In fact, I have a lead—not on her directly, but on some people who may know where she's gone."

"How far have you gone with them—these people?" he demanded sharply.

"As far as I could in the time I had. I don't drag cases on just to keep my expense bill mounting."

"Yeah, no one's accusing you of that. I just don't want you to go any further."

"What?" I said incredulously. "You started this whole chain of events and now you don't want me to find Anita? Or did she turn up?"

"No, she hasn't turned up. But I think I flew off the handle a bit when she left her apartment. I thought she might be wrapped up in young Thayer's murder somehow. Now the police have arrested this drug addict, I see the two weren't connected."

Some of my anger returned. "You do? By divine inspiration, maybe? There were no signs of robbery in that apartment, and no sign that Mackenzie had been there. I don't believe he did it."

"Look here, Warshawski, who are you to go around questioning the police? The goddamn punk has been held for two days now. If he hadn't done it, he'd have been let go by now. Now where the hell do you get off saying 'I don't believe it'?" he mimicked me savagely.

"Since you and I last talked, McGraw, I have been beaten and my apartment and office decimated by Earl Smeissen in an effort to get me off the case. If Mackenzie is the murderer, why does Smeissen care so much?"

"What Earl does has no bearing on anything I do," McGraw answered. "I'm telling you to stop looking for my daughter. I hired you and I can fire you. Send me a bill for your expenses—throw in your apartment if you want to. But quit."

"This is quite a change. You were worried sick about your daughter on Friday. What's happened since then?"

"Just get off the case, Warshawski," McGraw bellowed. "I've said I'll pay you—now stop fighting over it."

"Very well," I said in cold anger. "I'm off the payroll. I'll send you a bill. But you're wrong about one thing, McGraw—and you can tell Earl from me—you can fire me, but you can't get rid of me."

I hung up. Beautiful, Vic: beautiful rhetoric. It had just been possible that Smeissen believed he'd cowed me into quitting. So why be so full of female-chismo and yell challenges into the phone? I ought to write, "Think before acting" a hundred times on the blackboard.

At least McGraw had agreed to knowing Earl, or at least to knowing who he was. That had been a shot—not totally in the dark, however, since the Knifegrinders knew most of the hoods in Chicago. The fact that he knew Earl didn't mean he'd sikked him onto my apartment—or onto killing Peter Thayer—but it was sure a better connection than anything else I had.

I dialed Ralph's number. He wasn't home. I paced some more, but decided the time for action had arrived. I wasn't going to get any further thinking about the case, or worrying about intercepting a bullet from Tony's gun. I changed out of the green slacks into jeans and running shoes. I got out my collection of skeleton keys and put them in one pocket, car keys, driver's license, private investigator license, and fifty dollars in the other. I fastened the shoulder holster over a loose, man-tailored shirt and practiced drawing the gun until it came out quickly and naturally.

Before leaving Lotty's, I examined my face in the bathroom mirror. She was right—I did look better. The left side was still discolored—in fact it was showing some more yellow and green—but the swelling had gone down considerably. My left eye was completely open and not inflamed, even though the purple had spread farther. It cheered me up a bit; I switched on Lotty's telephone answering machine, slipped on a jean jacket and left, carefully locking the doors behind me.

The Cubs were playing a doubleheader with St. Louis, and Addison was filled with people leaving the first game and those arriving for the second. I turned on WGN radio just in time to hear DeJesus lead off the bottom of the first inning with a hard drive to the shortstop. He was cut down easily at first, but at least he hadn't hit into a double play.

Once clear of Wrigley Field traffic, it was a quick twenty-minute drive downtown. It being Sunday, I was able to park on the street outside my office. The police had left the area, but a patrolman came over as I entered the building.

"What's your business here, miss?" he asked sharply but not unpleasantly.

"I'm V. I. Warshawski," I told him. "I have an office here which was broken into earlier today and I've come to inspect the damage."

"I'd like to see some identification, please."

I pulled out my driver's license and my private investigator photo-ID. He examined them, nodded, and gave them back to me. "Okay, you can go on up. Lieutenant Mallory told me to keep an eye out and not let anyone but tenants into the building. He told me you'd probably stop by."

I thanked him and went inside. For once the elevator was working and I took it rather than the stairs—I could keep fit someday when I wasn't feeling quite so terrible. The office door was closed, but its upper glass half had been shattered. When I went inside, though, the damage wasn't as severe as to my apartment. True, all my files had been dumped onto the floor, but the furniture had been left intact. No safe is totally entry-proof: someone had been into the little one in back of the big one. But it must have taken five hours at least. No wonder they'd been so angry by the time they got to my apartment—all that effort for nothing. Fortunately I hadn't had any money or sensitive papers in the place at the time.

I decided to leave the papers where they were: tomorrow I'd get a Kelly Girl to come in and file them all for me again. But I'd better call a boarding service for the door, or the place would be ransacked by thieves. I'd lost one of Gabriella's glasses; I didn't want the Olivetti to go as well. I got a twenty-four-hour place to agree to send someone over, and went downstairs. The patrolman wasn't too happy when I explained what I'd done, but he finally agreed to check it with the lieutenant. I left him at the phone and continued on my way to the South Side.

The bright, cool weather was continuing, and I had a pleasant drive south. The lake was dotted with sailboats along the horizon. Nearer the shore were a few swimmers. The game was in the bottom of the third, and Kingman struck out. 2–0, St. Louis. The Cubs had bad days, too—in fact, more than I did, probably.

I parked in the shopping center lot behind the Thayer apartment and reentered the building. The chicken bones had disappeared, but the smell of urine remained. No one came out to question mv right to be in the building, and I had no trouble finding a key to open the third-floor apartment.

I should have been prepared for the shambles, but it took me by surprise. When I'd been here before, there had just been the typical disorder of a student apartment. Now, the same hand or hands that had been to my place had done a similar job here. I shook my head to clear it. Of course. They were missing something, and they had been here first. It was only after they hadn't found it that they had come to me. I whistled a bit between my teeth—the opening bars to the third act of *Simon Boccanegra*—and tried to decide what to do. I wondered what was missing and thought it most likely to be a piece of paper of some kind. It might be evidence of fraud or a picture, but I didn't think it would be an actual object.

It didn't seem too likely that it was still in the apartment. Young Thayer might have given it to Anita. If she had it, she was in worse danger than she seemed to be already. I scratched my head. It looked as though Smeissen's boys had covered all the possibilities—sofa cushions ripped, papers and books dumped on the floor. I decided to believe that they had gone through everything page by page—only if my search didn't turn up anything would I take that job on. In a student apartment with several hundred books it would take a sizable chunk of time to examine each one in detail. The only things that were still intact were appliances and floors. I made a methodical search of all the rooms for loose boards or tiles. I found a few and pried them up, using a hammer I found under the kitchen sink, but didn't turn up anything more interesting than some old termite damage. Then I went through the bathroom fixture by fixture, taking down the shower rod and looking into it, and the toilet and sink pipes. That was quite a job; I had to go to my car for tools and break into the basement to turn off the water. It took me more than an hour to get the rusted fittings loose enough to open them. I wasn't surprised to find nothing but water in them—if anyone had been into them, they would have opened more easily.

It was 6:30 and the sun was going down when I returned to the kitchen. The chair where Peter Thayer had been sitting had had its back to the stove. It was possible, of course, that the missing thing had not been hidden deliberately, but had dropped. A piece of paper might float unnoticed under the stove. I lay on my stomach and shone a flashlight under it. I couldn't see anything, and the opening was pretty small. How thorough did I want to be? My muscles were aching and I had left my phenylbutazone at Lotty's. But I went to the living room and got some bricks from a brick-and-board bookcase. Using the jack from my trunk as a lever and the bricks as a wedge, I slowly pried the stove off the floor. It was an impossible task; the jack would catch and raise the thing, and just as I was kicking a brick under the side, down it would slip again. Finally, by dint of pulling the table over and wedging the jack underneath it, I was able to get one brick under the right side. After that the left came up more easily. I checked the gas line to make sure it wasn't straining, and carefully raised the stove by another brick. I then got down on my stomach again and looked underneath. There it was, a piece of paper stuck by grease to the bottom of the stove. I peeled it slowly off in order not to tear it, and took it over to the window to examine.

It was a carbon copy about eight inches square. The top left corner had the Ajax logo on it. In the center it read, "Draft only: not negotiable," and it was made out to Joseph Gielczowski, of 13227 South Ingleside in Matteson, Illinois. He could take this to a bank and have it certified, at which point Ajax would pay the sum of $250 to the bank as a Workers Compensation indemnity payment. The name meant nothing to me and the transaction sounded perfectly straightforward. What was so important about it? Ralph would know, but I didn't want to call him from here—better get the stove down and leave while the leaving was good.

I levered up the stove, using the table again as a wedge, and pulled the bricks out. The stove made a dull thud as it dropped—I hoped the downstairs neighbors weren't home or were too self-engrossed to call the police. I gathered up my tools, folded the claim draft and put it in my shirt pocket, and left. A second-floor apartment door opened a crack as I went by. "Plumber," I called. "There won't be any water on the third floor tonight." The door closed again and I left the building quickly.

When I got back to my car, the game was long over and I had to wait for the eight o'clock news to come on to get the score. The Cubs had pulled it out in the eighth inning. Good old Jerry Martin had hit a double; Ontiveros had singled, and wonderful Dave Kingman had gotten all three of them home with his thirty-second homer of the season. And all this with two out. I knew how the Cubs were feeling tonight, and sang a little *Figaro* on the way home to show it.

TEN
BEAUTIFUL
PEOPLE

Lotty lifted her thick eyebrows as I came into the living room. "Ah," she said, "success shows in your walk. The office was all right?"

"No, but I found what they were looking for." I took out the draft and showed it to her. "Make anything of it?"

She put on a pair of glasses and looked at it intently, pursing her lips. "I see these from time to time, you understand, when I get paid for administering to industrial accident victims. It looks totally in order, as far as I can tell—of course, I don't read them for their content, just glance at them and send them to the bank. And the name Gielczowski means nothing to me, except that it is Polish: should it?"

I shrugged. "I don't know. Doesn't mean anything to me either. I'd better make a copy of it and get it stowed away, though. Have you eaten?"

"I was waiting for you, my dear," she answered.

"Then let me take you out to dinner. I need it—it took a lot of work finding this, physical I mean, although the mental process helped—nothing like a university education to teach you logic."

Lotty agreed. I showered and changed into a respectable pair of slacks. A dressy shirt and a loose jacket completed the outfit, and the shoulder holster fitted neatly under my left arm. I put the claim draft in my jacket pocket.

Lotty scrutinized me when I came back into the living room. "You hide it well, Vic." I looked puzzled and she laughed. "My dear, you left the empty box in the kitchen garbage, and I knew I had brought no Smith & Wesson into the house. Shall we go?"

I laughed but said nothing. Lotty drove us down to Belmont and Sheridan and we had a pleasant, simple dinner in the wine cellar at the Chesterton Hotel. An Austrian wine store, it had expanded to include a tiny restaurant. Lotty approved of their coffee and ate two of the rich Viennese pastries.

When we got home, I insisted on checking front and back entrances, but no one had been around. Inside, I called Larry Anderson, my cleaning friend, and arranged for him to right my apartment. Not tomorrow—he had a big job on, but he'd go over with his best crew personally on Tuesday. Not at all, he'd be delighted. I got hold of Ralph and agreed to meet him for dinner the next night at Ahab's. "How's your face?" he asked.

"Much better, thanks. I should look almost presentable for you tomorrow night."

At eleven I bade Lotty a very sleepy good night and fell into bed. I was instantly asleep, falling down a black hole into total oblivion. Much later I began dreaming. The red Venetian glasses were lined up on my mother's dining-room table. "Now you must hit high C, Vicki, and hold it," my mother said. I made a tremendous effort and sustained the note. Under my horrified eyes, the row of glasses dissolved into a red pool. It was my mother's blood. With a tremendous effort I pulled myself awake. The phone was ringing.

Lotty had answered it on her extension by the time I oriented myself in the strange bed. When I lifted the receiver, I could hear her crisp, soothing voice saying, "Yes, this is Dr. Herschel." I hung up and squinted at the little illuminated face of the bedside clock: 5:13. Poor Lotty, I thought, what a life, and rolled back over to sleep.

The ringing phone dragged me back to life again several hours later. I dimly remembered the earlier call and, wondering if Lotty were back yet, reached for the phone. "Hello?" I said, and heard Lotty on the other extension. I was about to hang up again when a tremulous little voice said, "Is Miss Warshawski there?"

"Yes, speaking. What can I do for you?" I heard the click as Lotty hung up again.

"This is Jill Thayer," the little voice quavered, trying to speak calmly. "Can you come out to my house, please?"

"You mean right now?" I asked.

"Yes," she breathed.

"Sure thing, honey. Be right out. Can you tell me the trouble now?" I had shoved the receiver between my right shoulder and my ear and was pulling on some clothes. It was 7:30 and Lotty's burlap curtains let in enough light to dress by without my having to fumble for the lamp switch.

"It's—I can't talk right now. My mother wants me. Just come, *please*."

"Okay, Jill. Hold the fort. I'll be there in forty minutes." I hung up and hurriedly finished dressing in the clothes I'd worn last night, not omitting the gun under my left shoulder. I stopped in the kitchen where Lotty was eating toast and drinking the inevitable thick Viennese coffee.

"So," she said, "the second emergency of the day? Mine was a silly hemorrhaging child who had a bad abortion because she was afraid to come to me in the first place." She grimaced. "And the mother was not to know, of course. And you?"

"Off to Winnetka. Another child, but pleasant, not silly." Lotty had the *Sun-Times* open in front of her. "Anything new about the Thayers? She sounded quite panicked."

Lotty poured me a cup of coffee, which I swallowed in scalding gulps while scanning the paper, but I found nothing. I shrugged, took a piece of buttered toast from Lotty, kissed her cheek, and was gone.

Native caution made me check the stairwells and the front walk carefully before going to the street. I even examined the backseat and the engine for untoward activity before getting into the car. Smeissen really had me spooked.

Traffic on the Kennedy was heavy with the Monday morning rush hour and people staggering home at the last minute from weekends in the country. Once I hit the outbound Edens, however, I had the road chiefly to myself. I had given Jill Thayer my card more to let her feel someone cared than because I expected an SOS, and with the half of my mind that wasn't looking for speed traps I wondered what had caused the cry for help. A suburban teen-ager who had never seen death might find anything connected with it upsetting, yet she had struck me as essentially levelheaded. I wondered if her father had gone off the deep end in a big way.

I had left Lotty's at 7:42, and turned onto Willow Road at 8:03. Pretty good time for fifteen miles, considering that three had been in the heavy city traffic on Addison. At 8:09 I pulled up to the gates of the Thayer house. That was as far as I got. Whatever had happened, it was excitement in a big way. The entrance was blocked by a Winnetka police car, lights flashing, and as far as I could see into the yard, it was filled with more cars and many policemen. I backed the Chevy down the road a bit and parked it on the gravel verge. It wasn't until I turned the motor off and got out that I noticed the sleek black Mercedes that had been in the yard on Saturday. Only it wasn't in the yard, it was tilted at a strange angle off the road. And it was no longer sleek. The front tires were flat, and the front windshield was a series of glass shards, fragments left from radiating circles. My guess was that bullets, and many of them, had caused the damage.

In my neighborhood a noisy crowd would have gathered to gape over the sight. This being the North Shore, a crowd had gathered, but a smaller and quieter one than Halsted and Belmont would have attracted. They were being held at bay by a lean young policeman with a mustache.

"Gee, they really got Mr. Thayer's car," I said to the young man, strolling over.

When disaster strikes, the police like to keep all the news to themselves. They never tell you what happened, and they never answer leading questions. Winnetka's finest were no exception. "What do you want?" the young man said suspiciously.

I was about to tell him the candid truth when it occurred to me that it would never get me past the herd in the driveway. "My name is V. I. Warshawski," I said, smiling in what I hoped was a saintly way. "I used to be Miss Jill Thayer's governess. When all the trouble started this morning, she called me and asked me to come out to be with her."

The young cop frowned. "Do you have any identification?" he demanded.

"Certainly," I said righteously. I wondered what use a driver's license would be in proving my story, but I obligingly dug it out and handed it to him.

"All right," he said after studying it long enough to memorize the number, "you can talk to the sergeant."

He left his post long enough to walk me to the gate. "Sarge!" he yelled. One of the men by the door looked up. "This is the Thayer girl's governess!" he called, cupping his hands.

"Thank you, Officer." I said, imitating Miss Jean Brodie's manner. I walked up the drive to the doorway and repeated my story to the sergeant.

He frowned in turn. "We didn't have any word about a governess showing up. I'm afraid no one is allowed in right now. You're not with a newspaper, are you?"

"Certainly not!" I snapped. "Look, Sergeant," I said, smiling a bit to show I could be conciliatory, "how about just asking Miss Thayer to come to the door. She can tell you if she wants me here or not. If she doesn't, I can leave again. But since she did ask for me, she's likely to be upset if I'm not allowed inside."

The upsetness of a Thayer, even one as young as Jill, seemed to concern the sergeant. I was afraid he might ring for Lucy, but instead he asked one of his men to fetch Miss Thayer.

Minutes went by without her appearance, and I began to wonder whether Lucy had seen me after all and set the police straight on my governess story. Eventually Jill arrived, however. Her oval face was pinched and anxious and her brown hair had not been brushed. Her face cleared a little when she saw me. "Oh, it's you!" she said. "They told me my governess was here and I thought it was old Mrs. Wilkens."

"Isn't this your governess?" the patrolman demanded.

Jill gave me an anguished look. I moved into the house. "Just tell the man you sent for me," I said.

"Oh, yes, yes, I did. I called Miss Warshawski an hour ago and begged her to come up here."

The patrolman was looking at me suspiciously, but I was in the house and one of the powerful Thayers wanted me to be there. He compromised by having me spell out my name, letter by laborious letter, for his notebook. Jill tugged on my arm while I was doing this, and as soon as we were through spelling, before he could ask more questions, I gave her a little pat and propelled her toward the hall. She led me to a little room near the big green statue and shut the door.

"Did you say you were my governess?" She was still trying to figure that one out.

"I was afraid they wouldn't let me inside if I told them the truth," I explained. "Police don't like private detectives on their turf. Now suppose you tell me what's going on."

The bleak look reappeared. She screwed up her face. "Did you see the car outside?" I nodded. "My father—that was him, they shot him."

"Did you see them do it?" I asked.

She shook her head and wiped her hand across her nose and forehead. Tears were suddenly streaming down her face. "I heard them," she wailed.

The little room had a settee and a table with some magazines on it. Two heavy-armed chairs stood on either side of a window overlooking the south lawn. I pulled them up to the table and sat Jill in one of them. I sat in the other, facing her. "I'm sorry to put you through it, but I'm going to have to ask you to tell me how it happened. Just take your time, though, and don't mind crying."

The story came out in little sobs. "My dad always leaves—leaves for work between seven and seven thirty," she said. "Sometimes he goes earlier. If something special—special is—going on at the bank. I'm usually asleep when he goes. Lucy makes—made him breakfast, then I get up and she makes another breakfast. Mother has toast and coffee in her room. She's—she's always on a—a diet."

I nodded to explain not only that I understood these details but why she was reporting them. "But today you weren't asleep."

"No," she agreed. "All this stuff about Pete—his funeral was yesterday, you know, and it shook me up so I couldn't—couldn't sleep very well." She'd stopped crying and was trying to control her voice. "I heard Daddy get up, but I didn't go down to eat with him. He'd been so strange, you know, and I didn't want to hear him say anything terrible about Pete." Suddenly she was sobbing, "I wouldn't eat with him, and now he's dead, and now I'll never have another chance." The words came out in great heaving bursts between sobs; she kept repeating them.

I took her hands. "Yes, I know, it's tough, Jill. But you didn't kill him by not eating with him, you know." I patted her hands but didn't say anything else for a while. Finally, though, as the sobs quieted a bit, I said, "Tell me what did happen, honey, and then we can try to figure out an answer to it."

She worked hard to pull herself together, and then said, "There's not much else to tell. My bedroom is above here and I can see the side of the house. I sort of—of wandered to the window and watched him—watched him drive his car down to the road." She stopped to swallow but she had herself in hand. "You can't see the road because of all the bushes in front of it, and anyway, you can't see all the way down to the bottom from my room, but I knew from the sound that he'd gotten down and turned onto Sheridan." I nodded encouragingly, still holding her hands tightly. "Well, I was sort of going back to my bed, I thought I might get dressed, when I heard all these shots. Only I didn't know—know what they were." She carefully wiped two new tears away. "It sounded horrid. I heard glass shattering, and then this squeal, you know, the way a car sounds when it's turning a corner too fast or something, and I thought, maybe Daddy had an accident. You know, he was acting so crazy, he could have gone charging down Sheridan Road and hit someone.

"So I ran downstairs without taking off my nightgown and Lucy came running from the back of the house. She was yelling something, and trying to get me to go back upstairs and get some clothes on, but I went outside anyway and ran down to the drive and found the car." She screwed up her face, shutting her eyes and fought against her tears again. "It was terrible. Daddy—Daddy was bleeding and lying all spread out on the steering wheel." She shook her head. "I still thought he'd been in an accident, but I couldn't see the other car. I thought maybe they'd driven off, you know, the ones with the squealing tires, but Lucy seemed to guess about the shooting. Anyway, she kept me from going over to the car—I didn't have any shoes on, and by then a whole lot of cars had stopped to stare at it and she—Lucy—made one of them call the police on his CB. She wanted me to come back to the house but I wouldn't, not until the police came." She sniffed. "I didn't like to leave him there all by himself, you know."

"Yeah, sure, honey. You did real well. Did your mother come out?"

"No, we went back to the house when the police came, and I came upstairs to get dressed and then I remembered you and called you. But you know when I hung up?" I nodded. "Well, Lucy went to wake up Mother and tell her, and she—she started crying and made Lucy get me, and she came in just then so I had to hang up."

"So you didn't get a glimpse of the people who killed your dad?" She shook her head. "Do the police believe he was in the car you heard taking off?"

"Yes, it's something to do with shells. I think there weren't any shells or something, so they think they must be in the car."

I nodded. "That makes sense. Now for the big question, Jill: Did you want me to come out for comfort and support—which I'm happy to provide—or to take some kind of action?"

She stared at me through gray eyes that had seen and heard too much for her age lately. "What can you do?" she asked.

"You can hire me to find out who killed your dad and your brother," I said matter-of-factly.

"I don't have any money, only my allowance. When I'm twenty-one I get some of my trust money, but I'm only four-teen now."

I laughed. "Not to worry. If you want to hire me, give me a dollar and I'll give you a receipt, and that will mean you've hired me. You'll have to talk to your mother about it, though."

"My money's upstairs," she said, getting up. "Do you think the same person killed Daddy who killed Pete?"

"It seems probable, although I don't really have any facts to go on."

"Do you think it's someone who might—well, is someone trying to wipe out my family?"

I considered that. It wasn't completely out of the question, but it was an awfully dramatic way to do it, and rather slow. "I doubt it," I said finally. "Not completely impossible—but if they wanted to do that, why not just get you all when you were in the car together yesterday?"

"I'll go get my money," Jill said, going to the door. She

opened it and Lucy appeared, crossing the hall. "So that's where you are," she said sharply. "How can you disappear like that and your mother wanting you?" She looked into the room. "Now don't tell me that detective woman got in here! Come on, you," she said to me. "Out you go! We've got trouble enough around here without you stirring it up."

"If you please, Lucy," Jill said in a very grown-up way, "Miss Warshawski came up here because I invited her, and she will leave when I ask her to."

"Well, your mother will have something to say about that," Lucy snapped.

"I'll talk to her myself," Jill snapped back. "Can you wait here, please, while I get my money," she added to me, "and then would you mind coming to see my mother with me? I don't think I can explain it to her by myself."

"Not at all," I said politely, giving her an encouraging smile.

After Jill had gone, Lucy said, "All I can say is that Mr. Thayer didn't want you here, and what he would say if he could see you—"

"Well, we both know he can't," I interrupted. "However, if he had been able to explain—to me or to anyone else—what was on his mind, he would very likely be alive this morning.

"Look. I like Jill and I'd like to help her out. She called me this morning not because she has the faintest idea of what I can do for her as a private detective, but because she feels I'm supporting her. Don't you think she gets left out around here?"

Lucy looked at me sourly. "Maybe so, Miss Detective, maybe so. But if Jill had any consideration for her mother, maybe she'd get a little consideration back."

"I see," I said dryly. Jill came back downstairs.

"Your mother is waiting for you," Lucy reminded her sharply.

"I know!" Jill yelled. "I'm coming." She handed me a dollar, and I gravely wrote out a receipt on a scrap of paper from my handbag. Lucy watched the whole thing angrily, her lips shut in a thin line. We then retraced the route I'd taken Saturday through the long hall. We passed the library door and went clear to the back of the house.

Lucy opened the door to a room on the left, saying, "Here she is, Mrs. Thayer. She's got some terrible detective with her who's trying to take money from her. Mr. Thayer threw her out of the house on Saturday, but now she's back."

A patrolman standing beside the door gave me a startled look.

"Lucy!" Jill stormed. "That's a lie." She pushed her way past the disapproving figure into the room. I stood behind Lucy, looking over her shoulder. It was a delightful room, completely windows on three sides. It overlooked the lake out the east side, and a beautiful lawn, complete with a grass tennis court, on the north. It was furnished with white bamboo furniture with cheerful color accents in reds and yellows in the cushions, lamp bases, and floor covering. A profusion of plants gave it a greenhouse effect.

In the middle of this charming setting was Mrs. Thayer. Even with no makeup and a few tearstains, she was very handsome, easily recognizable as the original of the picture in yesterday's *Herald-Star*. A very pretty young woman, an older edition of Jill, sat solicitously on one side of her, and a handsome young man in a polo shirt and checked trousers sat across from her, looking a little ill-at-ease.

"Please, Jill, I don't understand a word you or Lucy are saying, but don't shout, darling, my nerves absolutely won't stand it."

I moved past Lucy into the room and went over to Mrs. Thayer's couch. "Mrs. Thayer, I'm very sorry about your husband and your son," I said. "My name is V. I. Warshawski. I'm a private detective. Your daughter asked me to come up here this morning to see if I could help out."

The young man answered, sticking his jaw out. "I'm Mrs. Thayer's son-in-law, and I think I can safely say that if my father-in-law threw you out of the house on Saturday, that you're probably not wanted here."

"Jill, did you call her?" the young woman asked, shocked.

"Yes, I did," Jill answered, setting her jaw mulishly. "And you can't throw her out, Jack: it's not your house. I asked her to come up, and I've hired her to find out who killed Daddy and Pete. She thinks the same person did it both times."

"Really, Jill," the other woman said, "I think we can leave this to the police without upsetting Mother by bringing in hired detectives."

"Just what I tried telling her, Mrs. Thorndale, but of course she wouldn't listen." That was Lucy, triumphant.

Jill's face was screwed up again, as if she were going to cry. "Take it easy, honey," I said. "Let's not get everyone more worked up than they are already. Why don't you tell me who's who?"

"Sorry," she gulped. "This is my mother, my sister, Susan Thorndale, and her husband, Jack. And Jack thinks because he can boss Susan around he can do that to me, but—"

"Steady, Jill," I said, putting a hand on her shoulder.

Susan's face was pink. "Jill, if you hadn't been spoiled rotten all these years you would show a little respect to someone like Jack who has a lot more experience than you do. Do you have any idea what people are going to be saying about Daddy, the way he was killed and all? Why, why it looks like a gang killing, and it makes Daddy look as if he was involved with the gang." Her voice rose to a high pitch on the last sentence.

"Mob," I said. Susan looked at me blankly. "It looks like a mob killing. Some gangs may go in for that style of execution, but usually they don't have the resources."

"Now look here," Jack said angrily. "We've already asked you to leave. Why don't you go, instead of showing off your smart mouth! Like Susan said, it's going to be hard enough explaining away the way Mr. Thayer died, without having to explain why we got a private detective involved as well."

"Is that all you care about?" Jill cried. "What people will say? With Pete dead, and Daddy dead?"

"No one is sorrier than me that Peter was shot," Jack said, "but if he had done what your father wanted and lived in a proper apartment, instead of that slummy dump with that slut of a girl, he would never have been shot in the first place."

"Oh!" Jill screamed. "How can you talk about Peter that way! He was trying to do something warm and real instead of— You're such a fake. All you and Susan care about is how much money you make and what the neighbors will say! I hate you!" She ended on another flood of tears and flung herself into my arms. I gave her a hug and wrapped my right arm around her while I fished in my bag for some tissues with the left.

"Jill," her mother said in a soft, complaining voice, "Jill, honey, please don't shout like that in here. My nerves just absolutely cannot take it. I'm just as sorry as you are that Petey is dead, but Jack is right, honey: if he'd listened to your father all this wouldn't have happened, and your father wouldn't be—be . . ." Her voice broke off and she started weeping quietly.

Susan put an arm around her mother and patted her shoulder. "Now, see what you've done," she said venomously, whether to me or to her sister I wasn't sure.

"Now you've caused enough disturbance, you polack detective, whatever your name is," Lucy began.

"Don't you dare talk to her like that," Jill cried, her voice partly muffled by my shoulder. "Her name is Miss Warshawski, and you should call her Miss Warshawski!"

"Well, Mother Thayer," Jack said with a rueful laugh, "sorry to drag you into this, but since Jill won't listen to her sister or me, will you tell her that she has to get this woman out of the house?"

"Oh, please, Jack," his mother-in-law said, leaning on Susan. She stretched out a hand to him without looking at him, and I was interested to note that her eyes didn't turn red with crying. "I just don't have the strength to deal with Jill in one of her moods." However, she pulled herself into a sitting position, still holding on to Jack's hand, and looked at Jill earnestly. "Jill, I just cannot stand for you to have one of your temper tantrums right now. You and Peter never listen to what anyone has to say to you. If Petey had, he wouldn't be dead now. With Petey dead, and John, I just can't take anything else. So don't talk to this private detective any longer. She's taking advantage of you to get her name in the paper, and I can't bear another scandal about this family."

Before I could say anything, Jill tore herself away from me, her little face crimson. "Don't talk like that to me!" she screamed. "I care about Pete and Daddy and you don't! You're the one who's bringing scandals into the house. Everybody knows you didn't love Daddy! Everybody knows what you and Dr. Mulgrave were up to! Daddy was probably—"

Susan leaped up from the couch and slapped her sister hard on the face. "You goddamn brat, be quiet!" Mrs. Thayer started weeping in earnest. Jill, overcome by assorted strong and uncontrollable feelings, began sobbing again.

At that moment a worried-looking man in a business suit came into the room, escorted by one of the patrolmen. He crossed to Mrs. Thayer and clasped her hands. "Margaret! I came as soon as I heard the news. How are you?"

Susan blushed. Jill's sobs died away. Jack looked as though he had been stuffed. Mrs. Thayer turned large tragic eyes to the newcomer's face. "Ted. How kind of you," she said in a brave voice, barely above a whisper.

"Dr. Mulgrave, I presume," I said.

He dropped Mrs. Thayer's wrists and stood up straight. "Yes, I'm Dr. Mulgrave." He looked at Jack. "Is this a policewoman?"

"No," I said. "I'm a private investigator. Miss Thayer has hired me to find out who killed her father and brother."

"Margaret?" he asked incredulously.

"No. *Miss* Thayer. Jill," I said.

Jack said, "Mrs. Thayer just ordered you to leave her house and leave her daughter alone. I'd think even an ambulance chaser like you would know how to take a hint like that."

"Oh, cool it, Thorndale," I said. "What's eating you? Jill asked me to come up here because she's scared silly—as any normal person would be with all this going on. But you guys are so defensive you make me wonder what you're hiding."

"What do you mean?" he scowled.

"Well, why don't you want me looking into your father-in-law's death? What are you afraid I'll find out—that he and Peter caught you with your fingers in the till and you had them shot to shut them up?"

I ignored his outraged gasp. "What about you, Doctor? Did Mr. Thayer learn about your relations with his wife and threaten divorce—but you decided a wealthy widow was a better bet than a woman who couldn't make a very good case for alimony?"

"Now look here, whatever your name is. I don't have to listen to that kind of crap," Mulgrave started.

"Then leave," I said. "Maybe Lucy is using this house as a center for burglarizing wealthy homes on the North Shore—after all, as a maid, she probably hears a lot about where jewelry, documents, and so on are kept. When Mr. Thayer and his son got too hot on her trail, she hired a murderer." I smiled enthusiastically at Susan, who was starting to babble—I was getting carried away by my own fantasies. "I could probably think of a motive for you too, Mrs. Thorndale. All I'm trying to say is, you people are so hostile that it starts me wondering. The less you want me to undertake a murder investigation, the more I start thinking there might be something to my ideas."

When I stopped talking, they were silent for a minute. Mulgrave was clasping Mrs. Thayer's hands again, sitting next to her now. Susan looked like a kitten getting ready to spit at a dog. My client was sitting on one of the bamboo side chairs, her hands clenched in her lap, her face intent. Then Mulgrave said, "Are you trying to threaten us—threaten the Thayer family?"

"If you mean, am I threatening to find out the truth, the answer is yes; if that means turning up a lot of sordid junk along the way, tough."

"Just a minute, Ted," Jack said, waving an arm at the older man. "I know how to deal with her." He nodded at me. "Come on, name your price," he said, pulling out his checkbook.

My fingers itched to bring out the Smith & Wesson and pistol-whip him. "Grow up, Thorndale," I snapped. "There are things in this life that money can't buy. Regardless of what you, or your mother-in-law, or the mayor of Winnetka says, I am investigating this murder—these murders." I laughed a little, mirthlessly. "Two days ago, John Thayer tried to give me $5,000 to buy me out of this case. You guys up here on the North Shore live in some kind of dream world. You think you can buy a cover-up for anything that goes wrong in your lives, just like you hire the garbagemen to take away your filth, or Lucy here to clean it up and carry it outside for you. It doesn't work that way. John Thayer is dead. He couldn't pay enough to get whatever filth he was involved in away from him, nor away from his son. Now whatever it was that caused their deaths isn't private anymore. It doesn't belong to you. Anyone who wants it can find out about it. I intend to."

Mrs. Thayer was moaning softly. Jack looked uncomfortable. With an effort to save his dignity he said, "Naturally, if you choose to poke around in something that's none of your business we can't stop you. It's just that we think matters are better off left to the police."

"Yeah, well, they're not batting a thousand right now," I

said. "They thought they had a guy behind bars for the crime, but while he was eating his prison breakfast this morning John Thayer got killed."

Susan turned to Jill. "This is all your fault! You brought this person up here. Now we've been insulted and embarrassed—I've never been more ashamed in my life. Daddy's been killed and all you can think about is bringing in some outsider to call us names."

Mulgrave turned back to Mrs. Thorndale, and Jack and Susan both started talking to him at once. While this was going on, I walked over to Jill and knelt down to look her in the face. She was looking as though she might collapse or go into shock. "Look, I think you need to get away from all this. Is there any friend or relative you can visit until the worst of the fuss is over?"

She thought for a minute, then shook her head. "Not really. I've got lots of friends, you know, but I don't think any of their mothers would like having me around right now." She gave a wobbly smile. "The scandal, you know, like Jack said. I wish Anita were here."

I hesitated a minute. "Would you like to come back to Chicago with me? My apartment's been torn up, and I'm staying with a friend, but she'll be glad to have you, too, for a few days." Lotty would never mind another stray. I needed Jill where I could ask her some questions, and I wanted her away from her family. She was tough and could fight back, but she didn't need to do that kind of fighting on top of the shock of her father's death.

Her face lightened. "Do you really mean that?"

I nodded. "Why don't you run upstairs now and pack an overnight bag while everyone is still arguing here."

When she had left the room, I explained what I was doing to Mrs. Thayer. This, predictably, started a fresh uproar from the family. Finally, though, Mulgrave said, "It's important that Margaret—Mrs. Thayer—be kept absolutely quiet. If Jill really is worrying her, perhaps it would be better if she did leave for a few days. I can make some inquiries about this person, and if she's not reliable, we can always bring Jill back home."

Mrs. Thayer gave a martyred smile. "Thank you, Ted. If you say it's all right, I'm sure it will be. As long as you live in a safe neighborhood, Miss—"

"Warshawski," I said dryly. "Well, no one's been machine-gunned there this week."

Mulgrave and Jack decided I ought to give them some references to call. I saw that as a face-saving effort and gave them the name of one of my old law professors. He would be startled but supportive if he got an inquiry into my character.

When Jill came back, she'd brushed her hair and washed her face. She went over to her mother, who was still sitting on the couch. "I'm sorry, Mother," she muttered. "I didn't mean to be rude to you."

Mrs. Thayer smiled wanly. "It's all right, dear. I don't expect you to understand how I feel." She looked at me. "Take good care of her for me."

"Sure," I answered.

"I don't want any trouble," Jack warned me.

"I'll keep that in mind, Mr. Thorndale." I picked up Jill's suitcase and she followed me out the door.

She stopped in the doorway to look at her family. "Well, good-bye," she said. They all looked at her but no one said anything.

When we got to the front door, I explained to the sergeant that Miss Thayer was coming home with me for a few days to get a little rest and attention; had the police taken all the statements they needed from her? After some talk with his lieutenant over the walkie-talkie, he agreed that she could leave, as long as I gave him my address. I gave it to him and we walked down the drive.

Jill didn't say anything on the way over to the Edens. She looked straight ahead and didn't pay much attention to the countryside. As we joined the stop-and-go traffic on the southbound Kennedy, though, she turned to look at me. "Do you think I was wrong, leaving my mother like that?"

I braked to let a fifty-ton semi merge in front of me. "Well, Jill, it seemed to me that everyone there was trying to play on your guilt feelings. Now you're feeling guilty, so maybe they got what they wanted out of you."

She digested that for a few minutes. "Is that a scandal, the way my father was killed?"

"People are probably talking about it, and that will make Jack and Susan very uncomfortable. The real question, though, is why he was killed—and even the answer to that question doesn't have to be a scandal to you." I threaded my way around a *Herald-Star* delivery van. "Thing is, you have to have your own sense of what's right built inside you. If your father ran afoul of the type of people who do machine-gun-style executions, it may be because they tried to violate his sense of what's right. No scandal to that. And even if he happened to be involved in some kind of shady activity, it doesn't have to affect you unless you want it to." I changed lanes. "I don't believe in the visitation of the sins of the fathers, and I don't believe in people brooding over vengeance for twenty years."

Jill turned a puzzled face toward me. "Oh, it can happen. It's just that you've got to want to make it happen. Like your mother—unhappy woman—right?" Jill nodded. "And probably unhappy because of things that happened thirty years ago. That's her choice. You've got the same choice. Suppose your father did something criminal and we find that out? It's going to be rough, but it only has to be a scandal and make your life miserable if you let it. Lots of things in this life happen to you no matter what you do, or through no fault of your own—like your father and brother getting killed. But how you make those events part of your life is under your control. You can get bitter, although I don't think you have that kind of character, or you can learn and grow from it."

I realized that I'd passed the Addison exit and turned onto

the Belmont off-ramp. "Sorry—that answer turned into a sermon, and I got so carried away I missed my exit. Does it help any?"

Jill nodded and was quiet again as I drove north along Pulaski and then turned east on Addison. "It's lonely now, with Peter gone," she said finally. "He was the only one in the family who—who cared about me."

"Yeah, it's going to be rough, sweetie," I said gently, and squeezed her hand.

"Thank you for coming up, Miss Warshawski," she whispered.

I had to lean over to hear her. "My friends call me Vic," I said.

ELEVEN
FRIENDLY PERSUASION

I stopped at the clinic before going to the apartment to let Lotty know I'd made free with her hospitality and to see if she thought Jill needed anything for shock. A small group of women, most of them with young children, were waiting in the little anteroom. Jill looked around her curiously. I poked my head into the inner door, where Lotty's nurse, a young Puerto Rican woman, saw me. "Hello, Vic," she said. "Lotty's with a patient. Do you need something?"

"Hi, Carol. Tell her that I'd like to bring my young friend back to her apartment—the one I went out this morning to see. She'll know whom you mean. And ask her if she can take a quick look at her—healthy kid, but she's had a lot of stress lately."

Carol went into the tiny examining room where she spoke for a few minutes. "Bring her into the office. Lotty will take a quick look at her after Mrs. Segi has left. And of course, take her to the apartment."

I took Jill into Lotty's office, among disapproving frowns from those who had been waiting longer. While we waited, I told her a little bit about Lotty, Austrian war refugee, brilliant London University medical student, maverick doctor, warm friend. Lotty herself came bustling in.

"So, this is Miss Thayer," she said briskly. "Vic has brought you down for a little rest? That's good." She lifted

Jill's chin with her hand, looked at her pupils, made her do some simple tests, talking all the while.

"What was the trouble?" she asked.

"Her father was shot," I explained.

Lotty clicked her tongue and shook her head, then turned to Jill. "Now, open your mouth. No, I know you haven't got a sore throat, but it's free, I'm a doctor, and I have to look. Good. Nothing wrong with you, but you need some rest and something to eat. Vic, when you get her home, a little brandy. Don't talk too much, let her get some rest. Are you going out?"

"Yes, I've got a lot to do."

She pursed her lips and thought a minute. "I'll send Carol over in about an hour. She can stay with Jill until one of us gets home."

At that moment I realized how much I liked Lotty. I'd been a little uneasy about leaving Jill alone, in case Earl was close on my trail. Whether Lotty knew that, or simply felt a scared young girl should not be left alone, it was a worry I now did not have to speak aloud.

"Great. I'll wait until she gets there."

We left the clinic among more baleful stares while Carol summoned the next patient. "She's nice, isn't she?" Jill said as we got into the car.

"Lotty or Carol?"

"Both, but Lotty, I meant. She really doesn't mind me showing up like this, does she?"

"No," I agreed. "All of Lotty's instincts are directed at helping people. She's just not sentimental about it."

When we got back to the apartment, I made Jill stay in the car while I checked the street and the entrance way. I didn't want to add to her fears, but I didn't want anyone getting a shot at her, either. The coast was still clear. Maybe Earl really did believe he'd scared me off. Or maybe with the police arresting poor Donald Mackenzie, he was resting easy.

When we got inside, I told Jill to take a hot bath. I was going to prepare some breakfast, and I would have to ask her a few questions, but then she was to sleep. "I can tell by your eyes that you haven't been doing that for a while," I said.

Jill agreed shyly. I helped her unpack her small suitcase in the room I'd been sleeping in; I could sleep on the daybed in the living room. I got out one of Lotty's enormous white bath sheets and showed her the bathroom.

I realized that I was quite hungry; it was ten and I hadn't eaten the toast Lotty had thrust at me. I foraged in the refrigerator: no juice—Lotty never drank anything out of cans. I found a drawer full of oranges and squeezed a small pitcher of juice, and then took some of Lotty's thick light Viennese bread and turned it into French toast, whistling under my breath. I realized I felt good, despite Thayer's death and all the unexplained dangling pieces to the case. Some instinct told me that things were finally starting to happen.

When Jill emerged pink and sleepy from the bath, I set her to eating, holding my questions and telling her a little bit about myself in answer to her inquiries. She wanted to know if I always caught the killer.

"This is the first time I've ever really dealt directly with a killer," I answered. "But generally, yes, I do get to the root of the problems I'm asked to look into."

"Are you scared?" Jill asked. "I mean, you've been beaten up and your apartment got torn up, and they—they shot Daddy and Pete."

"Yes, of course I'm scared," I said calmly. "Only a fool would look at a mess like this and not be. It's just that it doesn't panic me—it makes me careful, being scared does, but it doesn't override my judgment.

"Now, I want you to tell me everything you can remember about whom your father talked to in the last few days, and what they said. We'll go sit on the bed, and you'll drink some hot milk with brandy as Lotty ordered, so that when I'm done you'll go to sleep."

She followed me into the bedroom and got into bed, obediently sipping at the milk. I had put in brown sugar and nutmeg and laced it heavily. She made a face but continued sipping it while we talked.

"When I came out on Saturday, you said your father at first didn't believe this Mackenzie they've arrested killed your brother, but the neighbors talked him out of it. What neighbors?"

"Well, a lot of people came by, and they all more or less said the same thing. Do you want all their names?"

"If you can remember them and remember what they said."

We went through a list of about a dozen people, which included Yardley Masters and his wife, the only name I recognized. I got some long histories of relations among the families, and Jill contorted her face in the effort of trying to remember exactly what they'd all said.

"You said they 'all more or less said the same thing,' " I repeated after a while. "Was anyone more emphatic about it than the others?"

She nodded at that. "Mr. Masters. Daddy kept raving that he was sure that Anita's father had done it, and Mr. Masters said something like, 'Look, John, you don't want to keep going around saying things like that. A lot of things could come out that you don't want to hear.' Then Daddy got mad and started yelling, 'What do you mean? Are you threatening me?' And Mr. Masters said, 'No, of course not, John. We're friends. Just giving you some advice,' or something like that."

"I see," I said. Very illuminating. "Was that all?"

"Yes, but it was after Mr. and Mrs. Masters left that Daddy said he guessed he was wrong, which made me glad at the time, because of course Anita wouldn't try to kill Peter. But then he started saying terrible things about Peter."

"Yeah, let's not talk about that now. I want you to calm down so you can sleep. Did anything happen yesterday?"

"Well, he got into a fight with someone on the phone, but

I don't know who, or what it was about. I think it was some deal going on at the bank, because he said, 'I won't be a party to it'—that's all I heard. He'd been so—strange." She gulped and swallowed some more milk. "At the funeral, you know, I sort of was staying out of his way. And when I heard him start yelling on the phone, I just went outside. Susan was after me anyway to put on a dress and sit in the living room entertaining all these gruesome people who came over after the funeral, so I just sort of left and went down to the beach."

I laughed a little. "Good for you. This fight on the telephone—did your father get a call or make a call?"

"I'm pretty sure he made it. At least, I don't remember hearing the phone ring."

"Okay, all that's a help. Now try to put it out of your mind. You finish your milk while I brush your hair, and then you sleep."

She was really very tired; between the hairbrushing and the brandy she relaxed and lay down. "Stay with me," she asked drowsily. I pulled the shades behind the burlap curtains and sat down beside Jill, holding her hand. Something about her pierced my heart, made me long for the child I'd never had, and I watched her carefully until she was in a deep sleep.

While I waited for Carol, I made some phone calls, first to Ralph. I had to wait a few minutes while a secretary hunted him down on the floor, but he was as cheerful as ever when he came on the line. "How's it going, Sherlock?" he asked breezily.

"Pretty well," I answered.

"You're not calling to cancel dinner tonight, are you?"

"No, no," I assured him. "I'd just like you to do something that you can find out more easily than I can."

"What's that?"

"Just find out if your boss has had any calls from a guy named Andrew McGraw. And do it without letting him know you're asking."

"Are you still flogging that dead horse?" he asked, a little exasperated.

"I haven't written anyone off, Ralph, not even you."

"But the police made an arrest."

"Well, in that case, your boss is innocent. Just look on it as a favor to a lady who's had a rough week."

"All right," he agreed, not too happily. "But I wish you could believe the police know as much about catching murderers as you do."

I laughed. "You're not the only one. . . . By the way, did you know young Peter's father was killed this morning?"

"What!" he exclaimed. "How did that happen?"

"Well, he was shot. Too bad Donald Mackenzie is already in jail, but there must be some dope dealers on the North Shore to take the blame for this one."

"You think Peter's death is connected to this?"

"Well, it staggers the imagination if two members of the same family are killed within a week of each other and those events are only randomly associated."

"All right, all right," Ralph said. "You've made your point— no need to be sarcastic. . . . I'll ask Yardley's secretary."

"Thanks, Ralph, see you tonight."

The claim draft, Masters's remarks to Thayer, which might or might not have been vague threats. It didn't add up to much, but it was worth pursuing. The other piece to the puzzle was McGraw and the fact that McGraw knew Smeissen. Now, if I could connect McGraw and Masters, or Masters and Smeissen. . . . I should have asked Ralph to check on Earl too. Well, I could do that tonight. Say McGraw and Masters were doing an unspecified something together. If they were smart, they wouldn't leave names when they called each other. Even McGraw's enchanting secretary might give him away to the police if the evidence was hot enough. But they might get together, meet for a drink. I might make a trip to bars in the Loop and near Knifegrinder headquarters to see if the two had ever been seen together. Or Thayer with

McGraw, for that matter. I needed some photographs, and I had an idea where to find them.

Carol arrived as I was looking a number up in the directory. "Jill's asleep," I told her. "I hope she'll sleep through the afternoon."

"Good," she answered. "I've brought all the old medical records over: we're always too busy at the clinic to get them updated, but this is a good opportunity."

We chatted for a few minutes about her mother, who had emphysema, and the prospects for finding the arsonists who were plaguing the neighborhood, before I went back to the phone.

Murray Ryerson was the crime reporter for the *Herald-Star* who interviewed me after the Transicon case broke. He'd had a by-line, and a lot of his stuff was good. It was getting close to lunch, and I wasn't sure he'd be in when I called the city desk, but my luck seemed to be turning.

"Ryerson," he rumbled into the phone.

"This is V. I. Warshawski."

"Oh, hi," he said, mind turning over competently and remembering me without trouble. "Got any good stories for me today?"

"Not today. But I might have later in the week. I need some help, though. A couple of pictures."

"Whose?"

"Look, if I tell you, will you promise not to put two and two together in the paper until I have some evidence?"

"Maybe. Depends on how close you're coming to a story that we know is happening anyway."

"Andrew McGraw on any of your hot lists?"

"Oh, he's a perennial favorite but we don't have anything breaking on him right now. Who's the other?"

"Guy named Yardley Masters. He's a vice-president over at Ajax, and you probably have something in your file from Crusade of Mercy publicity or something like that."

"You tying McGraw to Ajax?"

"Stop slobbering in the phone, Murray; Ajax doesn't do any business with the Knifegrinders."

"Well, are you tying McGraw to Masters?" he persisted.

"What is this, twenty questions?" I said irritably. "I need two pictures. If a story breaks, you can have it—you did all right from me on Transicon, didn't you?"

"Tell you what—you eaten yet? Good, I'll meet you at Fiorella's in an hour with the pictures, if any, and try to pick your brains over a beer."

"Great, Murray, thanks." I hung up and looked at my watch. An hour would give me time to stop and register the Smith & Wesson. I started humming *"Ch'io mi scordi di te"* again. "Tell Lotty I'll be back around six but I'll be eating dinner out," I called to Carol on my way out.

TWELVE
PUB CRAWL

The eager bureaucrats at City Hall took longer than I expected with forms, fees, incomprehensible directions, and anger at being asked to repeat them. I was already running late, but I decided to stop at my lawyer's office to drop off a Xerox of the claim draft I'd found in Peter Thayer's apartment. He was a dry, imperturbable man, and accepted without a blink my instructions to give the draft to Murray Ryerson should anything happen to me in the next few days.

By the time I got to Fiorella's, a pleasant restaurant whose outdoor tables overlooked the Chicago River, Murray was already finishing his second beer. He was a big man who looked like a red-haired Elliott Gould, and he waved a hand at me lazily when he saw me coming.

A high-masted sailboat was floating past. "You know, they're going to raise every drawbridge along here for that one boat. Hell of a system, isn't it," he said as I came up.

"Oh, there's something appealing about a little boat being able to stop all the traffic on Michigan Avenue. Unless, of course, the bridge gets stuck up just when you need to cross the river." This was an all-too-frequent happening: motorists had no choice but to sit and boil quietly while they waited. "Has there ever been a murder when one of these bridges is stuck—someone getting too angry and shooting the bridge tender or something?"

"Not yet," Murray said. "If it happens, I'll be on the spot to interview you. . . . What are you drinking?"

I don't like beer that well; I ordered a white wine.

"Got your pix for you." Murray tossed a folder over to me.

"We had a lot of choice on McGraw, but only dug one up for Masters—he's receiving some civic award out in Winnetka—they never ran the shot but it's a pretty good three-quarter view. I got you a couple of copies."

"Thanks," I said, opening the folder. The one of Masters was good. He was shaking hands with the Illinois president of the Boy Scouts of America. At his right was a solemn-faced youth in uniform who apparently was his son. The picture was two years old.

Murray had brought me several of McGraw, one outside a federal courtroom where he was walking pugnaciously in front of a trio of Treasury men. Another, taken under happier circumstances, showed him at the gala celebration when he was first elected president of the Knifegrinders nine years ago. The best for my purposes, though, was a close-up, taken apparently without his knowledge. His face was relaxed, but concentrating.

I held it out toward Murray. "This is great. Where was it taken?"

Murray smiled. "Senate hearings on racketeering and the unions."

No wonder he looked so thoughtful.

A waiter came by for our order. I asked for mostaccioli; Murray chose spaghetti with meatballs. I was going to have to start running again, sore muscles or not, with all the starch I was eating lately.

"Now, V. I. Warshawski, most beautiful detective in Chicago, what gives with these pictures," Murray said, clasping his hands together on the table and leaning over them toward me. "I recall seeing that dead young Peter Thayer worked for Ajax, in fact for Mr. Masters, an old family friend. Also, somewhere in the thousands of lines that have been churned out since he died, I recall reading that his girl friend, the lovely and dedicated Anita McGraw, was the daughter of well-known union leader Andrew McGraw. Now you want pictures of both of them. Is it possible that you are suggest-ing they colluded in the death of young Thayer, and possibly his father as well?"

I looked at him seriously. "It was like this, Murray: Mc-Graw has what amounts to a psychopathic hatred of capitalist bosses. When he realized that his pure young daughter, who had always been protected from any contact with manage-ment, was seriously considering marrying not just a boss, but the son of one of Chicago's wealthiest businessmen, he de-cided the only thing to do was to have the young man put six feet underground. His psychosis is such that he decided to have John Thayer eliminated as well, just for—"

"Spare me the rest," Murray said. "I can spell it out for myself. Is either McGraw or Masters your client?"

"You'd better be buying this lunch, Murray—it is definitely a business expense."

The waiter brought our food, slapping it down in the hur-ried, careless way that is the hallmark of business restaurants at lunch. I snatched the pictures back just in time to save them from spaghetti sauce and started sprinkling cheese on my pasta: I love it really cheesy.

"Do you have a client?" he asked, spearing a meatball.

"Yes, I do."

"But you won't tell me who it is?" I smiled and nodded agreement.

"You buy Mackenzie as Thayer Junior's murderer?" Mur-ray asked.

"I haven't talked to the man. But one does have to wonder who killed Thayer Senior if Mackenzie killed the son. I don't like the thought of two people in the same family killed in the same week for totally unconnected reasons by uncon-nected people: laws of chance are against that," I answered. "What about you?"

He gave a big Elliott Gould smile. "You know, I talked to Lieutenant Mallory after the case first broke, and he didn't say anything about robbery, either of the boy or of the apartment. Now, you found the body, didn't you? Well, did the apartment look ransacked?"

"I couldn't really tell if anything had been taken—I didn't know what was supposed to be there."

"By the way, what took you down there in the first place?" he asked casually.

"Nostalgia, Murray—I used to go to school down there and I got an itch to see what the old place looked like."

Murray laughed. "Okay, Vic, you win—can't fault me for trying though, can you?"

I laughed too. I didn't mind. I finished my pasta—no child had ever died in India because of my inhumane failure to clean my plate.

"If I find out anything you might be interested in, I'll let you know," I said.

Murray asked me when I thought the Cubs would break this year. They were looking scrappy right now—two and a half games out.

"You know, Murray, I am a person with very few illusions about life. I like to have the Cubs as one of them." I stirred my coffee. "But I'd guess the second week in August. What about you?"

"Well, this is the third week in July. I give them ten more games. Martin and Buckner can't carry that team."

I agreed sadly. We finished lunch on baseball and split the check when it came.

"There is one thing, Murray."

He looked at me intently. I almost laughed, the change in his whole posture had been so complete—he really looked like a bloodhound on the trail, now.

"I have what I think is a clue. I don't know what it means, or why it is a clue. But I've left a copy of it with my attorney. If I should be bumped off, or put out of action for any length of time, he has instructions to give it to you."

"What is it?" Murray asked.

"You ought to be a detective, Murray—you ask as many

questions and you're just as hot when you're on the trail. One thing I will say—Earl Smeissen's hovering around this case. He gave me this beautiful black eye which you've been too gentlemanly to mention. It wouldn't be totally out of the question for my body to come floating down the Chicago River—you might look out your office window every hour or so to see."

Murray didn't look surprised. "You already knew that?" I asked.

He grinned. "You know who arrested Donald Mackenzie?"

"Yes, Frank Carlson."

"And whose boy is Carlson?" he asked.

"Henry Vespucci."

"And do you know who's been covering Vespucci's back all these years?"

I thought about it. "Tim Sullivan?" I guessed.

"The lady wins a Kewpie doll," Murray said. "Since you know that much, I'll tell you who Sullivan spent Christmas in Florida with last year.

"Oh, Christ! Not Earl."

Murray laughed. "Yes. Earl Smeissen himself. If you're playing around with that crowd, you'd better be very, very careful."

I got up and stuck the folder in my shoulder bag. "Thanks, Murray, you're not the first one to tell me so. Thanks for the pictures. I'll let you know if anything turns up."

As I climbed over the barrier separating the restaurant from the sidewalk, I could hear Murray yelling a question behind me. He came pounding up to me just as I reached the top of the stairs leading from the river level to Michigan Avenue. "I want to know what it was you gave your lawyer," he panted.

I grinned. "So long, Murray," I said, and boarded a Michigan Avenue bus.

I had a plan that was really a stab in the dark more than anything else. I was assuming that McGraw and Masters worked together. And I was hoping they met at some point. They could handle everything over the phone or by mail. But McGraw might be wary of federal wiretaps and mail interception. He might prefer to do business in person. So say they met from time to time. Why not in a bar? And if in a bar, why not one near to one or the other of their offices? Of course, it was possible that they met as far from anyplace connected to either of them as they could. But my whole plan was based on a series of shots in the dark. I didn't have the resources to comb the whole city, so I'd just have to add one more assumption to my agenda, and hope that if they met, and if they met in a bar, they did so near where they worked. My plan might not net me anything, but it was all I could think of. I was pinning more hope on what I might learn about Anita from the radical women's group tomorrow night; in the meantime I needed to keep busy.

Ajax's glass-and-steel high-rise was on Michigan Avenue at Adams. In the Loop, Michigan is the easternmost street. The Art Institute is across the street, and then Grant Park goes down to the lake in a series of pleasant fountains and gardens. I decided to take the Fort Dearborn Trust on La Salle Street as my western border, and to work from Van Buren, two blocks south of Ajax, up to Washington, three blocks north. A purely arbitrary decision, but the bars in that area would keep me busy for some time; I could expand it in desperation if that was necessary.

I rode my bus south past the Art Institute to Van Buren and got off. I felt very small walking between the high-rises when I thought of the vast territory I had to cover. I wondered how much I might have to drink to get responses from the myriad bartenders. There probably is a better way to do this, I thought, but this was the only way that occurred to me. I had to work with what I could come up with—no Peter Wimsey at home thinking of the perfect logical answer for me.

I squared my shoulders and walked half a block along Van

Buren and went into the Spot, the first bar I came to. I'd debated about an elaborate cover story, and finally decided that something approximating the truth was best.

The Spot was a dark, narrow bar built like a railway caboose. Booths lined the west wall and a long bar ran the length of the east, leaving just enough room for the stout, bleached waitress who had to tend to orders in the booths.

I sat up at the bar. The bartender was cleaning glasses. Most of the luncheon trade had left; only a few diehard drinkers were sitting farther down from me. A couple of women were finishing hamburgers and daiquiris in one of the booths. The bartender continued his work methodically until the last glass was rinsed before coming down to take my order. I stared ahead with the air of a woman in no particular hurry.

Beer is not my usual drink, but it was probably the best thing to order on an all-day pub crawl. It wouldn't make me drunk. Or at least not as quickly as wine or liquor.

"I'd like a draft," I said.

He went to his spigots and filled a glass with pale yellow and foam. When he brought it back to me, I pulled out my folder. "You ever see these two guys come in here?" I asked.

He gave me a sour look. "What are you, a cop or something?"

"Yes," I said. "Have you ever seen these two guys in here together?"

"I'd better get the boss on this one," he said. Raising his voice, he called "Herman!" and a heavy man in a polyester suit got up from the booth at the far end of the room. I hadn't noticed him when I came in, but now I saw that another waitress was sitting in the booth. The two were sharing a late lunch after the hectic noon-hour rush.

The heavy man joined the bartender behind the bar.

"What's up, Luke?"

Luke jerked his head toward me. "Lady's got a question." He went back to his glasses, stacking them in careful pyramids on either side of the cash register. Herman came down toward me. His heavyset face looked tough but not mean. "What do you want, ma'am?"

I pulled my photos out again. "I'm trying to find out if these two men have ever been in here together," I said in a neutral voice.

"You got a legal reason for asking?"

I pulled my P.I. license from my handbag. "I'm a private investigator. There's a grand jury investigation and there's some question of collusion between a witness and a juror." I showed him the ID.

He looked at the ID briefly, grunted, and tossed it back to me. "Yeah, I see you're a private investigator, all right. But I don't know about this grand jury story. I know this guy." He tapped Masters's picture. "He works up at Ajax. Doesn't come in here often, maybe three times a year, but he's been doing it as long as I've owned the place."

I didn't say anything, but took a swallow of beer. Anything tastes good when your throat is dry from embarrassment.

"Tell you for free, though, this other fellow's never been in here. At least not when I've been here." He gave a shout of laughter and reached across the bar to pat my cheek. "That's okay, cookie, I won't spoil your story for you."

"Thanks," I said dryly. "What do I owe you for the beer?"

"On the house." He gave another snort of laughter and rolled back down the aisle to his unfinished lunch. I took another swallow of the thin beer. Then I put a dollar on the counter for Luke and walked slowly out of the bar.

I walked on down Van Buren past Sears's main Chicago store. A lot of short-order food places were on the other side, but I had to go another block to find another bar. The bartender looked blankly at the photos and called the waitress over. She looked at both of them doubtfully, and then picked up McGraw's. "He looks kind of familiar," she said. "Is he on TV or something?" I said no, but had she ever seen him in the bar. She didn't think so, but she couldn't swear to it. What about Masters? She didn't think so, but a lot of businessmen came in there, and all men with gray hair and business suits ran together in her mind after a while. I put two singles on the counter, one for her and one for the bartender, and went on down the street.

Her TV question gave me an idea for a better cover story. The next place I went to I said I was a market researcher looking for viewer recognition. Did anyone remember ever seeing these two people together? This approach got more interest, but drew another blank.

The game was on TV in this bar, bottom of the fourth with Cincinnati leading 4–0. I watched Biittner hit a single and then die on second after a hair-raising steal before I moved on. In all, I went to thirty-two bars that afternoon, catching most of the game in between. The Cubs lost, 6–2. I'd covered my territory pretty thoroughly. A couple of places recognized McGraw vaguely, but I put that down to the number of times his picture had been in the paper over the years. Most people probably had a vague recognition of Jimmy Hoffa, too. One other bar knew Masters by sight as one of the men from Ajax, and Billy's knew him by name and title as well. But neither place remembered seeing McGraw with him. Some places were hostile and took a combination of bribes and threats to get an answer. Some were indifferent. Others, like the Spot, had to have the manager make the decision. But none of them had seen my pair together.

It was after six by the time I got to Washington and State, two blocks west of Michigan. After my fifth bar I'd stopped drinking any of the beer I ordered, but I was feeling slightly bloated, as well as sweaty and depressed. I'd agreed to meet Ralph at Ahab's at eight. I decided to call it an afternoon and go home to wash up first.

Marshall Field occupies the whole north side of the street between State and Wabash. It seemed to me there might be one other bar on Washington, close to Michigan, if my memory of the layout was correct. That could wait until another day. I went down the stairs to the State Street subway and boarded a B train to Addison.

Evening rush hour was still in full force. I couldn't get a seat and had to stand all the way to Fullerton.

At Lotty's I headed straight for the bathroom and a cold shower. When I came out, I looked into the guest room; Jill was up, so I dumped my clothes in a drawer and put on a caftan. Jill was sitting on the living-room floor playing with two rosy-cheeked, dark-haired children who looked to be three or four.

"Hi, honey. You get a good rest?"

She looked up at me and smiled. A lot of color had returned to her face and she seemed much more relaxed. "Hi," she said. "Yes, I only woke up an hour ago. These are Carol's nieces. She was supposed to baby-sit tonight, but Lotty talked her into coming over here and making homemade enchiladas, yum-yum."

"Yum-yum," the two little girls chorused.

"That sounds great. I'm afraid I have to go back out tonight, so I'll have to give it a miss."

Jill nodded. "Lotty told me. Are you doing some more detecting?"

"Well, I hope so."

Lotty called out from the kitchen and I went in to say hi. Carol was working busily at the stove and turned briefly to flash me a bright smile. Lotty was sitting at the table reading the paper, drinking her ever-lasting coffee. She looked at me through narrowed eyes. "The detective work wasn't so agreeable this afternoon, eh?"

I laughed. "No. I learned nothing and had to drink too much beer doing so. This stuff smells great; wish I could cancel this evening out."

"Then do so."

I shook my head. "I feel as though I don't have much time—maybe this second murder. Even though I feel a little rocky—too long a day, too much heat, I can't stop. I just hope

I don't get sick at dinner—my date is getting fed up with me as it is. Although maybe if I fainted or something it would make him feel stronger, more protective." I shrugged. "Jill looks a lot better, don't you think?"

"Oh, yes. The sleep did her good. That was well thought of, to get her out of that house for a while. I talked to her a bit when I came in; she's very well behaved, doesn't whine and complain, but it's obvious the mother has no emotions to spare for her. As for the sister—" Lotty made an expressive gesture.

"Yeah, I agree. We can't keep her down here forever, though. Besides, what on earth can she do during the day? I've got to be gone again tomorrow, and not on the kind of errand that she can go along with."

"Well, I've been thinking about that. Carol and I had a bit of an idea, watching her with Rosa and Tracy—the two nieces. Jill is good with these children—took them on, we didn't ask her to look after them. Babies are good when you're depressed—something soft and unquestioning to cuddle. What would you think of her coming over to the clinic and minding children there for a day? As you saw this morning, they're always tumbling around the place—mothers who are sick can't leave them alone; or if one baby is sick, who looks after the other when Mama brings him in?"

I thought it over for a minute, but couldn't see anything wrong with it. "Ask her," I said. "I'm sure the best thing for her right now would be to have something to do."

Lotty got up and went to the living room. I followed. We stood for a minute, watching the three girls on the floor. They were terribly busy about something, although it wasn't clear what. Lotty squatted down next to them, moving easily. I moved into the background. Lotty spoke perfect Spanish, and she talked to the little girls in that language for a minute. Jill watched her respectfully.

Then Lotty turned to Jill, still balancing easily on her

haunches. "You're very good with these little ones. Have you worked with young children before?"

"I was a counselor at a little neighborhood day camp in June," Jill said, flushing a bit. "But that's all. I never baby-sit or anything like that."

"Well, I had a bit of a plan. See what you think. Vic must be gone all the time, trying to find out why your father and brother were killed. Now while you are visiting down here, you could be of great help to me at the clinic." She outlined her idea.

Jill's face lit up. "But you know," she said seriously, "I don't have any training. I might not know what to do if they all started to cry or something."

"Well, if that happens, that will be the test of your knack and patience," Lotty said. "I will provide you a little assistance by way of a drawerful of lollipops. Bad for the teeth, perhaps, but great for tears."

I went into the bedroom to change for dinner. Jill hadn't made the bed. The sheets were crumpled. I straightened them out, then thought I might just lie down for a minute to recover my equilibrium.

The next thing I knew Lotty was shaking me awake. "It's seven thirty, Vic: don't you have to be going?"

"Oh, hell!" I swore. My head was thick with sleep. "Thanks, Lotty." I swung out of bed and hurriedly put on a bright orange sundress. I stuck the Smith & Wesson in my handbag, grabbed a sweater, and ran out the door, calling good-bye to Jill as I went. Poor Ralph, I thought. I really am abusing him, keeping him waiting in restaurants just so that I can pick his brains about Ajax.

It was 7:50 when I turned south on Lake Shore Drive and just 8:00 when I got onto Rush Street, where the restaurant lay. One of my prejudices is against paying to park the car, but tonight I didn't waste time looking for street parking. I turned the car over to a parking attendant across from

Ahab's. I looked at my watch as I went in the door: 8:08. Damned good, I thought. My head still felt woolly from my hour of sleep, but I was glad I'd gotten it.

Ralph was waiting by the entrance. He kissed me lightly in greeting, then stood back to examine my face. "Definitely improving," he agreed. "And I see you can walk again."

The headwaiter came over. Monday was a light night and he took us directly to our table. "Tim will be your waiter," he said. "Would you like a drink?"

Ralph ordered a gin-and-tonic; I settled for a glass of club soda—Scotch on top of beer didn't sound too appetizing.

"One of the things about being divorced and moving into the city is all the great restaurants," Ralph remarked. "I've come to this place a couple of times, but there are a lot in my neighborhood."

"Where do you live?" I asked.

"Over on Elm Street, not too far from here, actually. It's a furnished place with a housekeeping service."

"Convenient." That must cost a fair amount, I thought. I wondered what his income was. "That's quite a lot of money with your alimony, too."

"Don't tell me." He grinned. "I didn't know anything about the city when I moved in here, barring the area right around Ajax, and I didn't want to get into a long lease in a place I'd hate. Eventually I expect I'll buy a condominium."

"By the way, did you find out whether McGraw had ever called Masters?"

"Yes, I did you that little favor, Vic. And it's just what I told you. He's never had a call from the guy."

"You didn't ask him, did you?"

"No." Ralph's cheerful face clouded with resentment. "I kept your wishes in mind and only talked to his secretary. Of course, I don't have any guarantee that she won't mention the matter to him. Do you think you could let this drop now?"

I was feeling a little angry, too, but I kept it under control: I still wanted Ralph to look at the claim draft.

Tim arrived to take our orders. I asked for poached salmon and Ralph took the scampi. We both went to the salad bar while I cast about for a neutral topic to keep us going until after dinner. I didn't want to produce the draft until we'd eaten.

"I've talked so much about my divorce I've never asked whether you were ever married," Ralph remarked.

"Yes, I was."

"What happened?"

"It was a long time ago. I don't think either of us was ready for it. He's a successful attorney now living in Hinsdale with a wife and three young children."

"Do you still see him?" Ralph wanted to know.

"No, and I really don't think about him. But his name is in the papers a fair amount. He sent me a card at Christmas, that's how I know about the children and Hinsdale—one of those gooey things with the children smiling sentimentally in front of a fireplace. I'm not sure whether he sent it to prove his virility or to let me know what I'm missing."

"Do you miss it?"

I was getting angry. "Are you trying to ask in a subtle way about whether I wish I had a husband and a family? I certainly do not miss Dick, nor am I sorry that I don't have three kids getting under my feet."

Ralph looked astonished. "Take it easy, Vic. Can't you miss having a family without confusing that with Dick's family? I don't miss Dorothy—but that doesn't mean I'm giving up on marriage. And I wouldn't be much of a man if I didn't miss my children."

Tim brought our dinners. The salmon had a very good pimento sauce, but my emotions were still riding me and I couldn't enjoy it properly. I forced a smile. "Sorry. Guess I'm overreacting to people who think a woman without a child is like Welch's without grapes."

"Well, please don't take it out on me. Just because I've been acting like a protective man, trying to stop you from running after gangsters, doesn't mean I think you ought to be sitting home watching soaps and doing laundry."

I ate some salmon and thought about Dick and our short, unhappy marriage. Ralph was looking at me, and his mobile face showed concern and a little anxiety.

"The reason my first marriage fell apart was because I'm too independent. Also, I'm not into housekeeping, as you noticed the other night. But the real problem is my independence. I guess you could call it a strong sense of turf. It's—it's hard for me—" I smiled. "It's hard for me to talk about it." I swallowed and concentrated on my plate for a few minutes. I bit my lower lip and continued. "I have some close women friends, because I don't feel they're trying to take over my turf. But with men, it always seems, or often seems, as though I'm having to fight to maintain who I am."

Ralph nodded. I wasn't sure he understood, but he seemed interested. I ate a little more fish and swallowed some wine.

"With Dick, it was worse. I'm not sure why I married him—sometimes I think it's because he represented the white Anglo-Saxon establishment, and part of me wanted to belong to that. But Dick was a terrible husband for someone like me. He was an attorney with Crawford, Meade—they're a very big, high-prestige corporate firm, if you don't know them—and I was an eager young lawyer on the Public Defender's roster. We met at a bar association meeting. Dick thought he'd fallen in love with me because I'm so independent; afterwards it seemed to me that it was because he saw my independence as a challenge, and when he couldn't break it down, he got angry.

"Then I got disillusioned with working for the Public Defender. The setup is pretty corrupt—you're never arguing for justice, always on points of law. I wanted to get out of it, but I still wanted to do something that would make me feel that I was working on my concept of justice, not legal point-scoring. I resigned from the Public Defender's office, and was wondering what to do next, when a girl came to me and asked me to clear her brother of a robbery charge. He looked hopelessly guilty—it was a charge of stealing video equipment from a big corporate studio, and he had access, opportunity, and so on, but I took the case on and I discovered he was innocent by finding out who the guilty person really was."

I drank some more wine and poked at my salmon. Ralph's plate was clean, but he was waving off Tim—"Wait until the lady's finished."

"Well, all this time, Dick was waiting for me to settle down to being a housewife. He was very supportive when I was worrying through leaving the Public Defender, but it turned out that that was because he was hoping I'd quit to stay home on the sidelines applauding him while he clawed his way up the ladder in the legal world. When I took on that case—although it didn't seem like a case at the time, just a favor to the woman who had sent the girl to me—" (That had been Lotty.) It had been awhile since I'd thought about all this and I started to laugh. Ralph looked a question. "Well, I take my obligations very seriously, and I ended up spending a night on a loading dock, which was really the turning point in the case. It was the same night that Crawford, Meade were having a big cocktail party, wives invited. I had on a cocktail dress, because I thought I'd just slip down to the dock and then go to the party, but the time slipped away, and Dick couldn't forgive me for not showing up. So we split up. At the time it was horrible, but when I look back on it, the evening was so ludicrous it makes me laugh."

I pushed my plate away. I'd only eaten half the fish, but I didn't have much of an appetite. "The trouble is, I guess I'm a bit gun-shy now. There really are times when I wish I did have a couple of children and was doing the middle-class family thing. But that's a myth, you know: very few people live like an advertisement, with golden harmony, and enough money, and so on. And I know I'm feeling a longing for a myth, not the reality. It's just—I get scared that I've made the wrong choice, or—I don't quite know how to say it. Maybe I should be home watching the soaps, maybe I'm not doing the best thing with my life. So if people try to suggest it, I bite their heads off."

Ralph reached across the table and squeezed my hand. "I think you're remarkable, Vic. I like your style. Dick sounds like an ass. Don't give up on us men just because of him."

I smiled and squeezed his hand in return. "I know. But— I'm a good detective, and I've got an established name now. And it's not a job that's easy to combine with marriage. It's only intermittently demanding, but when I'm hot after something, I don't want to be distracted by the thought of someone at home stewing because he doesn't know what to do about dinner. Or fussing at me because Earl Smeissen beat me up."

Ralph looked down at his empty plate, nodding thoughtfully. "I see." He grinned. "Of course, you might find a guy who'd already done the children-and-suburbia number who would stand on the sidelines cheering your successes."

Tim came back to take dessert orders. I chose Ahab's spectacular ice-cream-and-cordial dessert. I hadn't eaten all my fish, and I was sick of being virtuous anyway. Ralph decided to have some too.

"But I think this Earl Smeissen business would take a lot of getting used to," he added after Tim had disappeared again.

"Aren't there any dangers to claim handling?" I asked. "I would imagine you'd come across fraudulent claimants from time to time who aren't too happy to have their frauds uncovered."

"That's true," he agreed. "But it's harder to prove a fraudulent claim than you might think. Especially if it's an accident case. There are lots of corrupt doctors out there who will happily testify to nonprovable injuries—something like a strained back, which doesn't show up on an X ray—for a cut of the award.

"I've never been in any danger. Usually what happens if you know it's a blown-up claim, and they know you know, but no one can prove it either way, you give them a cash settlement considerably below what it would be if it came to court. That gets them off your back—litigation is very expensive for an insurance company, because juries almost always favor the claimant, so it's really not as shocking as it sounds."

"How much of there is that?" I asked.

"Well, everyone thinks the insurance company is there to give them a free ride—they don't understand that it all comes out in higher rates in the end. But how often do we really get taken to the cleaners? I couldn't say. When I was working in the field, my gut sense was that maybe one in every twenty or thirty cases was a phony. You handle so many, though, that it's hard to evaluate each one of them properly—you just concentrate on the big ones."

Tim had brought the ice cream, which was sinfully delicious. I scraped the last drops out of the bottom of my dish. "I found a claim draft lying around an apartment the other day. It was an Ajax draft, a carbon of one. I wondered if it was a real one."

"You did?" Ralph was surprised. "Where did you find it? In your apartment?"

"No. Actually, in young Thayer's place."

"Do you have it? I'd like to see it."

I picked my bag up from the floor and got the paper out of the zippered side compartment and handed it to Ralph. He studied it intently. Finally he said, "This looks like one of ours all right. I wonder what the boy was doing with that on him. No claim files are supposed to go home with you."

He folded it and put it in his wallet. "This should go back to the office."

I wasn't surprised, just pleased I'd had the forethought to make Xeroxes of it. "Do you know the claimant?" I asked.

He pulled out the paper again and looked at the name. "No, I can't even pronounce it. But it's the maximum indemnity payment for this state, so he must be on a total disability case—either temporary or permanent. That means there should be a pretty comprehensive file on him. How did it get so greasy?"

"Oh, it was lying on the floor," I said vaguely.

When Tim brought the check, I insisted on splitting it with Ralph. "Too many dinners like this and you'll have to give up either your alimony or your apartment."

He finally let me pay my part of the bill. "By the way, before they kick me out for not paying the rent, would you like to see my place?"

I laughed. "Sure, Ralph. I'd love to."

THIRTEEN
THE MARK OF ZAV

Ralph's alarm went off at 6:30; I cracked my eyes briefly to look at the clock and then buried my head under the pillows. Ralph tried burrowing in after me, but I kept the covers pulled around my ears and fought him off successfully. The skirmish woke me up more thoroughly. I sat up. "Why so early? Do you have to be at the office at seven thirty?"

"This isn't early to me, baby: when I lived in Downers Grove I had to get up at five forty-five every day—this is luxury. Besides, I like morning—best time of day."

I groaned and lay down again. "Yeah, I've often said God must have loved mornings, he made so many of them. How about bringing me some coffee?"

He got out of bed and flexed his muscles. "Sure thing, Miss Warshawski, ma'am. Service with a smile."

I had to laugh. "If you're going to be so full of pep this early in the day, I think I'll head back north for breakfast." I swung my legs out of bed. It was now the fourth morning since my encounter with Earl and his boys, and I scarcely felt a twinge. Clearly, exercising paid off. I'd better get at it again—it would be easy to get out of the habit on the excuse that I was an invalid.

"I can feed you," Ralph said. "Not lavishly, but I've got toast."

"Tell you the truth, I want to go running this morning before I eat. I haven't been out for five days, and it's easy to go downhill if you don't keep it up. Besides, I have a teen-age guest at Lotty's, and I ought to go see how she's doing."

"Just as long as you aren't importing teen-age boys for

some weird orgy or other, I don't mind. How about coming back here tonight?"

"Mmm, maybe not. I've got to go to a meeting tonight, and I want to spend some time with Lotty and my friend." I was still bothered by Ralph's persistence. Did he want to keep tabs on me, or was he a lonely guy going after the first woman he'd met who turned him on? If Masters were involved in the deaths of John and Peter Thayer, it wasn't impossible that his assistant, who had worked for him for three years, was involved as well.

"You get to work early every morning?" I asked.

"Unless I'm sick."

"Last Monday morning too?" I asked.

He looked at me, puzzled. "I suppose. Why do you ask—oh. When Peter was shot. No, I forgot: I wasn't in early that morning. I went down to Thayer's apartment and held him down while Yardley shot him."

"Yardley get in on time that morning?" I persisted.

"I'm not his goddamn secretary!" Ralph snapped. "He doesn't always show up at the same time—he has breakfast meetings and crap—and I don't sit with a stopwatch waiting for him to arrive."

"Okay, okay. Take it easy. I know you think Masters is purity personified. But if he were doing something illegal, wouldn't he call on you, his trusty henchman, for help? You wouldn't want him relying on someone else, someone less able than you, would you?"

His face relaxed and he gave a snort of laughter. "You're outrageous. If you were a man, you couldn't get away with crap like that."

"If I were a man, I wouldn't be lying here," I pointed out. I held out an arm and pulled him back down into the bed, but I still wondered what he'd been doing Monday morning.

Ralph went off to shower, whistling slightly. I pulled the curtains back to look outside. The air had a faint yellow tinge.

Even this early in the morning the city looked slightly baked. The break in the weather was over; we were in for another hot, polluted spell.

I showered and dressed and joined Ralph at the table for a cup of coffee. His apartment included one large room with a half wall making a partially private eating area. The kitchen must have once been a closet: stove, sink, and refrigerator were stacked neatly, allowing room to stand and work, but not enough space even for a chair. It wasn't a bad-looking place. A large couch faced the front entrance, and a heavy armchair stood pulled back from the windows at right angles to it. I'd read somewhere that people who lived in rooms with floor-to-ceiling windows keep the furniture pulled back away from them—some illusion of falling if you're right up against the glass. A good two feet lay between the chair back and the lightly curtained windows. All the upholstery and the curtains were in the same light floral pattern. Nice for a prefurnished place.

At 7:30 Ralph stood up. "I hear those claims calling me," he explained. "I'll get in touch with you tomorrow, Vic."

"Fine," I said. We rode down in the elevator in amiable silence. Ralph walked me to my car, which I'd had to park near Lake Shore Drive. "Want a ride downtown?" I asked. He declined, saying he got his exercise walking the mile and a half to Ajax each day.

As I drove off, I could see him moving down the street in my rearview mirror, a jaunty figure despite the close air.

It was only eight when I got back to Lotty's. She was having toast and coffee in the kitchen. Jill, her oval face alive and expressive, was talking animatedly, a half-drunk glass of milk in front of her. Her innocent good spirits made me feel old and decadent. I made a face at myself.

"Good morning, ladies. It's a stinker outside."

"Good morning, Vic," said Lotty, her face amused. "What a pity you had to work all night."

I gave her a playful punch on the shoulder. Jill asked, "Were you really working all night?" in a serious, worried voice.

"No, and Lotty knows it. I spent the night at a friend's place after doing a little work. You have a pleasant evening? How were the enchiladas?"

"Oh, they were great!" Jill said enthusiastically. "Did you know that Carol has been cooking since she was seven?" She giggled. "I don't know how to do one useful thing, like ironing or even making scrambled eggs. Carol says I'd better marry someone with lots of money."

"Oh, just marry someone who likes to cook and iron," I said.

"Well, maybe you can practice on some scrambled eggs tonight," Lotty suggested. "Are you going to be here tonight?" she asked me.

"Can you make it an early dinner? I've got a seven thirty meeting down at the University of Chicago—someone who may be able to help me find Anita."

"How about it, Jill?" Lotty asked.

Jill made a face. "I think I'll plan on marrying someone rich." Lotty and I laughed. "How about peanut butter sandwiches?" she suggested. "I already know how to make those."

"I'll make you a fritata, Lotty," I promised, "if you and Jill will pick up some spinach and onions on your way home."

Lotty made a face. "Vic is a good cook, but a messy one," she told Jill. "She'll make a simple dinner for four in half an hour, but you and I will spend the night cleaning the kitchen."

"Lotty!" I expostulated. "From a fritata? I promise you—" I thought a minute, then laughed. "No promises. I don't want to be late for my meeting. Jill, you can clean up."

Jill looked at me uncertainly: Was I angry because she didn't want to make dinner? "Look," I said, "you don't have to be perfect: Lotty and I will like you even if you have temper tantrums, don't make your bed, and refuse to cook dinner. Okay?"

"Certainly," Lotty agreed, amused. "I've been Vic's friend these last fifteen years, and I've yet to see her make a bed."

Jill smiled at that. "Are you going detecting today?"

"Yes, up to the North Side. Looking for a needle in a haystack. I'd like to have lunch with you, but I don't know what my timetable is going to be like. I'll call down to the clinic around noon, though."

I went into the guest room and changed into shorts, T-shirt, and running shoes. Jill came in as I was halfway through my warm-up stretches. My muscles had tightened up in response to their abuse, and I was having to go more slowly and carefully than normal. When Jill came in, I was sweating a little, not from exertion, but from the residual pain. She stood watching me for a minute. "Mind if I get dressed while you're in here?" she asked finally.

"No," I grunted. "Unless—you'd feel more—comfortable—alone." I pulled myself upright. "You thought about calling your mother?"

She made a face. "Lotty had the same idea. I've decided to be a runaway and stay down here." She put on her jeans and one of her man-sized shirts. "I like it here."

"It's just the novelty. You'll get lonesome for your private beach after a while." I gave her a quick hug. "But I invite you to stay at Lotty's for as long as you like."

She laughed at that. "Okay, I'll call my mom."

"Atta girl. 'Bye, Lotty," I called, and started out the door. Sheffield Avenue is about a mile from the lake. I figured if I ran over to the lake, eight blocks down to Diversey and back again, that would give me close to four miles. I went slowly, partly to ease my muscles and partly because of the stifling weather. I usually run seven-and-a-half-minute miles, but I tried to pace it at about nine minutes this morning. I was sweating freely by the time I got to Diversey, and my legs felt wobbly. I cut the pace going north, but I was so tired I wasn't paying too much attention to the traffic around me. As I left the lake path, a squad car pulled out in front of me. Sergeant McGonnigal was sitting in the passenger seat.

"Good morning, Miss Warshawski."

"Morning, Sergeant," I said, trying to breathe evenly.

"Lieutenant Mallory asked me to find you," he said, getting out of the car. "He got a call yesterday from the Winnetka police. Seems you fast-talked your way past them to get into the Thayer house."

"Oh, yeah?" I said. "Nice to see so much cooperation between the suburban and the city forces." I did a few toe touches to keep my leg muscles from stiffening.

"They're concerned about the Thayer girl. They think she should be home with her mother."

"That's thoughtful of them. They can call her at Dr. Herschel's and suggest that to her. Is that why you tracked me down?"

"Not entirely. The Winnetka police finally turned up a witness to the shooter's car, though not to the shooting." He paused.

"Oh, yeah? Enough of an ID to make an arrest?"

"Unfortunately the witness is only five years old. He's scared silly and his parents have roped him around with lawyers and guards. Seems he'd been playing in the ditch alongside Sheridan Road, which was a no-no, but his folks were asleep, so he sneaked out. That's apparently why he went—because it's off limits. He was playing some crazy game, you know how kids are, thought he was stalking Darth Vader or something, when he saw the car. Big, black car, he says, sitting outside the Thayer house. He decided to stalk it when he saw a guy in the passenger seat who scared the daylights out of him."

McGonnigal stopped again to make sure I was following. He emphasized his next words carefully. "He finally said—after hours of talk, and many promises to the parents that we wouldn't subpoena him or publish the news—that what scared him about the guy was that Zorro had got him. Why Zorro? It seems this guy had some kind of mark on his face. That's all he knows: He saw it, panicked, and ran for his life. Doesn't know if the guy saw him or not."

"Sounds like a good lead," I commented politely. "All you have to do is find a big black car and a man with a mark on his face, and ask him if he knows Zorro."

McGonnigal looked sharply at me. "We police are not total idiots, Miss Warshawski. It's not something we can take to court, because of promising the parents and the lawyers. Anyway, the testimony isn't very good. But Zorro—you know, Zorro's mark is a big Z, and the lieutenant and I wondered if you knew anyone with a big Z on his face?"

I felt my face twitch. Earl's gofer, Tony, had had such a scar. I shook my head. "Should I?"

"Not too many guys with that kind of mark. We thought it might be Tony Bronsky. He got cut like that by a guy named Zav who objected to Tony taking away his girl friend seven–eight years ago. He hangs around Earl Smeissen these days."

"Oh?" I said. "Earl and I aren't exactly social friends, Sergeant—I don't know all his companions."

"Well, the lieutenant thought you'd like to know about it. He said he knew you'd sure hate for anything to happen to the little Thayer girl while you were looking after her." He got back into his car.

"The lieutenant has a fine sense of drama," I called after him. "He's been watching too many *Kojak* reruns late at night. Tell him that from me."

McGonnigal drove off and I walked the rest of the way home. I'd completely lost interest in exercise. Lotty and Jill had already left. I took a long, hot shower, easing my leg muscles and thinking over McGonnigal's message. It didn't surprise me that Earl was involved in John Thayer's death. I wondered if Jill really was in any danger, though. And if she was, was she worse off with Lotty and me? I toweled dry and weighed myself. I was down two pounds, surprising with all the starch I'd been eating lately.

I went into the kitchen to squeeze some orange juice. There was one way in which Jill was worse off with me, I realized. If Earl decided I needed to be blown away completely, she'd make a perfect hostage for him. I suddenly felt very cold.

Nothing I was doing was getting me anyplace—unless Thayer's execution could be called a destination. I couldn't tie McGraw to Masters or Thayer. I didn't have a clue about Anita. The one person who might supply me with anything was McGraw, and he wouldn't. Why the hell had he come to me in the first place?

On impulse I looked up the Knifegrinders' number in the white pages and dialed. The receptionist transferred me to Mildred. I didn't identify myself but asked for McGraw. He was in a meeting and couldn't be disturbed.

"It's important," I said. "Tell him it concerns Earl Smeissen and John Thayer."

Mildred put me on hold. I studied my fingernails. They needed filing. At last the phone clicked and McGraw's husky voice came on the line.

"Yes? What is it?" he asked.

"This is V. I. Warshawski. Did you finger Thayer for Earl?"

"What the hell are you talking about? I told you to stay out of my business."

"You dragged me in in the first place, McGraw. You made it my business. Now I want to know, did you finger Thayer for Earl?"

He was quiet.

"One of Earl's men shot Thayer. You brought Thayer's name into this to begin with. You've hedged about why. Did you want to be sure he got dragged into the case from the beginning? You were afraid the police might jump on Anita, and you wanted to make sure his name got in the pot? Then what—he threatened to squeal, and you asked Earl to kill him just in case?"

"Warshawski, I got a tape running. You make any more accusations like this and I could see you in court."

"Don't try it, McGraw: They might subpoena the rest of your tapes."

He slammed the phone down. I didn't feel any better.

I dressed in a hurry, but checked the Smith & Wesson carefully before putting it in my shoulder holster. My continuing hope was that Earl thought he'd rendered me negligible, and that he'd continue thinking so until I'd unraveled enough of the truth to make it too late for any other action he might take. But I took no chances, leaving the apartment from the rear and circling the block to come to my car. The coast was still clear.

I decided to abandon Loop bars and go to the Knifegrinders' neighborhood. I could return to the Loop tomorrow if necessary. On my way north I stopped at the clinic. Although it was early in the day, the waiting room was already full. I again walked past the baleful glares from those who had been sitting for an hour.

"I need to talk to Lotty," I said abruptly to Carol. She took one look at my face and got Lotty out of the examining room. I quickly explained to her what had happened. "I don't want to get Jill upset," I said, "but I don't want to feel like we're sitting on a land mine here."

Lotty nodded. "Yes, but what's to stop them from taking her out of the Thayer house?" she asked. "If they decide she would be a good hostage, I'm afraid they could get her wherever she was. It is not your peace of mind, but Jill's we need to think of. And I think she's better down here for another couple of days. Until her father's funeral, anyway; she called the mother—the funeral won't be until Friday."

"Yes, but, Lotty, I'm running against the clock here. I've got to keep going, I can't sit guarding Jill."

"No." She frowned, then her face cleared. "Carol's brother.

Big, bruising, good-natured guy. He's an architecture student at Circle—maybe he can come and watch out for thugs." She called to Carol, who listened eagerly to the problem, threw up her hands at the thought of Jill in danger, but agreed that Paul would be glad to come and help. "He looks mean and stupid," she said. "A perfect disguise, since he is really friendly and brilliant."

I had to be satisfied with that, but I wasn't happy: I'd have liked to ship Jill up to Wisconsin until everything was over.

I went on north and drove around the Knifegrinder territory, staking out my route for the day. There weren't nearly as many bars here as there were in the Loop. I picked a twenty-block square and decided to keep the car. This morning, no matter what sort of ill will it raised in the bars, I was not going to drink. I cannot face beer before noon. Or even Scotch.

I started at the west end of my territory, along the Howard el tracks. The first place, Clara's, looked so down-at-the-heels, I wasn't sure I wanted to go into it. Surely someone as fastidious as Masters looked would not go to a dump like that. On the other hand, maybe that's the kind of place he'd want—something that no one would associate with him. I braced my shoulders and pushed into the gloom out of the sticky air.

By noon I'd drawn nine blanks and was beginning to think I'd come up with a truly rotten idea, one that was wasting a lot of valuable time as well. I would finish my present stint, but not go back for a second crack at the Loop. I called the clinic. Carol's brother was in residence, enchanted by Jill and helping entertain some seven toddlers. I told Lotty I was going to stay where I was and to give my apologies to Jill.

By now the humid, polluted heat was stifling. I felt as though I were being pushed to the earth by it every time I walked back outside. The smell of stale beer in the bars began to nauseate me. Everyplace I went into had a few pathetic souls riveted to their stools, sipping down one drink after another, even though it was only morning. I was meeting with the same variety of hostility, indifference, and cooperation that I'd found downtown, and the same lack of recognition of my photos.

After calling Lotty, I decided to get lunch. I wasn't far from Sheridan Road; I walked over and found a decent-looking steak house at the end of the block. I opted against lunch in a bar, and walked in thankfully out of the heat. The High Corral, as the place called itself, was small, clean, and full of good food smells, a welcome contrast to sour beer. About two thirds of the tables were filled. A plump, middle-aged woman came up with a menu and a cheerful smile and led me to a corner table. I began to feel better.

I ordered a small butt steak, an undressed salad, and a tall gin fizz and took my time over the food when it arrived. No one would ever write it up for *Chicago* magazine, but it was a simple, well-prepared meal and mellowed my spirits considerably. I ordered coffee, and lingered over that too. At 1:45 I realized I was procrastinating. " 'When duty beckons, "Lo thou must," Youth replies to Age, "I can," ' " I muttered encouragingly to myself. I put two dollars on the table and carried my bill over to the cash register. The plump hostess bustled up from the back of the restaurant to take my money.

"Very pleasant lunch," I said.

"I'm glad you enjoyed it. Are you new to this neighborhood?"

I shook my head. "I was just passing by and your sign looked inviting." On impulse I pulled out my folder, now grimy and wilted around the edges. "I wonder if these two men have ever come in here together."

She picked up the pictures and looked at them. "Oh, yes."

I couldn't believe it. "Are you sure?"

"I couldn't be mistaken. Not unless it's something I'd have to go to court for." Her friendly face clouded a bit. "If it's a legal matter you're talking about—" She shoved the pictures back at me.

"Not at all," I said hastily. "Or at least, not one that you'll have to be involved in." I couldn't think of a plausible story on the spur of the moment.

"If anyone sends me a summons, I never saw either of them," she reiterated.

"But off the record, just for my ears, how long have they been coming here?" I said, in what I hoped was a sincere, persuasive voice.

"What's the problem?" She was still suspicious.

"Paternity suit," I said promptly, the first thing that came into my mind. It sounded ridiculous, even to me, but she relaxed.

"Well, that doesn't sound too dreadful. I guess it's been about five years. This is my husband's restaurant, and we've been working it together for eighteen years now. I remember most of my regular customers."

"Do they come in often?" I asked.

"Oh, maybe three times a year. But over a period of time, you get to recognize your regulars. Besides, this man"—she tapped McGraw's picture—"comes in a lot. I think he's with that big union down the road."

"Oh, really?" I said politely. I pulled Thayer's picture out. "What about him?" I asked.

She studied it. "It looks familiar," she said, "but he's never been in here."

"Well, I certainly won't spread your name any further. And thanks for a very nice lunch."

I felt dizzy walking out into the blinding heat. I couldn't believe my luck. Every now and then you get a break like that as a detective, and you start to think maybe you're on the side of right and good after all and a benevolent Providence is guiding your steps. Hot damn! I thought. I've got Masters tied to McGraw. And McGraw knows Smeissen. And the twig is on the branch, the branch is on the tree, the tree is on the hill. Vic, you are a genius, I told myself. The only question is, what is tying these two guys together? It must be that beautiful claim draft I found in Peter Thayer's apartment, but how?

I found a pay phone and called Ralph to see if he had tracked down the Gielczowski file. He was in a meeting. No, I wouldn't leave a message, I'd call later.

There was another question too. What was the connection among Thayer, McGraw, and Masters? Still, that shouldn't be too difficult to find out. The whole thing probably revolved around some way to make money, maybe nontaxable money. If that were so, then Thayer came in naturally as Masters's neighbor and good friend and vice-president of a bank. He could probably launder money in a dozen different ways that I couldn't begin to imagine. Say he laundered the money and Peter found out. McGraw got Smeissen to kill Peter. Then Thayer was overcome with remorse. "I won't be a party to it," he said—to Masters? to McGraw? and they got Earl to blow him away too.

Steady, Vic, I told myself, getting into the car. So far you only have one fact: McGraw and Masters know each other. But what a beautiful, highly suggestive fact.

It was the bottom of the fifth inning at Wrigley Field, and the Cubs were rolling over Philadelphia. For some reason, smoggy, wilting air acted on them like a tonic; everyone else was dying, but the Cubs were leading 8–1. Kingman hit his thirty-fourth homer. I thought maybe I'd earned a trip to the park to see the rest of the game, but sternly squashed the idea.

I got back to the clinic at 2:30. The outer room was even more crowded than it had been in the morning. A small window air conditioner fought against the heat and the combined bodies and lost. As I walked into the room, the inner door opened and a face looked around. "Mean and stupid" summed it up exactly. I went on across the room. "You must be Paul," I said, holding out a hand. "I'm Vic."

He smiled. The transformation was incredible. I could see the bright intelligence in his eyes, and he looked handsome rather than brutish. I wondered fleetingly if Jill was old enough to fall in love.

"Everything's quiet here," he said. "Everything but the babies, of course. Do you want to come out and see how Jill is doing?"

I followed him to the back. Lotty had moved the steel table out of her second examining room. In this tiny space Jill sat playing with five children between the ages of two and seven. She had the self-important look of someone coping with a major crisis. I grinned to myself. A baby was asleep in a basket in the corner. She looked up when I came in, and said hello, but her smile was for Paul. Was that an unnecessary complication or a help? I wondered.

"How's it going?" I asked.

"Great. Whenever things get too hectic, Paul makes a quick trip to the Good Humor man. I'm just afraid they'll catch on and squawk all the time."

"Do you think you could leave them for a few minutes? I'd like to ask you a few questions."

She looked at the group doubtfully. "Go ahead," Paul said cheerfully. "I'll fill in for you—you've been at it too long, anyway."

She got up. One of the children, a little boy, protested. "You can't go," he said in a loud, bossy voice.

"Sure, she can," Paul said, squatting easily in her place. "Now where were you?"

I took Jill into Lotty's office. "Looks like you're a natural," I said. "Lotty will probably try to talk you into spending the rest of the summer down here."

She flushed. "I'd like to. I wonder if I really could."

"No reason not, once we get this other business cleared up. Have you ever met Anita's father?"

She shook her head. I pulled out my package of pictures and took out the ones of McGraw. "This is he. Have you ever seen him, either with your dad, or maybe in the neighborhood?"

She studied them for a while. "I don't think I've ever seen him before. He doesn't look at all like Anita."

I stopped for a minute, not sure of the least hurting way to say what I wanted. "I think Mr. McGraw and Mr. Masters are partners in some scheme or other—I don't know what. I believe your father must have been involved in some way, maybe without realizing what it was he was involved in." In fact, I suddenly thought, if Thayer had been obviously a party to it, wouldn't Peter have confronted him first? "Do you remember Peter and your father fighting in the last week or two before Peter's death?"

"No. In fact, Peter hadn't been home for seven weeks. If he and Daddy had a fight, it had to be over the telephone. Maybe at the office, but not out at the house."

"That's good. Now, going back to this other business, I've got to know what it is your father knew about their deal. Can you think of anything that might help me? Did he and Mr. Masters lock themselves up in the study for long talks?"

"Yes, but lots of men do that—did that. Daddy did business with lots of people, and they would often come over to the house to talk about it."

"Well, what about money?" I asked. "Did Mr. Masters ever give your father a lot of money? or the other way around?"

She laughed embarrassedly and shrugged her shoulders. "I just don't know about any of that kind of stuff. I know Daddy worked for the bank and was an officer and all, but I don't know what he did exactly, and I don't know anything about the money. I guess I should. I know my family is well off, we've all got these big trusts from my grandparents, but I don't know anything about Daddy's money."

That wasn't too surprising. "Suppose I asked you to go back to Winnetka and look through his study to see if he had any papers that mention McGraw or Masters or both. Would that make you feel dishonest and slimy?"

She shook her head. "If it would help I'll do it. But I don't want to leave here."

"That is a problem," I agreed. I looked at my watch and calculated times. "I don't think we could fit it in before dinner this evening, anyway. But how about first thing tomorrow morning? Then we could come back here to the clinic in time for the baby rush hour."

"Sure," she agreed. "Would you want to come along? I mean, I don't have a car or anything, and I would like to come back, and they might try to talk me into staying up there once I got there."

"I wouldn't miss it." By tomorrow morning the house probably wouldn't be filled with police anymore, either.

Jill got up and went back to the nursery. I could hear her saying in a maternal voice, "Well, whose turn is it?" I grinned, popped my head in Lotty's door, and told her I was going home to sleep.

FOURTEEN
IN THE HEAT
OF THE NIGHT

I set off for the University Women United meeting at seven. I'd slept for three hours and felt on top of the world. The fritata had turned out well—an old recipe of my mother's, accompanied by lots of toast, a salad constructed by Paul, and Paul's warm appreciation. He'd decided his bodyguarding included spending the night, and had brought a sleeping bag. The dining room was the only place with space for him, Lotty warned him. "And I want you to stay in it," she added. Jill was delighted. I could just imagine her sister's reaction if she came back with Paul as a boyfriend.

It was an easy drive south, a lazy evening with a lot of people out cooling off. This was my favorite time of day in the summer. There was something about the smell and feel of it that evoked the magic of childhood.

I didn't have any trouble parking on campus, and got into the meeting room just before things began. About a dozen women were there, wearing work pants and oversized T-shirts, or denim skirts made out of blue jeans with the legs cut apart and restitched, seams facing out. I was wearing jeans and a big loose shirt to cover the gun, but I was still dressed more elegantly than anyone else in the room.

Gail Sugarman was there. She recognized me when I came in, and said, "Hi, I'm glad you remembered the meeting." The others stopped to look at me. "This is—" Gail stopped, embarrassed. "I've forgotten your name—it's Italian, I remember you told me that. Anyway, I met her at the Swift coffee shop last week and told her about the meetings and here she is."

"You're not a reporter, are you?" one woman asked.

"No, I'm not," I said neutrally. "I have a B.A. from here, pretty old degree at this point. I was down here the other day talking to Harold Weinstein and ran into Gail."

"Weinstein," another one snorted. "Thinks he's a radical because he wears work shirts and curses capitalism."

"Yeah," another agreed. "I was in his class on 'Big Business and Big Labor.' He felt the major battle against oppression had been won when Ford lost the battle with the UAW in the forties. If you tried to talk about how women have been excluded not just from big business but from the unions as well, he said that didn't indicate oppression, merely a reflection of the current social mores."

"That argument justifies all oppression," a plump woman with short curling hair put in. "Hell, the Stalin labor camps reflected Soviet mores of the 1930s. Not to mention Scheransky's exile with hard labor."

Thin, dark Mary, the older woman who'd been with Gail at the coffee shop on Friday, tried to call the group to order. "We don't have a program tonight," she said. "In the summer our attendance is too low to justify a speaker. But why don't we get in a circle on the floor so that we can have a group discussion." She was smoking, sucking in her cheeks with her intense inhaling. I had a feeling she was eyeing me suspiciously, but that may have just been my own nerves.

I obediently took a spot on the floor, drawing my legs up in front of me. My calf muscles were sensitive. The other women straggled over, getting cups of evil-looking coffee as they came. I'd taken one look at the overboiled brew on my way in and decided it wasn't necessary to drink it to prove I was one of the group.

When all but two were seated, Mary suggested we go around the circle and introduce ourselves. "There are a couple of new people here tonight," she said. "I'm Mary Annasdaughter." She turned to the woman on her right, the one who'd protested women's exclusion from big unions. When they got to me, I said, "I'm V. I. Warshawski. Most people call me Vic."

When they'd finished, one said curiously, "Do you go by your initials or is Vic your real name?"

"It's a nickname," I said. "I usually use my initials. I started out my working life as a lawyer, and I found it was harder for male colleagues and opponents to patronize me if they didn't know my first name."

"Good point," Mary said, taking the meeting back. "Tonight I'd like to see what we can do to support the ERA booth at the Illinois State Fair. The state NOW group usually has a booth where they distribute literature. This year they want to do something more elaborate, have a slide show, and they need more people. Someone who can go down to Springfield for one or more days the week of August fourth to tenth to staff the booth and the slide show."

"Are they sending a car down?" the plump, curly-haired one asked.

"I expect the transportation will depend on how many people volunteer. I thought I might go. If some of the rest of you want to, we could all take the bus together—it's not that long a ride."

"Where would we stay?" someone wanted to know.

"I plan to camp out," Mary said. "But you can probably find some NOW people to share a hotel room with. I can check back at the headquarters."

"I kind of hate doing anything with NOW," a rosy-cheeked woman with waist-long hair said. She was wearing a T-shirt and bib overalls; she had the face of a peaceful Victorian matron.

"Why, Annette?" Gail asked.

"They ignore the real issues—women's social position, inequities of marriage, divorce, child care—and go screwing around supporting establishment politicians. They'll support a candidate who does one measly little thing for child care, and overlook the fact that he doesn't have any women on his staff, and that his wife is a plastic mannequin sitting at home supporting his career."

"Well, you're never going to have social justice until you get some basic political and economic inequalities solved," a stocky woman, whose name I thought was Ruth, said. "And political problems can be grappled with. You can't go around trying to uproot the fundamental oppression between men and women without some tool to dig with: laws represent that tool."

This was an old argument; it went back to the start of radical feminism in the late sixties: Do you concentrate on equal pay and equal legal rights, or do you go off and try to convert the whole society to a new set of sexual values? Mary let the tide roll in for ten minutes. Then she rapped the floor with her knuckles.

"I'm not asking for a consensus on NOW, or even on the ERA," she said. "I just want a head count of those who'd like to go to Springfield."

Gail volunteered first, predictably, and Ruth. The two who'd been dissecting Weinstein's politics also agreed to go.

"What about you, Vic?" Mary said.

"Thanks, but no," I said.

"Why don't you tell us why you're really here," Mary said in a steely voice. "You may be an old UC student, but no one stops by a rap group on Tuesday night just to check out politics on the old campus."

"They don't change that much, but you're right: I came here because I'm trying to find Anita McGraw. I don't know anyone here well, but I know this is a group she was close to, and I'm hoping that someone here can tell me where she is."

"In that case, you can get out," Mary said angrily. The group silently closed against me; I could feel their hostility like a physical force. "We've all had the police on us—now I guess they thought a woman pig could infiltrate this meeting and worm Anita's address out of one of us—assuming we had it to worm. I don't know it myself—I don't know if anyone in here knows it—but you pigs just can't give up, can you?"

I didn't move. "I'm not with the police, and I'm not a reporter. Do you think the police want to find Anita so that they can lay Peter Thayer's death on her?"

"Of course," Mary snorted. "They've been poking around trying to find if Peter slept around and Anita was jealous or if he'd made a will leaving her money. Well, I'm sorry—you can go back and tell them that they just cannot get away with that."

"I'd like to present an alternative scenario," I said.

"Screw yourself," Mary said. "We're not interested. Now get out."

"Not until you've listened to me."

"Do you want me to throw her out, Mary?" Annette asked.

"You can try," I said. "But it'll just make you madder if I hurt one of you, and I'm still not going to leave until you've listened to what I have to say."

"All right," Mary said angrily. She took out her watch. "You can have five minutes. Then Annette throws you out."

"Thank you. My tale is short: I can embellish it later if you have questions.

"Yesterday morning, John Thayer, Peter's father, was gunned down in front of his home. The police presume, but cannot prove, that this was the work of a hired killer known to them. It is my belief, not shared by the police, that this same killer shot Peter Thayer last Monday.

"Now, why was Peter shot? The answer is that he knew something that was potentially damaging to a very powerful and very corrupt labor leader. I don't know what he knew, but I assume it had something to do with illegal financial transactions. It is further possible that his father was a party to these transactions, as was the man Peter worked for."

I stretched my legs out and leaned back on my hands. No

one spoke. "These are all assumptions. I have no proof at the moment that could be used in court, but I have the proof that comes from watching human relationships and reactions. If I am correct in my assumptions, then I believe Anita Mc-Graw's life is in serious danger. The overwhelming probability is that Peter Thayer shared with her the secret that got him killed, and that when she came home last Monday evening to find his dead body, she panicked and ran. But as long as she is alive, and in lonely possession of this secret—whatever it is—then the men who have killed twice to protect it will not care about killing her as well."

"You know a lot about it," Ruth said. "How do you happen to be involved if you're not a reporter and not a cop?"

"I'm a private investigator," I said levelly. "At the moment my client is a fourteen-year-old girl who saw her father murdered and is very frightened."

Mary was still angry. "You're still a cop, then. It doesn't make any difference who is paying your salary."

"You're wrong," I said. "It makes an enormous difference. I'm the only person I take orders from, not a hierarchy of officers, aldermen, and commissioners."

"What kind of proof do you have?" Ruth asked.

"I was beaten up last Friday night by the man who employs the killer who probably killed the two Thayers. He warned me away from the case. I have a presumption, not provable, of who hired him: a man who got his name from an associate on speaking terms with many prominent criminals. This man is the person Peter Thayer was working for this summer. And I know the other guy, the one with the criminal contacts, has been seen with Peter's boss. Ex-boss. I don't know about the money, that's just a guess. No one in that crowd would be hurt by sex scandals, and spying is very unlikely."

"What about dope?" Gail asked.

"I don't think so," I said. "But anyway, that is certainly an illegal source of income for which you might kill to cover up."

"Frankly, V.I., or Vic, or whatever your real name is, you haven't convinced me. I don't believe Anita's life could be in danger. But if anyone disagrees with me and knows where Anita is, go ahead and betray her."

"I have another question," Ruth said. "Assuming we did know where she is and told you, what good would that do her—if everything you're saying is true?"

"If I can find out what the transaction is, I can probably get some definite proof of who the murderer is," I said. "The more quickly that happens, the less likely it is that this hired killer can get to her."

No one said anything else. I waited a few minutes. I kind of hoped Annette would try to throw me out: I felt like breaking someone's arm. Radicals are so goddamn paranoid. And radical students combine that with isolation and pomposity. Maybe I'd break all their arms, just for fun. But Annette didn't move. And no one chirped up with Anita's address.

"Satisfied?" Mary asked triumphantly, her thin cheeks pulled back in a smirk.

"Thanks for the time, sisters," I said. "If any of you changes her mind, I'm leaving some business cards with my phone number by the coffee." I put them down and left.

I felt very depressed driving home. Peter Wimsey would have gone in and charmed all those uncouth radicals into slobbering all over him. He would never have revealed he was a private detective—he would have started some clever conversation that would have told him everything he wanted to know and then given two hundred pounds to the Lesbian Freedom Fund.

I turned left onto Lake Shore Drive, going much too fast and getting a reckless pleasure from feeling the car careening, almost out of control. I didn't even care at this point if someone stopped me. I did the four miles between Fifty-seventh Street and McCormick Place in three minutes. It was at that point that I realized someone was following me.

The speed limit in that area is forty-five and I was doing

eighty, yet I was holding the same pair of headlights in my rearview mirror that had been behind me in the other lane when I got on the Drive. I braked quickly, and changed to the outside lane. The other car didn't change lanes, but slowed down also.

How long had I been carrying a tail, and why? If Earl wanted to blow me away, he had unlimited opportunities, no need to waste manpower and money on a tail. He might not know where I'd gone after leaving my apartment, but I didn't think so. My answering service had Lotty's phone number, and it's a simple matter to get an address from the phone company if you have the number.

Maybe they wanted Jill and didn't realize I'd taken her to Lotty's. I drove slowly and normally, not trying to change lanes or make an unexpected exit. My companion stayed with me, in the center lane, letting a few cars get between us. As we moved downtown, the lights got brighter and I could see the car better—a mid-sized gray sedan, it looked like.

If they got Jill, they would have a potent weapon to force me off the case. I couldn't believe that Earl thought I had a case. He'd given me the big scare, he'd torn my apartment apart, and he'd gotten the police to make an arrest. As far as I could tell, despite John Thayer's death, Donald Mackenzie was still in jail. Perhaps they thought I could lead them to the document they had overlooked at Peter Thayer's, and not found in my apartment.

The phrase "lead them to" clicked in my brain. Of course. They weren't interested in me, or in Jill, or even in that claim draft. They wanted Anita McGraw, just as I did, and they thought I could lead them to her. How had they known I was going to the campus tonight? They hadn't: they'd followed me there. I'd told McGraw I had a lead on a lead to Anita and he had told—Smeissen?—Masters? I didn't like the thought of McGraw fingering his daughter. He must have told someone he thought he could trust. Surely not Masters, though.

If my deduction was correct, I ought to keep them guessing. As long as they thought I knew something, my life was probably safe. I got off the Drive downtown, going past Buckingham Fountain as it shot up jets of colored water high into the night. A large crowd had gathered to see the nightly show. I wondered if I could lose myself in it, but didn't think much of my chances. I went on over to Michigan Avenue, and parked across the street from the Conrad Hilton Hotel. I locked the car door and leisurely crossed the street. I stopped inside the glass doors for a glance outside, and was pleased to see the gray sedan pull up next to my car. I didn't wait to see what the occupants would do, but moved quickly down the hotel's long corridor to the side entrance on Eighth Street.

This part of the hotel had airline ticket offices, and as I walked past them, a doorman was calling, "Last call for the airport bus. Nonstop to O'Hare Field." Without thinking or stopping to look behind me, I pushed in front of a small crew of laughing flight attendants and got on the bus. They followed me more slowly; the conductor checked his load and got off, and the bus started moving. As we turned the corner onto Michigan, I could see a man looking up and down the street. I thought it might be Freddie.

The bus moved ponderously across the Loop to Ontario Street, some twelve blocks north, and I kept an anxious lookout through the rear window, but it seemed as though Freddie's slow wits had not considered the possibility of my being on the bus.

It was 9:30 when we got to O'Hare. I moved from the bus to stand in the shadow of one of the giant pillars supporting the terminal, but saw no gray sedan. I was about to step out when I thought perhaps they had a second car, so I looked to see if any vehicle repeated its circuit more than once, and scanned the occupants to see if I recognized any of Smeissen's crew. By ten I decided I was clear and caught a cab back to Lotty's.

I had the driver drop me at the top of her street. Then I went down the alley behind her building, keeping a hand close to my gun. I didn't see anyone but a group of three teen-age boys, drinking beer and talking lazily.

I had to pound on the back door for several minutes before Lotty heard and came to let me in. Her thick black eyebrows went up in surprise. "Trouble?" she said.

"A little, downtown. I'm not sure whether anyone is watching the front."

"Jill?" she asked.

"I don't think so. I think they're hoping I'll lead them to Anita McGraw. Unless I do, or unless they find her first, I think we're all pretty safe." I shook my head in dissatisfaction. "I don't like it, though. They could snatch Jill and hold her to ransom if they thought I knew where Anita was. I didn't find out tonight. I'm sure one of those goddamned radical women knows where she is, but they think they're being noble and winning a great war against the pigs, and they won't tell me. It's so frustrating."

"Yes, I see," Lotty said seriously. "Maybe it's not so good for the child to be here. She and Paul are watching the movie on television," she added, jerking her head toward the living room.

"I left my car downtown," I said. "Someone was following me back from the university and I shook them off in the Loop—took the bus out to O'Hare—long and expensive way to shake a tail, but it worked.

"Tomorrow, Jill's taking me out to Winnetka to go through her father's papers. Maybe she should just stay there."

"We'll sleep on it," Lotty suggested. "Paul is loving his guard duty, but he couldn't do much against men with machine guns. Besides, he is an architecture student and should not miss too many of his classes."

We went back into the living room. Jill was curled up on the daybed, watching the movie. Paul was lying on his stomach, looking up at her every few minutes. Jill didn't seem aware of the impression she was creating—this seemed to be her first conquest—but she glowed with contentment.

I went into the guest room to make some phone calls. Larry Anderson said they'd finished my apartment. "I didn't think you'd want that couch, so I let one of the guys take it home. And about the door—I've got a friend who does some carpentry. He has a beautiful oak door, out of some mansion or other. He could fix it up for you and put some dead bolts in it, if you'd like."

"Larry, I can't begin to thank you," I said, much moved. "That sounds like a beautiful idea. How did you close the place up today?"

"Oh, we nailed it shut," he said cheerfully. Larry and I had gone to school together years ago, but he'd dropped out earlier and further than I had. We chatted for a few minutes, then I hung up to call Ralph.

"It's me, Sherlock Holmes," I said. "How did your claim files go?"

"Oh, fine. Summer is a busy time for accidents with so many people on the road. They should stay home, but then they'd cut off their legs with lawnmowers or something and we'd be paying just the same."

"Did you refile that draft without any trouble?" I asked.

"Actually not, I couldn't find the file. I looked up the guy's account, though: he must have been in a doozy of an accident—we've been sending him weekly checks for four years now." He chuckled a little. "I was going to inspect Yardley's face today to see if he looked guilty of multiple homicide, but he's taking the rest of the week off—apparently cut up about Thayer's death."

"I see." I wasn't going to bother telling him about the link I'd found between Masters and McGraw; I was tired of arguing with him over whether I had a case or not.

"Dinner tomorrow night?" he asked.

"Make it Thursday," I suggested. "Tomorrow's going to be pretty open-ended."

As soon as I put the phone down, it rang. "Dr. Herschel's residence," I said. It was my favorite reporter, Murray Ryerson.

"Just got a squeal that Tony Bronsky may have killed John Thayer," he said.

"Oh, really? Are you going to publish that?"

"Oh, I think we'll paint a murky picture of gangland involvement. It's just a whiff, no proof, he wasn't caught at the scene, and our legal people have decided mentioning his name would be actionable."

"Thanks for sharing the news," I said politely.

"I wasn't calling out of charity," Murray responded. "But in my lumbering Swedish way it dawned on me that Bronsky works for Smeissen. We agreed yesterday that his name has been cropping up here and there around the place. What's his angle, Vic—why would he kill a respectable banker and his son?"

"Beats the hell out of me, Murray," I said, and hung up.

I went back and watched the rest of the movie, *The Guns of Navarone*, with Lotty, Jill, and Paul. I felt restless and on edge. Lotty didn't keep Scotch. She didn't have any liquor at all except brandy. I went into the kitchen and poured myself a healthy slug. Lotty looked questioningly at me, but said nothing.

Around midnight, as the movie was ending, the phone rang. Lotty answered it in her bedroom and came back, her face troubled. She gave me a quiet signal to follow her to the kitchen. "A man," she said in a low voice. "He asked if you were here; when I said yes, he hung up."

"Oh, hell," I muttered. "Well, nothing to be done about it now. . . . My apartment will be ready tomorrow night—I'll go back and remove this powder keg from your home."

Lotty shook her head and gave her twisted smile. "Not to worry, Vic—I'm counting on you fixing the AMA for me someday."

Lotty sent Jill unceremoniously off to bed. Paul got out his sleeping bag. I helped him move the heavy walnut dining-room table against the wall, and Lotty brought him a pillow from her bed, then went to sleep, herself.

The night was muggy; Lotty's brick, thick-walled building kept out the worst of the weather, and exhaust fans in the kitchen and dining rooms moved the air enough to make sleep possible. But the air felt close to me anyway. I lay on the daybed in a T-shirt, and sweated, dozed a bit, woke, tossed, and dozed again. At last I sat up angrily. I wanted to do something, but there was nothing for me to do. I turned on the light. It was 3:30.

I pulled on a pair of jeans and tiptoed out to the kitchen to make some coffee. While water dripped through the white porcelain filter, I looked through a bookcase in the living room for something to read. All books look equally boring in the middle of the night. I finally selected *Vienna in the Seventeenth Century* by Dorfman, fetched a cup of coffee, and flipped the pages, reading about the devastating plague following the Thirty Years War, and the street now called Graben—"the grave"—because so many dead had been buried there. The terrible story fit my jangled mood.

Above the hum of the fans I could hear the phone ring faintly in Lotty's room. We'd turned it off next to the spare bed where Jill was sleeping. I told myself it had to be for Lotty—some mother in labor, or some bleeding teen-ager—but I sat tensely anyway and was somehow not surprised when Lotty came out of her room, wrapped in a thin, striped cotton robe.

"For you. A Ruth Yonkers."

I shrugged my shoulders; the name meant nothing to me. "Sorry to get you up," I said, and went down the short hall-way to Lotty's room. I felt as if all the night's tension had had its focus in waiting for this unexpected phone call from an unknown woman. The instrument was on a small Indonesian table next to Lotty's bed. I sat on the bed and spoke into it.

"This is Ruth Yonkers," a husky voice responded. "I talked to you at the UWU meeting tonight."

"Oh, yes," I said calmly. "I remember you." She'd been the stocky, square young woman who'd asked me all the questions at the end.

"I talked to Anita after the meeting. I didn't know how seriously to take you, but I thought she ought to know about it." I held my breath and said nothing. "She called me last week, told me about finding Peter's—finding Peter. She made me promise not to tell anyone where she was without checking with her first. Not even her father, or the police. It was all rather—bizarre."

"I see," I said.

"Do you?" she asked doubtfully.

"You thought she'd killed Peter, didn't you," I said in a comfortable tone. "And you felt caught by her choosing you to confide in. You didn't want to betray her, but you didn't want to be involved in a murder. So you were relieved to have a promise to fall back on."

Ruth gave a little sigh, half laugh, that came ghostily over the line. "Yes, that was it exactly. You're smarter than I thought you were. I hadn't realized Anita might be in danger herself—that was why she sounded so scared. Anyway, I called her. We've been talking for several hours. She's never heard of you and we've been debating whether we can trust you." She paused and I was quiet. "I think we have to. That's what it boils down to. If it's true, if there really are some mob people after her—it all sounds surreal, but she says you're right."

"Where is she?" I asked gently.

"Up in Wisconsin. I'll take you to her."

"No. Tell me where she is, and I'll find her. I'm being followed, and it'll just double the danger to try to meet up with you."

"Then I won't tell you where she is," Ruth said. "My agreement with her was that I would bring you to her."

"You've been a good friend, Ruth, and you've carried a heavy load. But if the people who are after Anita find out you know where she is, and suspect you're in her confidence, your own life is in danger. Let me run the risk—it's my job, after all."

We argued for several more minutes, but Ruth let herself be persuaded. She'd been under a tremendous strain for the five days since Anita had first called her, and she was glad to let someone else take it over. Anita was in Hartford, a little town northwest of Milwaukee. She was working as a waitress in a café. She'd cut her red hair short and dyed it black, and she was calling herself Jody Hill. If I left now, I could catch her just as the café opened for breakfast in the morning.

It was after four when I hung up. I felt refreshed and alert, as if I'd slept soundly for eight hours instead of tossing miserably for three.

Lotty was sitting in the kitchen, drinking coffee and reading. "Lotty, I do apologize. You get little enough sleep as it is. But I think this is the beginning of the end."

"Ah, good," she said, putting a marker in her book and shutting it. "The missing girl?"

"Yes. That was a friend who gave me the address. All I have to do now is get away from here without being seen."

"Where is she?" I hesitated. "My dear, I've been questioned by tougher experts than these Smeissen hoodlums. And perhaps someone else should know."

I grinned. "You're right." I told her, then added, "The question is, what about Jill? We were going to go up to Winnetka tomorrow—today, that is—to see if her father had any papers that might explain his connection with Masters and McGraw. Now maybe Anita can make that tie-in for me. But I'd still be happier to get Jill back up there. This whole arrangement—Paul under the dining-room table, Jill and the babies—makes me uncomfortable. If she wants to come back for the rest of the summer, sure—she can stay with me once this mess is cleared up. But for now—let's get her back home."

Lotty pursed her lips and stared into her coffee cup for several minutes. Finally she said, "Yes. I believe you're right. She's much better—two good nights of sleep, with calm people who like her—she can probably go back to her family. I agree. The whole thing with Paul is too volatile. Very sweet, but too volatile in such a cramped space."

"My car is across from the Conrad Hilton downtown. I can't take it—it's being watched. Maybe Paul can pick it up tomorrow, take Jill home. I'll be back here tomorrow night, say good-bye, and give you a little privacy."

"Do you want to take my car?" Lotty suggested.

I thought it over. "Where are you parked?"

"Out front. Across the street."

"Thanks, but I've got to get away from here without being seen. I don't know that your place is being watched—but these guys want Anita McGraw very badly. And they did call earlier to make sure I was here."

Lotty got up and turned out the kitchen light. She looked out window, concealed partly by a hanging geranium and thin gauze curtains. "I don't see anyone. . . . Why not wake up Paul? He can take my car, drive it around the block a few times. Then, if no one follows him, he can pick you up in the alley. You drop him down the street."

"I don't like it. You'll be without a car, and when he comes back on foot, if there is someone out there, they'll be suspicious."

"Vic, my dear, it's not like you to be so full of quibbles. We won't be without a car—we'll have yours. As for the second—" She thought a minute. "Ah! Drop Paul at the clinic. He can finish his sleep there. We have a bed, for nights when Carol or I have to stay over."

I laughed. "Can't think of any more quibbles, Lotty. Let's wake up Paul and give it a try."

Paul woke up quickly and cheerfully. When the plan was

explained to him, he accepted it enthusiastically. "Want me to beat up anyone hanging around outside?"

"Unnecessary, my dear," said Lotty, amused. "Let's try not to attract too much attention to ourselves. There's an all-night restaurant on Sheffield off Addison—give us a call from there."

We left Paul to dress in privacy. He came out to the kitchen a few minutes later, pushing his black hair back from his square face with his left hand and buttoning a blue workshirt with the right. Lotty gave him her car keys. We watched the street from Lotty's dark bedroom. No one attacked Paul as he got into the car and started it; we couldn't see anyone follow him down the street.

I went back to the living room and dressed properly. Lotty watched me without speaking while I loaded the Smith & Wesson and stuck it into the shoulder holster. I was wearing well-cut jeans and a blouson jacket over a ribbed knit shirt.

About ten minutes later Lotty's phone rang. "All clear," Paul said. "There is someone out front, though. I think I'd better not drive down the alley—it might bring him around to the rear. I'll be at the mouth of the alley at the north end of the street."

I relayed this to Lotty. She nodded. "Why don't you leave from the basement? You can go down there from inside, and outside the door is hidden by stairs and garbage cans." She led me downstairs. I felt very alert, very keyed up. Through a window on the stairwell we could see the night clearing into a predawn gray. It was 4:40 and the apartment was very quiet. A siren sounded in the distance, but no traffic was going down Lotty's street.

Lotty had brought a flashlight with her, rather than turn on a light that might show through the street-side window. She pointed it down the stairs so I could see the way, then turned it off. I padded down after her. At the bottom she seized my wrist, led me around bicycles and a washing machine, and very slowly and quietly drew back the dead bolts in the outside door. There was a little *click* as they snapped open. She waited several minutes before pulling the door open. It moved into the basement, quietly, on oiled hinges. I slipped out up the stairs in crepe-soled shoes.

From behind the screen of garbage cans I peered into the alley. Freddie sat propped against the back of the wall at the south end of the alley two buildings down. As far as I could tell, he was asleep.

I moved quietly back down the stairs. "Give me ten minutes," I mouthed into Lotty's ear. "I may need a quick escape route." Lotty nodded without speaking.

At the top of the stairs I checked Freddie again. Did he have the subtlety to fake sleep? I moved from behind the garbage cans into the shadow of the next building, my right hand on the revolver's handle. Freddie didn't stir. Keeping close to the walls, I moved quickly down the alley. As soon as I was halfway down, I broke into a quiet sprint.

FIFTEEN
THE UNION MAID

Paul was waiting as promised. He had a good head—the car was out of sight of the alley. I slid into the front seat and drew the door closed. "Any trouble?" he said, starting the engine and pulling away from the curb.

"No, but I recognized a guy asleep in the alley. You'd better call Lotty from the clinic. Tell her not to leave Jill alone in the apartment. Maybe she can get a police escort to the clinic. Tell her to call a Lieutenant Mallory to request it."

"Sure thing." He was very likable. We drove the short way to the clinic in silence. I handed him my car keys, and reiterated where the car was. "It's a dark blue Monza."

"Good luck," he said in his rich voice. "Don't worry about Jill and Lotty—I'll take care of them."

"I never worry about Lotty," I said, sliding into the driver's seat. "She's a force unto herself." I adjusted the side mirror and the rearview mirror, and let in the clutch: Lotty drove a small Datsun, as practical and unadorned as she was.

I kept checking the road behind me as I drove across Addison to the Kennedy, but it seemed to be clear. The air was clammy, the damp of a muggy night before the sun would rise and turn it into smog again. The eastern sky was light now, and I was moving quickly through the empty streets. Traffic was light on the expressway, and I cleared the suburbs to the northbound Milwaukee toll road in forty-five minutes.

Lotty's Datsun handled well, although I was out of practice with a standard shift and ground the gears a bit changing down. She had an FM radio, and I listened to WFMT well past the Illinois border. After that the reception grew fuzzy so I switched it off.

It was six in clear daylight when I reached the Milwaukee bypass. I'd never been to Hartford, but I'd been to Port Washington, thirty miles to the east of it on Lake Michigan, many times. As far as I could tell, the route was the same, except for turning west onto route 60 instead of east when you get twenty miles north of Milwaukee.

At 6:50 I eased the Datsun to a halt on Hartford's main street, across from Ronna's Café—Homemade Food, and in front of the First National Bank of Hartford. My heart was beating fast. I unbuckled the seat belt and got out, stretching my legs. The trip had been just under 140 miles; I'd done it in two hours and ten minutes. Not bad.

Hartford is in the beautiful moraine country, the heart of Wisconsin dairy farming. There's a small Chrysler plant there that makes outboard motors, and up the hill I could see a Libby's cannery. But most of the money in the town comes from farming, and people were up early. Ronna's opened at 5:30, according to the legend on the door, and at seven most of the tables were full. I bought the *Milwaukee Sentinel* from a coin box by the door, and sat down at an empty table near the back.

One waitress was taking care of the crowd at the counter. Another covered all the tables. She was rushing through the swinging doors at the back, her arms loaded up with plates. Her short, curly hair had been dyed black. It was Anita McGraw.

She unloaded pancakes, fried eggs, toast, hash browns, at a table where three heavyset men in bib overalls were drinking coffee, and brought a fried egg to a good-looking young guy in a dark blue boiler suit at the table next to me. She looked at me with the harassment common to all overworked waitresses in coffee shops. "I'll be right with you. Coffee?"

I nodded. "Take your time," I said, opening the paper. The men in the bib overalls were kidding the good-looking guy—

he was a veterinarian, apparently, and they were farmers who'd used his services. "You grow that beard to make everyone think you're grown up, Doc?" one of them said.

"Naw, just to hide from the FBI," the vet said. Anita was carrying a cup of coffee to me; her hand shook and she spilled it on the veterinarian. She flushed and started apologizing. I got up and took the cup from her before any more spilled, and the young man said good-naturedly, "Oh, it just wakes you up faster if you pour it all over yourself—especially if it's still hot. Believe me, Jody," he added as she dabbed ineffectually at the wet spot on his arm with a napkin, "this is the nicest stuff that's likely to spill on this outfit today."

The farmers laughed at that, and Anita came over to take my order. I asked for a Denver omelette, no potatoes, wholewheat toast, and juice. When in farm country, eat like a farmer. The vet finished his egg and coffee. "Well, I hear those cows calling me," he said, put some money on the table, and left. Other people began drifting out too: It was 7:15—time for the day to be under way. For the farmers this was a short break between morning milking and some business in town. They lingered over a second cup of coffee. By the time Anita brought back my omelette, though, only three tables had people still eating, and just a handful were left at the counter.

I ate half the omelette, slowly, and read every word in the paper. People kept drifting in and out; I had a fourth cup of coffee. When Anita brought my bill, I put a five on it and, on top of that, one of my cards. I'd written on it: "Ruth sent me. I'm in the green Datsun across the street."

I went out and put some money in the meter, then got back in the car. I sat for another half hour, working the crossword puzzle, before Anita appeared. She opened the passenger door and sat down without speaking. I folded up the paper and put it in the backseat and looked at her gravely. The picture I'd found in her apartment had shown a laughing young woman, not precisely beautiful, but full of the vitality that is better than beauty in a young woman. Now her face was strained and gaunt. The police would never have found her from a photograph—she looked closer to thirty than twenty—lack of sleep, fear, and tension cutting unnatural lines in her young face. The black hair did not go with her skin, the delicate creamy skin of a true redhead.

"What made you choose Hartford?" I asked.

She looked surprised—possibly the last question she'd expected. "Peter and I came up here last summer to the Washington County Fair—just for fun. We had a sandwich in that café, and I remembered it." Her voice was husky with fatigue. She turned to look at me and said rapidly, "I hope I can trust you—I've got to trust someone. Ruth doesn't know—doesn't know the kind of people who—who might shoot someone. I don't either, really, but I think I have a better idea than she does." She gave a bleak smile. "I'm going to lose my mind if I stay here alone any longer. But I can't go back to Chicago. I need help. If you can't do it, if you blow it and I get shot—or if you're some clever female hit man who fooled Ruth into giving you my address—I don't know. I have to take the chance." She was holding her hands together so tightly that the knuckles were white.

"I'm a private investigator," I said. "Your father hired me last week to find you, and I found Peter Thayer's body instead. Over the weekend, he told me to stop looking. I have my own guesses as to what all that was about. That's how I got involved. I agree that you're in a pretty tough spot. And if I blow it, neither of us will be in very good shape. You can't hide here forever, though, and I think that I'm tough enough, quick enough, and smart enough to get things settled so that you can come out of hiding. I can't cure the pain, and there's more to come, but I can get you back to Chicago—or wherever else you want so that you can live openly and with dignity."

She thought about that, nodding her head. People were walking up and down the sidewalk; I felt as if we were in a fishbowl. "Is there somewhere we can go to talk—somewhere with a little more room?"

"There's a park."

"That'd be fine." It was back along route 60 toward Milwaukee. I parked the Datsun out of sight of the road and we walked down to sit on the bank of a little stream that ran through the park, dividing it from the back wall of the Chrysler plant on the other side. The day was hot, but here in the country the air was clear and sweet.

"You said something about living with dignity," she said, looking at the water, her mouth twisted in a harsh smile. "I don't think I'll ever do that again. I know what happened to Peter, you see. In a way, I guess you could say I killed him."

"Why do you say that?" I asked gently.

"You say you found his body. Well, so did I. I came home at four and found him. I knew then what had happened. I lost my head and ran. I didn't know where to go—I didn't come here until the next day. I spent the night at Mary's house, and then I came up here. I couldn't figure out why they weren't waiting for me, but I knew if I went back they'd get me." She was starting to sob, great dry sobs that heaved her shoulders and chest. "Dignity!" she said in a hoarse voice. "Oh, Christ! I'd settle for a night's sleep." I didn't say anything, but sat watching her. After a few minutes she calmed down a bit. "How much do you know?" she asked.

"I don't know much for certain—that I can prove, I mean. But I've got some guesses. What I know for certain is that your father and Yardley Masters have a deal going. I don't know what it is, but I found a claim draft from Ajax in your apartment. I presume that Peter brought it home, so one of my guesses is that the deal has to do with claim drafts. I know that your father knows Earl Smeissen, and I know that someone wanted something very badly that they thought was in your apartment and then thought that I had taken it and put in mine. They wanted it badly enough to ransack both places. My guess is that they were looking for the claim draft, and that it was Smeissen, or one of his people, who did the ransacking."

"Is Smeissen a killer?" she asked in her harsh, strained voice.

"Well, he's doing pretty well these days: he doesn't kill, himself, but he's got muscle to do it for him."

"So my father had him kill Peter, didn't he?" She stared at me challengingly, her eyes hard and dry, her mouth twisted. This was the nightmare she'd been lying down with every night. No wonder she wasn't sleeping.

"I don't know. This is one of my guesses. Your father loves you, you know, and he's going nuts right now. He would never knowingly have put your life in danger. And he would never knowingly have let Peter be shot. I think what happened was that Peter confronted Masters, and Masters panicked and called your dad." I stopped. "This isn't pretty and it's hard to say to you. But your dad knows the kind of people who will put someone away for a price. He's made it to the top of a rough union in a rough industry, and he's had to know those kinds of people."

She nodded wearily, not looking at me. "I know. I never wanted to know it in the past, but I know it now. So my—my father, gave him this Smeissen's name. Is that what you're getting at?"

"Yes. I'm sure Masters didn't tell him who it was who'd crossed his path—just that someone had tumbled to the secret, and had to be eliminated. It's the only thing that explains your father's behavior."

"What do you mean?" she asked, not very interested.

"Your father came to me last Wednesday, gave me a fake name and a phony story, but he wanted me to find you. He knew about Peter's death at that point, and he was upset because you'd run away. You called and accused him of killing Peter, didn't you?"

She nodded again. "It was too stupid for words. I was off

my head, with anger, and fear, and—and grief. Not just for Peter, you know, but for my father, and the union, and everything I'd grown up thinking was fine and—and worth fighting for."

"Yes that was tough." She didn't say anything else, so I went on. "Your father didn't know at first what had happened. It was only a few days later that he connected Peter with Masters. Then he knew that Masters had had Peter killed. Then he knew that you were in trouble, too. And that's when he fired me. He didn't want me to find you because he didn't want anyone else to find you, either."

She looked at me again. "I hear you," she said in that same weary voice. "I hear you, but it doesn't make it any better. My father is the kind of man who gets people killed, and he got Peter killed."

We sat looking at the stream for a few minutes without talking. Then she said, "I grew up on the union. My mother died when I was three. I didn't have any brothers or sisters, and my dad and I—we were very close. He was a hero, I knew he was in a lot of fights, but he was a hero. I grew up knowing he had to fight because of the bosses, and that if he could lick them, America would be a better place for working men and women everywhere." She smiled mirthlessly again. "It sounds like a child's history book, doesn't it? It was child's history. As my dad moved up in the union, we had more money. The University of Chicago—that was something I'd always wanted. Seven thousand dollars a year? No problem. He bought it for me. My own car, you name it. Part of me knew that a working-class hero didn't have that kind of money, but I pushed it aside. 'He's entitled,' I'd say. And when I met Peter, I thought, why not? The Thayers have more money than my father ever dreamed of, and they never worked for it." She paused again. "That was my rationalization, you see. And guys like Smeissen. They're around the house—not much, but some. I just wouldn't believe any of it.

You read about some mobster in the paper, and he's been over drinking with your father? No way." She shook her head.

"Peter came home from the office, you see. He'd been working for Masters as a favor to his dad. He was sick of the whole money thing—that was before we fell in love, even, although I know his father blamed me for it. He wanted to do something really fine with his life—he didn't know what. But just to be nice, he agreed to work at Ajax. I don't think my father knew. I didn't tell him. I didn't talk to him about Peter much—he didn't like me going around with the son of such an important banker. And he is kind of a Puritan—he hated my living with Peter like that. So like I said, I didn't talk to him about Peter.

"Anyway, Peter knew who some of the big shots in the union are. You know, when you're in love, you learn that kind of thing about each other. I knew who the chairman of the Fort Dearborn Trust is, and that's not the kind of thing I know as a rule."

The story was starting to come easily now. I didn't say anything, just made myself part of the landscape that Anita was talking to.

"Well, Peter did rather boring things for Masters. It was a kind of make-work job in the budget department. He worked for the budget director, a guy he liked, and one of the things they asked him to do was check records of claim drafts against claim files—see if they matched, you know. Did Joe Blow get fifteen thousand dollars when his file shows he should only have gotten twelve thousand dollars. That kind of thing. They had a computer program that did it, but they thought there was something wrong with the program, so they wanted Peter to do a manual check." She laughed, a laugh that was really a sob. "You know, if Ajax had a good computer system, Peter would still be alive. I think of that sometimes, too, and it makes me want to shoot all their programmers. Oh, well. He started with the biggest ones—there were thousands and thousands—they have three hundred thousand Workers Compensation claims every year, but he was only going to do a spot check. So he started with some of the really big ones—total disability claims that had been going on for a while. At first it was fun, you know, to see what kinds of things had happened to people. Then one day he found a claim set up for Carl O'Malley. Total disability, lost his right arm and been crippled by a freak accident with a conveyor belt. That happens, you know—someone gets caught on a belt and pulled into a machine. It's really terrible."

I nodded agreement.

She looked at me and started talking to me, rather than just in front of me. "Only it hadn't happened, you see. Carl is one of the senior vice-presidents, my dad's right-hand man—he's been part of my life since before I can remember. I call him Uncle Carl. Peter knew that, so he brought home the address, and it was Carl's address. Carl is as well as you or me—he's never been in an accident, and he's been away from the assembly line for twenty-three years."

"I see. You didn't know what to think, but you didn't ask your father about it?"

"No, I didn't know what to ask. I couldn't figure it out. I guess I thought Uncle Carl had put in for a fake accident, and we kind of treated it like a joke, Peter and I did. But he got to thinking about it; he was like that, you know, he really thought things through. And he looked up the other guys on the executive board. And they all had indemnity claims. Not all of them for total disability, and not all of them permanent, but all of them good-sized sums. And that was the terrible thing. You see, my dad had one, too. Then I got scared, and I didn't want to say anything to him."

"Is Joseph Gielczowski on the executive board?" I asked.

"Yes, he's one of the vice-presidents, and president of Local 3051, a very powerful local in Calumet City. Do you know him?"

"That was the name of the claim draft I found." I could see why they didn't want that innocent little stick of dynamite in my hands. No wonder they'd torn my place apart looking for it. "So Peter decided to talk to Masters? You didn't know Masters was involved, did you?"

"No, and Peter thought he owed it to him, to talk to him first, you know. We weren't sure what we would do next— talk to my dad, we had to. But we thought Masters should know." Her blue eyes were dark pools of fear in her face. "What happened was, he told Masters, and Masters told him it sounded really serious, and that he'd like to talk it over with Peter in private, because it might have to go to the State Insurance Commission. So Peter said sure, and Masters said he would come down Monday morning before work." She looked at me. "That was strange, wasn't it? We should have known it was strange, we should have known a vice-president doesn't do that, he talks to you in his office. I guess we just assumed it was Peter being a friend of the family." She looked back at the stream. "I wanted to be there, but I had a job, you see, I was doing some research for one of the guys in the Political Science Department."

"Harold Weinstein?" I guessed.

"Yeah. You really have been detecting me, haven't you? Well, I had to be there at eight thirty, and Masters was coming by around nine, so I left Peter to it. I really left him to it, didn't I? Oh, God, why did I think that job was so goddamn important? Why didn't I stay there with him?" Now she was crying, real tears, not the dry heaves. She hid her face in her hands and sobbed. She kept repeating that she'd left Peter alone to be killed, and she should have been the one that died; her father was the one with all the criminal friends, not his. I let her go on for several minutes.

"Listen, Anita," I said in a clear sharp voice, "you can blame yourself for this for the rest of your life. But you didn't kill Peter. You didn't abandon him. You didn't set him up. If you had been there, you'd be dead, too, and the truth of what happened might never come out."

"I don't care about the truth," she sobbed. "I know it. It doesn't matter whether the rest of the world knows it or not."

"If the rest of the world doesn't know it, then you're as good as dead," I said brutally. "And the next nice young boy or girl who goes through those files and learns what you and Peter learned is dead, too. I know this is rotten. I know you've been through hell and more besides, and you've got worse ahead. But the quicker we get going and finish off this business, the quicker you can get that part over with. It will only get more unbearable, the longer you have to anticipate it."

She sat with her head in her hands, but her sobs died down. After a while she sat up and looked at me again. Her face was tear-streaked and her eyes red, but some of the strain had gone out of it, and she looked younger, less like a death mask of herself. "You're right. I was brought up not to be afraid of dealing with people. But I don't want to go through this with my dad."

"I know," I said gently. "My father died ten years ago. I was his only child, and we were very close. I know what you must be feeling."

She was wearing a ridiculous waitress costume, black rayon with a white apron. She blew her nose into the apron.

"Who cashed the drafts?" I asked. "The people they were made out to?"

She shook her head. "There's no way of telling. You don't cash drafts, you see: you present them to the bank and the bank verifies you have an account there and tells the insurance company to send a check to that account. You'd have to know what bank the drafts were presented to, and that information wasn't in the files—only carbons of the drafts were there. I don't know if they kept the originals or if they went to the controller's department, or what. And Peter—Peter didn't like to probe too far without Masters knowing."

"How was Peter's father involved?" I asked.

Her eyes opened at that. "Peter's father? He wasn't."

"He had to be: he was killed the other day—Monday."

Her head started moving back and forth and she looked ill. "I'm sorry," I said. "That was thoughtless, to spring it on you like that." I put an arm around her shoulders. I didn't say anything more. But I bet Thayer had helped Masters and McGraw cash in on the drafts. Maybe some of the other Knifegrinders were involved, but they wouldn't share a kitty like that with the whole executive board. Besides, that was the kind of secret that everyone would know if that many people knew. Masters and McGraw, maybe a doctor, to put a bonafide report in the files. Thayer sets up an account for them. Doesn't know what it is, doesn't ask any questions. But they give him a present every year, maybe, and when he threatens to push the investigation into his son's death, they stick in the knife: he's been involved, and he can be prosecuted. It looked good to me. I wondered if Paul and Jill would find anything in Thayer's study. Or if Lucy would let either of them into the house. Meanwhile there was Anita to think of.

We sat quietly for a while. Anita was off in her own thoughts, sorting out our conversation. Presently she said, "It makes it better, telling someone else about it. Not quite so horrible."

I grunted agreement. She looked down at her absurd outfit. "Me, dressed up like this! If Peter could see me, he'd—" The sentence trailed off into a sniff. "I'd like to leave here, stop doing the Jody Hill thing. Do you think I can go back to Chicago?"

I considered this. "Where were you planning to go?"

She thought for a few minutes. "That's a problem, I guess. I can't involve Ruth and Mary any more."

"You're right. Not just because of Ruth and Mary, but also because I was followed to the UWU meeting last night, so chances are Earl will keep an eye on some of the members for a while. And you know you can't go home until this whole business is cleared up."

"Okay," she agreed. "It's just—it's so hard—it was smart in a way, coming up here, but I'm always looking over my shoulder, you know, and I can't talk to anyone about what's really going on in my mind. They're always teasing me about boyfriends, like that nice Dr. Dan, the one I spilled coffee on this morning, and I can't tell them about Peter, so they think I'm unfriendly."

"I could probably get you back to Chicago," I said slowly. "But you'd have to hole up for a few days—until I get matters straightened out. . . . We could publish an account of the insurance scheme, but that would get your dad in trouble without necessarily getting Masters. And I want him implicated in a way he can't slide out of before I let everything else out. Do you understand?" She nodded. "Okay, in that case, I can see that you get put up in a Chicago hotel. I think I can fix it so that no one will know you are there. You wouldn't be able to go out. But someone trustworthy would stop by every now and then to talk to you so you won't go completely stir crazy. That sound all right?"

She made a face. "I guess I don't have any choice, do I? At least I'd be back in Chicago, closer to the things I know. . . . Thanks," she added belatedly. "I didn't mean to sound so grudging—I really appreciate everything you're doing for me."

"Don't worry about your party manners right now; I'm not doing it for the thanks, anyway."

We walked slowly back to the Datsun together. Little insects hummed and jumped in the grass and birds kept up an unending medley. A woman with two young children had come into the park. The children were rooting industriously in the dirt. The woman was reading a book, looking up at them every few minutes. They had a picnic basket propped under a tree. As we walked by, the woman called, "Matt! Eve! How about a snack?" The children came running up. I felt a small stirring of envy. On a beautiful summer day it might be nice to be having a picnic with my children instead of hiding a fugitive from the police and the mob.

"Is there anything you want to collect in Hartford?" I asked.

She shook her head. "I should stop at Ronna's and tell them I'm leaving."

I parked in front of the restaurant and she went in while I used a phone on the corner to call the *Herald-Star*. It was almost ten and Ryerson was at his desk.

"Murray, I've got the story of a lifetime for you if you can keep a key witness on ice for a few days."

"Where are you?" he asked. "You sound like you're calling from the North Pole. Who's the witness? The McGraw girl?"

"Murray, your mind works like a steel trap. I want a promise and I need some help."

"I've already helped you," he protested. "Lots. First by giving you those photos, and then by not running a story that you were dead so I could collect your document from your lawyer."

"Murray, if there was another soul on earth I could turn to right now, I would. But you are absolutely incorruptible if faced with the promise of a good story."

"All right," he agreed. "I'll do what I can for you."

"Good. I'm in Hartford, Wisconsin, with Anita McGraw. I want to get her back to Chicago and keep her under close wraps until this case blows over. That means no one must have a whiff of where she is, because if they do, you'll be covering her obituary. I can't bring her down myself because I'm a hot property now. What I want to do is take her to Milwaukee and put her on a train and have you meet her at Union Station. When you do, get her into a hotel. Some place far enough from the Loop that some smart bellhop on Smeissen's payroll won't put two and two together when she comes in. Can do?"

"Jesus, Vic, you don't do anything in a small way, do you?

Sure. What's the story? Why is she in danger? Smeissen knock off her boyfriend?"

"Murray, I'm telling you, you put any of this in print before the whole story is finished, and they're going to be fishing *your* body out of the Chicago River: I guarantee I'll put it there."

"You have my word of honor as a gent who is waiting to scoop the City of Chicago. What time is the train coming in?"

"I don't know. I'll call you again from Milwaukee."

When I hung up, Anita had come back out and was waiting by the car. "They weren't real happy about me quitting," she said.

I laughed. "Well, worry about that on the way down. It'll keep your mind off your troubles."

SIXTEEN
PRICE OF A CLAIM

We had to wait in Milwaukee until 1:30 for a Chicago train. I left Anita at the station and went out to buy her some jeans and a shirt. When she had washed up in the station rest room and changed, she looked younger and healthier. As soon as she got that terrible black dye out of her hair, she'd be in good shape. She thought her life was ruined, and it certainly didn't look great at the moment. But she was only twenty; she'd recover.

Murray agreed to meet the train and get her to a hotel. He'd decided on the Ritz. "If she's going to be holed up for a few days, it might as well be someplace where she'll be comfortable," he explained. "The *Star* will share the bill with you."

"Thanks, Murray," I said dryly. He was to call my answering service and leave a message: "yes" or "no"—no name. "No" meant something had gone wrong with pickup or delivery and I would get back to him. I wasn't going to go near the hotel. He'd stop by a couple of times a day with food and chat—we didn't want Anita calling room service.

As soon as the train pulled out, I headed back to the tollway and Chicago. I had almost all the threads in my hands now. The problem was, I couldn't prove that Masters had killed Peter Thayer. Caused him to be killed. Of course, Anita's story confirmed it: Masters had had an appointment with Peter. But there was no proof, nothing that would make Bobby swear out a warrant and bring handcuffs to a senior vice-president of an influential Chicago corporation. Somehow I had to stir around in the nest enough to make the king hornet come out and get me.

As I left the toll road for the Edens Expressway, I made a detour to Winnetka to see if Jill had gone home, and if she had turned up anything among her father's papers. I stopped at a service station on Willow Road and called the Thayer house.

Jack answered the phone. Yes, Jill had come home, but she wasn't talking to reporters. "I'm not a reporter," I said. "This is V. I. Warshawski."

"She certainly isn't talking to you. You've caused Mother Thayer enough pain already."

"Thorndale, you are the stupidest SOB I have ever met. If you don't put Jill on the phone, I will be at the house in five minutes. I will make a lot of noise, and I will go and bother all the neighbors until I find one who will put a phone call through to Jill for me."

He banged the receiver down hard, on a tabletop I guessed, since the connection still held. A few minutes later Jill's clear, high voice came onto the line. "What did you say to Jack?" she giggled. "I've never seen him so angry."

"Oh, I just threatened to get all your neighbors involved in what's going on," I answered. "Not that they aren't anyway—the police have probably been visiting all of them, asking questions. . . . You get out to Winnetka all right?"

"Oh, yes. It was very exciting. Paul got a police escort for us to the clinic. Lotty didn't want to do it, but he insisted. Then he went and got your car and we got a blast-off with sirens from the clinic. Sergeant McGonnigal was really, really super."

"Sounds good. How are things on the home front?"

"Oh, they're okay. Mother has decided to forgive me, but Jack is acting like the stupid phony he is. He keeps telling me I've made Mother very, very unhappy. I asked Paul to stay to lunch, and Jack kept treating him as if he were the garbage collector or something. I got really mad, but Paul told me he was used to it. I hate Jack," she concluded.

I laughed at this outburst. "Good girl! Paul's a neat guy—

worth standing up for. Did you have a chance to look through your father's papers?"

"Oh, yes. Of course, Lucy had a fit. But I just pretended I was Lotty and didn't pay any attention to her. I didn't really know what I was looking for," she said, "but I found some kind of document that had both Mr. Masters's and Mr. McGraw's names on it."

I suddenly felt completely at peace, as though I'd been through a major crisis and come out whole on the other side. I found myself grinning into the telephone. "Did you now," I said. "What was it?"

"I don't know," Jill said doubtfully. "Do you want me to get it and read it to you?"

"That's probably the best thing," I agreed. She put the phone down. I started singing under my breath. What will you be, O document? What kind of laundry ticket?

"It's a Xerox," Jill announced, back at the phone. "My dad wrote the date in ink at the top—March eighteenth, 1974. Then it says: 'Agreement of Trust. The Undersigned, Yardley Leland Masters and Andrew Solomon McGraw, are herein granted fiduciary responsibility for any and all monies submitted to this account under their authority for the following.'" She stumbled over *fiduciary*. "Then it gives a list of names—Andrew McGraw, Carl O'Malley, Joseph Giel— I can't pronounce it. There are about—let's see—" I could hear her counting under her breath: "—twenty-three names. Then it adds, 'and any other names as shall be added at their discretion under my countersignature.' Then Daddy's name, and a place for him to sign it. Is that what you were looking for?"

"That's what I was looking for, Jill." My voice was as calm and steady as if I were announcing that the Cubs had won the World Series.

"What does it mean?" she asked. She was sobering up from her glee at triumphing over Jack and Lucy. "Does it mean Daddy killed Peter?"

"No, Jill, it does not. Your father did not kill your brother. What it means is that your father knew about a dirty scheme that your brother found out about. Your brother was killed because he found out about it."

"I see." She was quiet for a few minutes. "Do you know who killed him?" she asked presently.

"I think so. You hang loose, Jill. Stay close to the house and don't go out with anyone but Paul. I'll come up to see you tomorrow or the next day—everything should be over by then." I started to hang up, then thought I should warn her to hide the paper. "Oh, Jill," I said, but she had hung up. Oh, well, I thought. If anyone suspected it was there, they would have been around looking by now.

What that document meant was that Masters could set up fake claims for anyone; then he and McGraw could cash the drafts, or whatever one did with them. Put them into the trust account, which Thayer ostensibly oversaw. In fact, I wondered why they even bothered to use real names. Why not just made-up people—easier to disguise. If they'd done that, Peter Thayer and his father would still be alive. Maybe they'd gotten to that later. I'd have to see a complete list of the names on the account and check them against the Knifegrinders' roster.

It was almost four. Anita should have made it to Chicago by now. I called my answering service, but no one had rung up with the message of "yes" or "no." I got back in the car and returned to the Edens. Inbound traffic moved at a crawl. Repairs on two of the lanes turned rush hour into a nightmare. I oozed slowly onto the Kennedy, irate and impatient, although I didn't have an agenda. Just an impatience. I didn't know what to do next. I could certainly expose the fake claim drafts. But as I'd pointed out to Anita, Masters would certainly disclaim all knowledge: the Knifegrinders might well have set them up, with complete doctors' reports. Did claim handlers actually physically look at accident victims? I wondered. I'd better talk to Ralph, explain what I'd learned today, and see if there was some legal angle that would link Masters irretrievably with the fraud. Even that wasn't good enough, though. I had to link him with the killing. And I couldn't think of a way.

It was 5:30 by the time I exited at Addison, and then I had to fight my way across town. I finally swung off onto a small side street, full of potholes, but not much traffic. I was about to turn up Sheffield to Lotty's, when I thought that might mean walking open-armed into a setup. I found the all-night restaurant on the corner of Addison and gave her a call.

"My dear Vic," she greeted me. "Can you believe, those Gestapo actually had the effrontery to break into this apartment? Whether they were looking for you, Jill, or the Mc-Graw girl, I couldn't say, but they have been here."

"Oh, my God, Lotty," I said, my stomach sinking. "I am so sorry. How bad is the damage?"

"Oh, it's nothing—just the locks, and Paul is here now replacing them; it's just the wantonness of it that makes me so angry."

"I know," I said remorsefully. "I'll certainly repair whatever damage has been done. I'll come by to get my stuff right now, and be gone."

I hung up and decided to take my chances on a trap. It would be just as well if Smeissen knew I had gone back home—I didn't want Lotty put in any more danger, or to suffer any more invasions. I raced up the street to her building, and only gave cursory attention to potential marksmen in the street. I didn't see anyone I knew, and no one opened fire as I dashed up the stairs.

Paul was in the doorway, screwing a dead-bolt lock into the door. His square face looked very mean. "This is pretty bad, Vic—you think Jill is in any danger?"

"Not too likely," I said.

"Well, I think I should go up there and see."

I grinned. "Sounds like a good idea to me. Be careful though, you hear?"

"Don't worry." His breathtaking smile came. "But I'm not sure whether I'm protecting her from that brother-in-law or from a gunman."

"Well, do both." I went on into the apartment. Lotty was at the back, trying to reattach a screen to the back door. For a woman with such skillful medical fingers she was remarkably inept. I took the hammer from her and quickly finished the job. Her thin face was set and hard, her mouth in a fine line.

"I am glad you gave the warning to Paul and had that Sergeant Mc-Whatever take us to the clinic. At the time, I was annoyed, with you and with Paul, but clearly it saved the child's life." Her Viennese accent was very heavy in her anger. I thought she was exaggerating about the danger to Jill but didn't want to argue the point. I went through the apartment with her but had to agree that there really had been no damage. Not even the medical samples, some of which had great street value, had been removed.

Lotty kept up a stream of invective during the inspection which became heavily laden with German, a language I don't speak. I gave up trying to calm her down and merely nodded and grunted agreement. Paul finally brought it to a halt by coming in to say that the front door was now secure, and did she want him to do anything else?

"No, my dear, thank you. Go out and visit Jill, and take very good care of her. We don't want her harmed."

Paul agreed fervently. He gave me my car keys, and told me the Chevy was over on Seminary off Irving Park Road. I'd thought about leaving him the car, but felt I'd better hang on to it: I didn't know what the evening would bring in the way of action.

I called Larry to see if my apartment was ready for occupation. It was; he'd left the keys to the new locks with the first-floor tenants; they'd seemed a bit friendlier than Mrs. Alvarez on the second floor.

"Well, everything is all set, Lotty: I can go home. Sorry I

didn't yesterday, and sleep with the place nailed shut—it would have spared you this invasion."

Her mouth twisted in her sardonic smile. "Ah, forget it, Vic, my anger storm has passed, blown over. Now I am feeling a little melancholy at being alone—I shall miss those two children. They are very sweet together. . . . I forgot to ask: Did you find Miss McGraw?"

"I forgot to tell you—I did. And I should check to see whether she is safely ensconced in her new hiding place." I put in a call to my answering service; yes, that long-suffering outfit reported, someone had called up and left a message "yes." They had not left a name, but said I would know what it meant. I told them they could switch my office calls to my own home number. In the activity of the last few days I'd forgotten to get a Kelly Girl to tidy my office, but at least it was boarded shut. I'd wait until tomorrow to go down there.

I tried Ralph, but there was no answer. He wasn't at the office, either. Out for dinner? Was I jealous? "Well, Lotty, this is it. Thanks for letting me disrupt your life for a few days. You've made a major impression on Jill—she told me the maid up there was trying to hassle her but she 'pretended she was Lotty' and didn't pay her any mind."

"I'm not sure that's such a good idea—to model herself on me, that is. A very attractive girl—amazing that she's avoided all that suburban insularity." She sat on the daybed to watch me pack. "What now? Can you expose the killer?"

"I've got to find a lever," I said. "I know who did it—not who fired the actual shot, that's probably a guy named Tony Bronsky, but it could have been any one of several of Smeissen's crew. But who desired that shot to be fired—that I know but can't prove. I know what the crime was, though, and I know how it was worked." I zipped the canvas bag shut. "What I need is a lever, or maybe a wedge." I was talking to myself more than to Lotty. "A wedge to pry this guy apart a bit. If I can find out that the fiddle couldn't be worked without his involvement, then maybe I can force him into the open."

I was standing with one foot on the bed, absentmindedly tapping the suitcase with my fingers while I thought. Lotty said, "If I were a sculptor, I would make a statue of you—Nemesis come to life. You will think of a way—I see it in your face." She stood on tiptoe and gave me a kiss. "I'll walk you to the street—if anyone shoots at you, then I can patch you up quickly, before too much blood is lost."

I laughed. "Lotty, you're wonderful. By all means, cover my back for me."

She walked me to the corner of Seminary, but the street was clear. "That's because of that Sergeant Mc-Something," she said. "I think he's been driving around here from time to time. Still, Vic, be careful: you have no mother, but you are a daughter of my spirit. I should not like anything to happen to you."

"Lotty, that's melodrama," I protested. "Don't start getting old, for God's sake." She shrugged her thin shoulders in a way wholly European and gave me a sardonic smile, but her eyes were serious as I walked up the street to my car.

SEVENTEEN

SHOOT-OUT ON ELM STREET

Larry and his friend the carpenter had done a beautiful job on my apartment. The door was a masterpiece, with carved flowers on the panels. The carpenter had installed two dead bolts, and the action on them was clean and quiet. Inside, the place shone as it had not for months. Not a trace of the weekend ravage remained. Although Larry had sent the shredded couch away, he had moved chairs and an occasional table around to fill the empty space. He had left a bill in the middle of the kitchen table. Two people for two days at $8.00 an hour, $256.00. The door, locks, and installation, $315.00. New supplies of flour, sugar, beans, and spices; new pillows for the bed: $97.00. It seemed like a pretty reasonable bill to me. I wondered who was going to pay me, though. Maybe Jill could borrow from her mother until her trust fund matured.

I went to look through my jewelry box. By some miracle the vandals had not taken my mother's few valuable pieces, but I thought I'd better lock them in a bank vault and not leave them around for the next invader. Larry seemed to have thrown out the shards of the broken Venetian glass. I should have told him to save them, but that couldn't be helped; it was beyond restoration, anyway. The other seven held pride of place in the built-in china cupboard, but I couldn't look at them without a thud in my stomach.

I tried Ralph again. This time he answered on the fourth

ring. "What's up, Miss Marple?" he asked. "I thought you were out after Professor Moriarty until tomorrow."

"I found him earlier than I expected. In fact, I found out the secret that Peter Thayer died to protect. Only he didn't want to protect it. You know that claim draft I gave you? Did you ever find the file?"

"No. I told you I put it on the missing-file search, but it hasn't turned up."

"Well, it may never. Do you know who Joseph Gielczowski is?"

"What is this? Twenty questions? I've got someone coming over in twenty minutes, Vic."

"Joseph Gielczowski is a senior vice-president of the Knifegrinders union. He has not been on an assembly line for twenty-three years. If you went to visit him in his home, you would find he was as healthy as you are. Or you could go see him at Knifegrinders headquarters where he is able to work and draw a salary without needing any indemnity payments."

There was a pause. "Are you trying to tell me that that guy is fraudulently drawing Workers Compensation payments?"

"No," I said.

"Goddamnit, Vic, if he's healthy and is getting indemnity drafts, then he's drawing them fraudulently."

"No," I reiterated. "Sure, they're fraudulent, but he's not drawing them."

"Well, who is, then?"

"Your boss."

Ralph exploded into the phone. "You've got this damned bee in your bonnet about Masters, Vic, and I'm sick of it! He's one of the most respected members of a highly respected company in a very respectable industry. To suggest that he's involved in something like that—"

"I'm not suggesting it, I know it," I said coldly. "I know that he and Andrew McGraw, head of the Knifegrinders union, set up a fund with themselves as joint trustees, enabling them to cash drafts, or whatever it is you do to get payments on drafts, drawn to Gielczowski and at least twenty-two other healthy people."

"How can you possibly know something like that?" Ralph said, furious.

"Because, I just listened to someone read a copy of the agreement to me over the phone. I've also found someone who has seen Masters with McGraw on numerous occasions up near Knifegrinder headquarters. And I know that Masters had an appointment with Peter Thayer—at his apartment—at nine on the morning he was killed."

"I still don't believe it. I have worked for Yardley for three years, and been in his organization for ten years before that, and I'm sure there's a different explanation for everything you've found out—if you've found it out. You haven't seen this trust agreement. And Yardley may have eaten with McGraw, or drunk with him or something—maybe he was checking out some coverage or claims, or something. We do do that from time to time."

I felt like screaming with frustration. "Just let me know ten minutes before you go to Masters to check the story with him, will you? So I can get there in time to save your ass."

"If you think I'm going to jeopardize my career by telling my boss that I've been listening to that kind of rumor about him, you're nuts," Ralph roared. "As a matter of fact, he's coming over here in a few minutes, and I promise you, without any difficulty, that I am not such an ass as to tell him about it. Of course, if that Gielczowski claim is fraudulent, that explains a lot. I'll tell him that."

My hair seemed to stand straight up on my head. "What? Ralph, you are so goddamn naive it's unbelievable. Why the hell is he coming over?"

"You really don't have any right to ask me that," he snapped, "but I'll tell you anyway, since you started the whole uproar by finding that draft. Claims that big are handled out of the home office, not by a field adjustor. I went around to the guys today and asked who'd handled the file.

No one remembered it. If anyone had been handling such a big file for so many years, there's no way they would forget it. This puzzled me, so when I called Yardley this afternoon—he hasn't been in the office this week—I call him at home once a day—I mentioned it to him."

"Oh, Christ! That is the absolute end. So he told you it sounded like a serious problem, didn't he? And that since he had to come down to the city tonight for some other reason, he'd just drop by and talk it over with you? Is that right?" I said savagely.

"Why, yes, it is," he shouted. "Now go find someone's missing poodle and stop screwing around in the Claim Department."

"Ralph, I'm coming over. Tell Yardley *that* when he walks in the door, as soon as he walks in, and maybe it will save your goddamn ass for a few minutes." I slammed down the phone without waiting for his answer.

I looked at my watch. 7:12. Masters was due there in twenty minutes. Roughly. Say he got there around 7:30, maybe a few minutes earlier. I put my driver's license, my gun permit, and my P.I. license in my hip pocket with some money—I didn't want a purse in my way at this point. Checked the gun. Put extra rounds in my jacket pocket. Wasted forty-five seconds changing to running shoes. Locked the new, oiled dead bolts behind me and sprinted down the stairs three at a time. Ran the half-block to my car in fifteen seconds. Put it in gear and headed for Lake Shore Drive.

Why was every goddamn person in Chicago out tonight, and why were so many of them on Belmont Avenue? I wondered savagely. And why were the lights timed so that every time you hit a corner they turned and some asshole grandfather wouldn't clear the intersection in front of you on the yellow? I pounded the steering wheel in impatience, but it didn't make the traffic flow faster. No point in sitting on the horn, either. I took some deep diaphragm breaths to steady myself. Ralph, you stupid jerk. Making a present of your life to a man who's had two people killed in the last two weeks. Because Masters wears the old-boy network tie and you're on his team he couldn't possibly do something criminal. Naturally not. I swooped around a bus and got a clear run to Sheridan Road and the mouth of the Drive. It was 7:24. I prayed to the patron saint who protects speeders from speed traps and floored the Monza. At 7:26 I slid off the Drive onto La Salle Street, and down the inner parallel road to Elm Street. At 7:29 I left the car at a fireplug next to Ralph's building and sprinted inside.

The building didn't have a doorman. I pushed twenty buttons in quick succession. Several people squawked "Who is it?" through the intercom, but someone buzzed me in. No matter how many break-ins are executed this way, there is always some stupid idiot who will buzz you into an apartment building without knowing who you are. The elevator took a century or two to arrive. Once it came, though, it carried me quickly to the seventeenth floor. I ran down the hall to Ralph's apartment and pounded on the door, my Smith & Wesson in my hand.

I flattened myself against the wall as the door opened, then dove into the apartment, gun out. Ralph was staring at me in amazement. "What the hell do you think you're doing?" he said. No one else was in the room.

"Good question," I said, standing up.

The bell rang and Ralph went to push the buzzer. "I wouldn't mind if you left," he remarked. I didn't move. "At least put that goddamn gun away." I put it in my jacket pocket but kept my hand on it.

"Do me one favor," I said. "When you open the door, stand behind it, don't frame yourself in the doorway."

"You are the craziest goddamn—"

"If you call me a crazy broad I will shoot you in the back. Block your damned body with the door when you open it."

Ralph glared at me. When the knocking came a few minutes later, he went straight to the door and deliberately opened it so that it would frame his body squarely. I moved to the side of the room parallel with the door and braced myself. No shots sounded.

"Hello, Yardley, what's all this?" Ralph was saying.

"This is my young neighbor, Jill Thayer, and these are some associates who've come along with me."

I was stunned and moved toward the door to look. "Jill?" I said.

"Are you here, Vic?" the clear little voice quavered a bit. "I'm sorry. Paul called to say he was coming up on the train and I started to walk into town to meet him at the station. And Mr.—Mr. Masters passed me in his car and stopped to give me a lift—and—and I asked him about that paper and he made me come along with him. I'm sorry, Vic, I know I shouldn't have said anything."

"That's okay, honey—" I started to say, but Masters interrupted with "Ah, you're here, are you? We thought we'd come visit you and that Viennese doctor Jill admires so much a little later, but you've saved us a trip." He looked at my gun, which I'd pulled out, and smiled offensively. "I would put that away if I were you. Tony here is pretty trigger-happy and I know you'd hate to watch anything happen to Jill."

Tony Bronsky had come into the room behind Masters. With him was Earl. Ralph was shaking his head, like a man trying to wake up from a dream. I put the gun back into my pocket.

"Don't blame the girl," Masters said to me. "But you really shouldn't have gotten her involved, you know. As soon as Margaret Thayer told me she had come back home, I tried finding a way of talking to her without anyone in the house knowing about it. Sheer luck, really, that she walked down Sheridan just at that time. But we got her to explain quite a bit, didn't we, Jill?"

I could see now that there was an ugly bruise on the side of her face. "Cute, Masters," I said. "You're at your best when you're beating up little girls. I'd like to see you with a grandmother." He was right: I'd been stupid to bring her down to Lotty's and get her involved in things that Masters and Smeissen didn't want anyone to know about. I'd save my self-reproach for later, though—I didn't have time for it now.

"Want me to put her away?" Tony breathed, his eyes glistening with happiness, his Z-shaped scar vivid as a wound.

"Not yet, Tony," Masters said. "We want to find out how much she knows and who she's told it to. . . . You, too, Ralph. It's really a shame you got this Polish gal over here— we weren't going to shoot you unless it was absolutely necessary, but now I'm afraid we'll have to." He turned to Smeissen. "Earl, you've had more experience at this kind of thing than I have. What's the best way to set them up?"

"Get the Warchoski broad's gun away from her," Earl said in his squeaky voice. "Then have her and the guy sit together on the couch so that Tony can cover them both."

"You heard him," Masters said. He started toward me.

"No," Earl squeaked. "Don't go close to her. Make her drop it. Tony, cover the kid."

Tony pointed his Browning at Jill. I dropped the S&W on the floor. Earl came and kicked it into the corner. Jill's little face was white and pinched.

"Over to the couch," Masters said. Tony continued to cover Jill. I went and sat down. The couch was firm, one good thing—one didn't sink into it. I kept my weight distributed forward onto my legs and feet. "Move," Earl squeaked at Ralph. Ralph was looking dazed. Little drops of sweat covered his face. He stumbled a bit on the thick carpet as he came to sit next to me.

"You know, Masters, this cesspool you've built is stinking so high you're going to have to kill everyone in Chicago to cover it up," I said.

"You think so, do you? Who knows about it besides you?" He was still smiling unpleasantly. My hand itched to break his lower jaw.

"Oh, the *Star* has a pretty good idea. My attorney. A few others. Even little Earl over here isn't going to be able to buy off the cops if you shoot down an entire newspaper crew."

"Is this true, Yardley?" Ralph asked. His voice came out in a hoarse whisper and he cleared his throat. "I don't believe it. I wouldn't believe Vic when she tried to tell me. You didn't shoot Peter, did you?"

Masters gave a superior little laugh. "Of course not. Tony here shot him. I had to go along, though, just as I did to-night—to get Tony into the building. And Earl came along as an accessory. Earl doesn't usually get involved, do you, Earl? But we don't want any blackmail after this."

"That's good, Masters," I praised him. "The reason Earl's ass is so fat is because he's been protecting it all these years."

Earl turned red. "You two-cent bitch, just for that, I'm going to let Tony work you over again before he shoots you!" he squeaked.

"Attaboy, Earl." I looked at Masters. "Earl never beats any-one up himself," I explained. "I used to think it was because he didn't have any balls, but last week I found out that wasn't true, right, Earl?"

Earl started for me, as I hoped he would, but Masters held him back. "Calm down, Earl, she's just trying to ride you. You can do whatever you want to her—after I find out how much she knows and where Anita McGraw is."

"I don't know, Yardley," I said brightly.

"Don't give me that," he said, leaning forward to hit me on the mouth. "You disappeared early this morning. That heap of shit Smeissen had watching the back alley went to sleep and you got away. But we questioned some of the girls you talked to at the UWU meeting last night and Tony here—persuaded—one of them to tell him where Anita had gone. But when we got to Hartford, Wisconsin, at noon, she'd dis-appeared. And the woman at the restaurant described you pretty well. An older sister, she thought, who'd come to take Jody Hill away with her. Now where is she?"

I uttered a silent prayer of thanks for the urge that had prompted Anita to want to leave Hartford. "There's got to be more to this racket than just those twenty-three names on the original deed of trust Jill found," I said. "Even at two hundred fifty dollars a week apiece, that isn't paying for the services of a guy like Smeissen. Round-the-clock surveillance on me? That must have cost you a bundle, Masters."

"Tony," Masters said conversationally, "hit the girl. Hard."

Jill gave a gasp, a scream held back. Good girl. Lots of guts. "You kill the girl, Masters, you got nothing to stop me," I said. "You're in a little ol' jam. The minute Tony takes that gun off her, she's going to roll on the floor and get behind that big chair, and I'm going to jump Tony and break his neck. And if he kills her, the same thing will happen. So sure, I don't want to watch you rough up Jill, but you're using up your weapon doing it."

"Go ahead and kill Warchoski," Earl squeaked. "You're going to sooner or later anyway."

Masters shook his head. "Not until we know where the McGraw girl is."

"Tell you what, Yardley," I offered. "I'll trade you Jill for Anita. You send the kid outside, let her go home, and I'll tell you where Anita is."

Masters actually wasted a minute thinking about it. "You do think I'm dumb, don't you? If I let her go, all she'll do is call the police."

"Of course I think you're dumb. As Dick Tracy once put it so well, all crooks are dumb. How many fake claimants do you have pulling indemnity payments into that dummy account?"

He laughed, his fake-hearty laugh again. "Oh, close to three hundred now, set up in different parts of the country. That deed of trust is quite outdated, and I see John never bothered to go back and check the original to see how it was growing."

"What was his cut for overseeing the account?"

"I really didn't come here to answer a smart-mouthed broad's questions," Yardley said, still good-natured, still in control. "I want to know how much you know."

"Oh, I know quite a bit," I said. "I know that you called McGraw and got Earl's name from him when Peter Thayer came to you with those incriminating files. I know you didn't tell McGraw who you were having put away, and when he found out, he panicked. You've got him in a cleft stick, haven't you: he knows you're gunning for his kid, but he can't turn state's evidence, or he hasn't got the guts to, anyway, because then he'll be an accessory before the fact, sending a professional killer to you. Let's see. I also know that you talked Thayer out of continuing the investigation into his son's death by telling him he'd been a party to the crime for which Peter died. And that if he pushed the investigation, the Thayer name would be mud and he'd lose his position at the bank. And I know he wrestled with that grim news for two days, then decided he couldn't live with himself and called you and told you he wouldn't be a party to his son's death. So you got cute little Tony here to gun him down the next morning before he could get to the state's attorney." I turned to Tony. "You aren't as good as you used to be, Tony, my boy: someone saw you waiting outside the Thayer place. That witness is on ice now—you didn't get him when you had the opportunity."

Earl's face turned red again. "You had a witness and you didn't see him?" he screeched, as much of a shout as his high voice could manage. "Goddamnit, what do I pay you for? I want amateurs, I pull one off the street. And what about Freddie? He's paid to watch—he doesn't see anyone? Goddamn dumb bastards, all of you!" He was pumping his fat little arms up and down in his rage. I glanced at Ralph; his face was gray. He was in shock. I couldn't do anything about that now. Jill gave me a little smile. She'd caught the message. As soon as Tony lifted the gun, she'd roll behind the chair.

"See," I said disgustedly, "you guys have made so many mistakes that piling up three more corpses isn't going to help you one bit. I told you before, Earl: Bobby Mallory's no dummy. You can't knock off four people in his territory and get away with it forever."

Earl smirked. "They never hung one on me yet, Warchoski, you know that."

"It's Warshawski, you goddamn kraut. You know why Polish jokes are so short?" I asked Masters. "So the Germans can remember them."

"This is enough, Warchoski or whatever your name is," Masters said. He used a stern voice, the kind that got him heard with his junior staff. "You tell me where the McGraw girl is. You're right—Jill is as good as dead. I hate to do it, I've known that girl since she was born, but I just can't take the risk. But you've got a choice. I can have Tony kill her, one clean shot and it's done, or I can have him rape her while you watch, and then kill her. You tell me where the McGraw girl is, and you'll save her a lot of grief."

Jill was very white; her gray eyes looked huge and black in her face. "Oh, jeez, Yardley," I said. "You big he-men really impress the shit out of me. Are you telling me Tony's going to rape that girl on your command? Why do you think the boy carries a gun? He can't get it up, never could, so he has a big old penis he carries around in his hand."

I braced my hands on the couch at my sides as I spoke. Tony turned crimson and gave a primitive shriek in the back of his throat. He turned to look at me.

"Now!" I yelled, and jumped. Jill dived behind the armchair. Tony's bullet went wide and I reached him in one spring and chopped his gun arm hard enough to break the bone. He screamed in pain and dropped the Browning. As I spun away, Masters lunged over for it. I made a diving slide, but he got there first, sitting down hard. He brandished the Browning at me while he got up and I backed away a few paces.

The report from Tony's shot had brought Ralph back to life. Out of the corner of my eye I saw him move over on the couch toward the phone and lift the receiver. Masters saw it, too, and turned and shot him. In the second he turned, I made a rolling fall into the corner of the room and got the Smith & Wesson. As Masters turned to fire at me, I shot him in the knee. He wasn't used to pain: he fell with a great cry of surprised agony and dropped the gun. Earl, who'd been dancing in the background, pretending he was part of the fight, moved forward to get it. I shot at his hand. I was out of practice and missed, but he jumped back anyway.

I pointed the Smith & Wesson at Tony. "Onto the couch. Move." Tears were running down his cheeks. His right arm hung in a funny way: I'd broken the ulna. "You guys are worse than trash and I'd love to shoot the three of you dead. Save the state a lot of money. If any of you goes for that gun, I'll kill you. Earl, get your fat little body over on the couch next to Tony." He looked like a two-year-old whose mother has unexpectedly spanked him; his whole face was squashed up as if he, too, were about to burst into tears. But he moved over next to Tony. I picked up the Browning, continuing to cover the two on the couch. Masters was bleeding into the carpet. He wasn't in any shape to move. "The police are going to love this gun," I said. "I bet it fired the bullet that shot Peter Thayer, didn't it, Tony?"

I called to Jill, "You still alive back there, honey?"

"Yes, Vic," she said in a little voice.

"Good. You come on out now and call the number I'm going to give you. We're going to call the police and have them collect this garbage. Then maybe you'd better call Lotty, get her over here to look at Ralph." I hoped there was something left of him for Lotty to work on. He wasn't moving, but I couldn't go to him—he'd fallen on the far side of the room, and the couch and phone table would block me if I went over to where he lay.

Jill came out from behind the big armchair where she'd

been crouching. The little oval face was still very white, and she was shaking a bit. "Walk behind me, honey," I told her. "And take a couple of deep breaths. In a few minutes you can relax and let it all out, but right now you've got to keep on going."

She turned her head away from the floor where Masters lay bleeding and walked over to the phone. I gave her Mallory's office number and told her to ask for him. He'd gone home for the day, she reported. I gave her the home number. "Is Lieutenant Mallory there, please?" she asked in her clear, polite voice. When he came on the line, I told her to bring the phone over to me, but not to get in front of me at all.

"Bobby? Vic. I'm at two-oh-three East Elm with Earl Smeissen, Tony Bronsky, and a guy from Ajax named Yardley Masters. Masters has a shattered knee, and Bronsky a broken ulna. I also have the gun that was used to shoot Peter Thayer."

Mallory made an explosive noise into the phone. "Is this some kind of joke, Vicki?"

"Bobby, I'm a cop's daughter. I never make that kind of joke. Two-oh-three East Elm. Apartment seventeen-oh-eight. I'll try not to kill the three of them before you get here."

EIGHTEEN

BLOOD IS THICKER THAN GOLD

It was ten, and the short black nurse said, "You shouldn't be here at all, but he won't go to sleep until you stop by." I followed her into the room where Ralph lay, his face very white, but his gray eyes alive. Lotty had made a good job of bandaging him up and the surgeon at Passavant had only changed the dressing without disturbing her work. As Lotty said, she'd done a lot of bullet wounds.

Paul had come with Lotty to Ralph's apartment, frantic. He'd gotten to Winnetka and forced his way past Lucy about twenty minutes after Masters had picked up Jill. He went straight from there to Lotty's. The two of them had called me, called the police to report Jill missing, but fortunately had stayed at Lotty's close to the phone.

Jill ran sobbing into Paul's arms when they arrived and Lotty had given a characteristic shake of the head. "Good idea. Get her out of here, get her some brandy," then turned her attention to Ralph, who lay unconscious and bleeding in the corner. The bullet had gone through his right shoulder, tearing up a lot of bone and muscle, but coming out clean on the other side.

Now I looked down at him on the hospital bed. He took hold of my right hand with his left and squeezed it weakly; he was pretty drugged. I sat on the bed.

"Get off the bed," the little nurse said.

I was exhausted. I wanted to tell her to go to hell, but I didn't feel like fighting the hospital on top of everything else. I stood up.

"I'm sorry," Ralph said, his words slightly slurred.

"Don't worry about it. As it turned out, that was probably the best thing that could have happened. I couldn't figure out how to get Masters to show his hand."

"No, but I should have listened to you. I couldn't believe you knew what you were talking about. I guess deep down I didn't take your detecting seriously. I thought it was a hobby, like Dorothy's painting."

I didn't say anything.

"Yardley shot me. I worked for him for three years and didn't see that about him. You met him once and knew he was that kind of guy." His words were slurred but his eyes were hurt and angry.

"Don't keep hitting yourself with that," I said gently. "I know what it means to be a team player. You don't expect your teammates, your quarterback, to do that kind of thing. I came at it from the outside, so I was able to see things differently."

He was quiet again, but the hold on my fingers tightened, so I knew he wasn't sleeping. Presently he said, "I've been falling in love with you, Vic, but you don't need me." His mouth twisted and he turned his head to one side to hide some tears.

My throat was tight and I couldn't get any words out. "That's not true," I tried to say, but I didn't know if it was or not. I swallowed and cleared my throat. "I wasn't just using you to get Masters." My words came out in a harsh squawk. "I liked you, Ralph."

He shook his head slightly; the movement made him wince. "It's not the same thing. It just wouldn't work out."

I squeezed his hand painfully. "No. It would never work out." I wished I didn't feel so much like crying.

Gradually the hold on my fingers relaxed. He was asleep. The little nurse pulled me away from the bed; I didn't look around before leaving the room.

I wanted to go home and get drunk and go to bed or pass

out or something but I owed Murray his story, and Anita should be let out of captivity. I called Murray from the Passavant lobby.

"I was beginning to wonder about you, Vic," he said. "The news about Smeissen's arrest just came in, and my gofer at the police station says Bronsky and an Ajax executive are both in the police ward at Cook County."

"Yeah." I was bone tired. "Things are mostly over. Anita can come out of hiding. I'd like to pick her up and take her down to see her dad. That's something that's got to be done sooner or later, and it might as well be now." Masters was sure to squeal on McGraw as soon as he started talking, and I wanted to see him before Mallory did.

"Tell you what," Murray said. "I'll meet you in the lobby at the Ritz, and you can tell me about it on the way down. Then I can get a few heartrending shots of the crusty old union guy being reunited with his daughter."

"Bad idea, Murray. I'll meet you in the lobby and fill you in on the broad outline. If Anita wants you to come along, you can, but don't bet on it. Don't worry about your story, though: you'll still scoop the town."

I hung up and walked out of the hospital. I was going to have to talk to Bobby myself. I'd gone with Lotty and Ralph when the ambulance came, and Mallory had been too busy to do more than shout, "I need to talk to you!" at me as I went out the door. I didn't feel like doing it tonight. Jill was going to be okay, that was one good thing. But poor Anita— Still, I owed it to her to get her down to her father before the police got to him.

It was only four blocks from the hospital to the Ritz. The night was clear and warm and caressing. I needed a mother just now, and mother night felt like a good companion, folding dark arms around me.

The lobby of the Ritz, plush and discreet, hovered twelve stories above the street. The rich atmosphere jarred on my mood. I didn't fit in too well with it, either. In the mirrored walls of the elevator riding up, I'd seen myself disheveled, with blood on my jacket and jeans, my hair uncombed. As I waited for Murray, I half expected the house detective. Murray and he arrived at the same time.

"Excuse me, madam," he said urbanely, "I wonder if you'd mind coming with me."

Murray laughed. "Sorry, Vic, but you earned that." He turned to the house detective. "I'm Murray Ryerson, with the *Star*. This is V. I. Warshawski, a private investigator. We've come to pick up a guest of yours, and then we'll be gone."

The detective frowned over Murray's press card, then nodded. "Very well, sir. Madam, I wonder if you would mind waiting near the desk."

"Not at all," I said politely. "I understand that most of your guests never see any more blood than is contained by the average steak tartare. . . . Actually, maybe I could wash up while Mr. Ryerson waits for Miss McGraw?"

The detective ushered me happily to a private washroom in the manager's office. I scrubbed off the worst of the mess and washed my face. I found a brush in the cabinet over the sink and got my hair shaped up. On the whole I looked a lot better. Maybe not material for the Ritz, but not someone to be thrown out on sight.

Anita was waiting with Murray in the lobby when I got back. She looked at me doubtfully. "Murray says I'm out of danger?"

"Yes. Smeissen, Masters, and Smeissen's gunman have been arrested. Do you want to talk to your dad before he's arrested, too?" Murray's mouth dropped open. I put a hand on his arm to keep him from talking.

Anita thought for a minute. "Yes," she finally said. "I've been thinking it over today. You're right—the longer I put it off the worse it will be."

"I'm coming along," Murray announced.

"No," Anita said. "No, I'm not showing all that to the newspapers. Vic will give you the story later. But I'm not having reporters hanging around for this."

"You got it, Murray," I said. "Catch up with me later on tonight. I'll be—I don't know. I'll be at my bar downtown."

Anita and I started for the elevator. "Where's that?" he demanded, catching up with us.

"The Golden Glow on Federal and Adams."

I called a cab to take us back to my car. A zealous officer, possibly one who'd been left guarding the lobby, had put a parking ticket on the windshield. Twenty dollars for blocking a fire hydrant. They serve and protect.

I was so tired I didn't think I could drive and talk at the same time. I realized that this was the same day that I'd made the three-hundred-mile round trip to Hartford, and that I hadn't slept the night before. It was all catching up with me now.

Anita was preoccupied with her private worries. After giving me directions on how to get to her father's Elmwood Park house, she sat quietly, staring out the window. I liked her, I felt a lot of empathy with her, but I was too drained to reach out and give her anything at the moment.

We were on the Eisenhower Expressway, the road that runs from the Loop to the western suburbs, and had gone about five miles before Anita spoke. "What happened to Masters?"

"He showed up with his hired help to try to blow me and Ralph Devereux away. They had Jill Thayer with them—they were using her as a hostage. I managed to jump the gunman and break his arm, and disable Masters. Jill is all right."

"Is she? She's such a good kid. I'd hate like hell for anything to happen to her. Have you met her at all?"

"Yes, she spent a few days with me. She's a great kid, you're right."

"She's a lot like Peter. The mother is very self-centered, into clothes and the body beautiful, and the sister is incredible, you'd think someone made her up for a book. But Jill and Peter both are—are . . ." She groped for words. ". . . Self-assured, but completely turned out on the world. Everything always is—was—so interesting to Peter—what makes it work, how to solve the problem. Every person was someone he might want to be best friends with. Jill's a lot the same."

"I think she's falling in love with a Puerto Rican boy. That should keep things stirred up in Winnetka."

Anita gave a little chuckle. "For sure. That'll be worse than me—I was a labor leader's daughter, but at least I wasn't black or Spanish." She was quiet for a while. Then she said, "You know, this week has changed my life. Or made it seem upside-down. My whole life was directed to the union. I was going to go to law school and be a union lawyer. Now—it doesn't seem worth a lifetime. But there's a big empty hole. I don't know what to put there instead. And with Peter gone—I lost the union and Peter all at the same time. I was so busy last week being terrified that I didn't notice it. Now I do."

"Oh, yes. That's going to take a while. All mourning takes a long time, and you can't rush it along. My dad's been dead ten years now, and every now and then, something comes up that lets me know that the mourning is still going on, and another piece of it is in place. The hard part doesn't last so long. While it is going on, though, don't fight it—the more you poke away the grief and anger, the longer it takes to sort it out."

She wanted to know more about my dad and our life together. The rest of the way out I spent telling her about Tony. Funny that he should have the same name as that stupid gunman of Earl's. My father, my Tony, had been a bit of a dreamer, an idealist, a man who had never shot another human being in all his years on the force—warning shots in the air, but no one killed because of Tony Warshawski. Mallory couldn't believe it—I remember that, as Tony was dying. They were talking one evening, Bobby came over a lot at night those days, and Bobby asked him how many people he'd killed in his years on the force. Tony replied he'd never even wounded a man.

After a few minutes of silence, I thought of a small point that had been bothering me. "What's with this fake-name business? When your father first came to me he called you Anita Hill. Up in Wisconsin you were Jody Hill. I can see he gave you a false name in a not-too-bright effort to keep you out of things—but why'd you both use Hill?"

"Oh, not collusion. But Joe Hill has always been a big hero of ours. Jody Hill just came to me subconsciously. He probably picked it for the same reason."

We had reached our exit, and Anita started giving me detailed directions. When we pulled up in front of the house, she sat for a bit without speaking. Finally she said, "I couldn't decide whether to ask you to come in with me or not. But I think you should. This whole thing got started—or your involvement got started—because he came to you. Now I don't know whether he'll believe it's over without your story."

"Okay." We walked up to the house together. A man was sitting outside the front door.

"Bodyguard," Anita murmured to me. "Daddy's had one as long as I can remember." Aloud she said, "Hi, Chuck. It's me, Anita—I've dyed my hair."

The man was taken aback. "I heard you ran off, that someone was gunning for you. You okay?"

"Oh, yes, I'm fine. My dad home?"

"Yup, he's in there alone."

We went into the house, a small ranch house on a large plot. Anita led me through the living room to a sunken family room. Andrew McGraw was watching television. He turned as he heard us coming. For a second he didn't recognize Anita with her short black hair. Then he jumped up.

"Annie?"

"Yes, it's me," she said quietly. "Miss Warshawski here

found me, as you asked her to. She shot Yardley Masters, and broke the arm of Earl Smeissen's hired gunman. They're all three in jail now. So we can talk."

"Is that true?" he demanded. "You disabled Bronsky and shot Masters?"

"Yes," I said. "But your troubles aren't over, you know: as soon as Masters has recovered somewhat, he's going to talk."

He looked from me to Anita, the heavy square face uncertain. "How much do you know?" he finally said.

"I know a lot," Anita said. Her voice wasn't hostile, but it was cold, the voice of someone who didn't know the person she was talking to very well and wasn't sure she'd want to. "I know you've been using the union as a front for collecting money on illegal insurance claims. I know that Peter found that out and went to Yardley Masters about it. And Masters called you and got the name of a hit man."

"Listen, Annie," he said in a low urgent tone, much different from the angry bluster I'd heard before. "You've got to believe I didn't know it was Peter when Yardley called."

She stayed in the doorway to the room, looking down at him as he stood in his shirt-sleeves. I moved over to one side. "Don't you see," she said, her voice breaking a little, "it doesn't matter. It doesn't matter whether you knew who it was or not. What matters is that you were using the union for fraud, and that you knew a killer when Masters needed one. I know you wouldn't have had Peter shot in cold blood. But it's because you knew how to get people shot that it happened at all."

He was silent, thinking. "Yes, I see," he said finally, in that same low voice. "Do you think I haven't seen it, sitting here for ten days wondering if I'd see you dead, too, and know that I had killed you?" She said nothing. "Look, Annie. You and the union—that's been my whole life for twenty years. I thought for ten days that I'd lost both of you. Now you're back. I'm going to have to give up the union—are you going to make me do without you as well?"

Behind us an insanely grinning woman on TV was urging the room to buy some kind of shampoo. Anita stared at her father. "It can never be the same, you know. Our life, you know, the foundation's broken."

"Look at me, Annie," he said hoarsely. "I haven't slept for ten days, I haven't eaten. I keep watching television, expecting to hear that they've found your dead body someplace. . . . I asked Warshawski here to find you when I thought I could keep a step ahead of Masters. But when they made it clear you'd be dead if you showed up, I had to call her off."

He looked at me. "You were right—about almost everything. I used Thayer's card because I wanted to plant the idea of him in your mind. It was stupid. Everything I've done this last week's been stupid. Once I realized Annie was in trouble, I just lost my head and acted on crazy impulses. I wasn't mad at you, you know. I was just hoping to God you'd stop before you found Annie. I knew if Earl was watching you you'd lead him straight to her."

I nodded.

"Maybe I should never have known any gangsters," he said to Anita. "But that started so long ago. Before you were born. Once you get in bed with those boys, you don't get out again. The Knifegrinders were a pretty rough bunch in those days— you think we're tough now, you should have seen us then. And the big manufacturers, they all hired hooligans to kill us and keep the union out. We hired muscle to get the union in. Only once we were in, we couldn't get rid of the muscle. If I'd wanted to get away, the only way I could have done it was to leave the Knifegrinders. And I couldn't do that. I was a shop steward when I was fifteen. I met your mother when I was picketing Western Springs Cutlery and she was a kid herself screwing scissors together. The union was my life. And guys like Smeissen were the dirty part that came along with it."

"But you betrayed the union. You betrayed it when you

started dealing with Masters on those phony claims." Anita was close to tears.

"Yeah, you're right." He ran a hand through his hair. "Probably the dumbest thing I ever did. He came up to me at Comiskey Park one day. Someone pointed me out to him. He'd been looking for years, I guess—he'd figured out the deal, you see, but he needed someone on the outside to send the claims into him.

"All I saw was the money. I just didn't want to look down that road. If I had . . . It's like some story I heard once. Some guy, Greek I think, was so greedy he begged the gods to give him a gift—everything he touched would turn to gold. Only thing is, these gods, they zap you: they always give you what you ask for but it turns out not to be what you want. Well, this guy was like me: he had a daughter that he loved more than life. But he forgot to look down the road. And when he touched her, she turned to gold, too. That's what I've done, haven't I?"

"King Midas," I said. "But he repented, and the gods forgave him and brought his daughter back to life."

Anita looked uncertainly at her father; he looked back, his harsh face stripped and pleading. Murray was waiting for his story. I didn't say good-bye.